Serpent's Dance

Serpent's Dance

Prism of Truth: Book 3

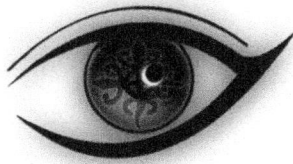

Shivon Mirza Sudesh

This one is for my parents.
I love you, Dada and Amma

Table of Contents

Shiva Varnam

Om

O' Lord Shiva, the eternally pure Universal father,
One without beginning or end, the destroyer.
As Shiva Linga, you are centre of the Universe, O' Jagadishwara,
Bless us Na Ma Shi Va Ya, a five-syllable panchakshara.

As Yogi Raj the ascetic, resides in Mount Kailasha,
With lustrous Parvati and sons Kartikeya and Ganesha.
Child warrior Kartikeya demolished asura Taraka,
Ganesha, the Lord of obstacles, is also known as Vinayaka.

By nature a loner with a disposition that calms,
Into fierce, ruthless Virabadra Sati's death transforms.
His inconsolable grief shook the worlds three,
Death of her father, Daksha, set his wrath free.

As cosmic dancer Nataraja, on demon of ignorance balances,
Matted locks whirling, cycles of life and death he dances.
The powerful masculine Rudra Tandava, the rumble of
destruction,
Or, the gentle feminine Lasya Tandava, the rhythm of creation.

As Thriambaka has a third eye like the bud of a flower,
The all-seeing eye of spiritual wisdom and power.

Blazed fire in anger to Lord of Desire, Kama, eliminate,
While his right and left eye, the sun and moon illuminate.

Crescent moon shimmering on his head, a decoration,
Waxing and waning, with onset and end of creation.
The hour-glass Damaru equalise male and female,
And give root to languages from its 'om' sound wave.

Serpentine tresses glowing like molten gold,
Swings and gathers to give mighty Ganga an abode.
Lets her out gently, as a cascade in earthly descent,
To flow as Nectar of Immortality for heavenly ascent
.

Called Neelakanta, as his throat is blue-hued,
From the poison the churning of the ocean spewed.
Parvati's nimble fingers stopped its further descent,
Thus, saving the Universe, within him resident.

Five glistening snakes, on his glorious body hover,
Showing he is wise, eternal and beyond death's power.
One, hood spread wide, slithers around with intent,
To coil as three chains, past, present and future represent.

Rules the three worlds, being the Thrishul holder,
Destroying the evils of pride, lust and anger.
Using the powers of knowledge, action and devotion,
As the three sharp points represent, paths of self-realisation.

The Lord of Winds, Vayu, sends his knotted curls streaming,
To exist in all living things as the air they are breathing.
Meditates and conquers love on a tiger skin seat,
His Bhootha Ganas tend to devotees, who fall at his feet.

On Chief of his army, Nandi the white bull he is borne,
Garland of Rudrasha, the chain of never ending knowledge worn.
Dusted by ashes, purified by the flames ultimate,
Material things you hold dear, remember this is their fate.

Out of the sacrificial pyre made to destroy the destroyer,
Sprang a ferocious tiger he slew, as the conqueror.
He held firmly the antelope that jumped out leaping,
Showing maturity and firmness in his way of thinking.

Scantily attired, with torso bhasma (ashes) sprinkled,
Married Parvati, who like the sunlight sparkled.
She won his mighty love through penances severe,
Shiva gave her his half, becoming Ardhanarishwara in revere.

Sudeshni Mirza

Behold, I send you forth as sheep in the midst of wolves: be ye therefore wise as serpents, and harmless as doves.

Matthew 10:16

.

Prologue

The Chief knew something was not right.

It was in the way the wind blew; in how the dark clouds covered the crescent moon like a murky veil. Small animals rustled uneasily among the foliage as he and his men marched deeper into the woods for the evening hunt. An owl hooted, and the Chief turned his head sharply towards the sound.

His right-hand-man caught his eye in concern. 'Is everything all right, Chief?

'I hope so.'

His men said nothing in reply. The hunting party proceeded silently for a few minutes, keeping their ears sharp for the tell-tale noises that would promise them a full stomach that night. When sounds of movement came, however, it was from behind them.

'Chief!'

One of his men – no more than a boy – ran up to him, panting. 'Chief, you must return.'

'What has happened?'

The boy hesitated, and he knew then that his premonitions had been accurate. 'Tell me!' the Chief commanded.

'It is your son. He has been bitten by a cobra.'

As they hurried back to the huts, the Chief cursed himself for not listening to his instincts. He should not have left today; he should have stayed behind and protected his family. When they approached his hut, the people gathered around it made way for their Chief. More swarmed inside the hut and spilled out of the doorway, avid with gossip. The women wailed and keened, each one competing to make her sorrow heard above the rest.

Seeing their Chief, they hurried to tell him what had happened. 'It was the naga king, Chief! He bit your boy in revenge.'

'But why?' a crone lamented. 'We have always offered prayers to the snake gods. Why would they do this?'

The men who had accompanied him on the hunt wordlessly began ushering the people out of the hut, clearing the room so that the Chief could see his son stretched out on a mat on the floor, pale with approaching death. His wife did not look up as the Chief approached the boy, her thin body still with grief as she clutched their son's limp hand. The Chief knelt beside the boy and reached out to stroke his son's eyelids; for now closed in sleep but awaiting a more permanent slumber.

The snakebite was near the boy's ankle; the puncture wound was a gruesome blemish against his young skin.

'How long?' he asked hoarsely.

When his wife did not reply, his right-hand-man answered. 'Too much time has elapsed. I am sorry. He will be dead within the hour.'

His wife closed her eyes and her lips moved silently as if in prayer. Tears rolled down her cheeks as she cradled their only child's head in her arms.

'No!' the Chief shouted, rising to his feet. He turned to his men, who stood at a respectful distance behind them. 'Find the snake and bring it here,' he ordered.

'But Chief –'

'Now!'

Without further argument, his men dispersed. Time trickled by slowly as they waited and watched their son edge closer to death.

Finally, the men returned. Two of them carried a long stick to which was tied a writhing, undulating cobra, trying desperately to slither free. The Chief watched on stonily as the men lowered the snake onto the floor next to the boy, its head near the wound on his leg. The serpent seemed to instinctively understand what they wanted of it.

Hissing, it stared around balefully before lowering its head to the boy's ankle. It began to slowly suck out the poison from the wound, its forked tongue flicking out now and then. After what seemed like an eternity, it drew back and spat out blue-black venom. Once it had expelled every last drop, it began to try to squirm free again.

The snake's vain efforts were the only sounds as they waited with bated breath, all eyes fixed on the boy's face. Slowly the colour began to return to it, and death's mark lifted from the child. He opened his eyes, stared upwards into his mother's face, and smiled.

'Thank God!' she exclaimed, sobbing and hugging her son.

A cheer went up among the men that spread like a wave out to the rest of the people gathered outside the hut, celebrating the news that the Chief's son lived. The Chief used the uproar to mask the shaky breath he'd just exhaled.

The two men who had brought the snake lifted it up and looked to the Chief. 'Shall we kill it now?'

The Chief shook his head. 'No. Take it deep into the woods and then release it. Its venom cannot hurt us now.'

PART ONE

Chapter One

Dance Master

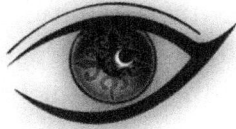

Zakiy had many problems in his life.

One was his brother, who had suffered from schizophrenia for most of his life and was only just recovering through sustained treatment. Another was the fact that his best friend's mother had been murdered eighteen years ago and she and Zakiy were in the middle of a quest to find the person responsible.

But right now, the most annoying obstacle before him was said best friend's father.

'I am not comfortable with the idea of the two of you trekking out to another district,' Nakul repeated, running his hand through his hair in agitation.

'Technically we won't be "trekking" anywhere,' Zakiy said helpfully, gesturing to Toothless, his trusty Jeep.

Okay, so maybe he was being helpfully unhelpful on purpose. Maybe.

Nakul threw him a glare while Sathi sighed. 'Dad, I don't know why you're getting so worked up about this. This isn't the first time Zakiy and I have gone on a long journey together.'

'We're kind of known for our tendency to do that,' Zakiy put in.

Nakul ignored him. 'Well, why can't I come with you then?'

'We've been over this!' Sathi exclaimed, her patience apparently running out. 'Dad, I need you to stay here in case Vee– Vidhya comes back. She may claim she's innocent, but I don't trust her, and if she decides to show her face again, I don't want to miss her.'

The two of them had a silent standoff as Zakiy considered his best friend's words. Sathi had come to India in search of her Amma's murderer and thought she'd found her in Vidhya Raman, her mother's ex-best friend, who'd been driven to violence by a jealous and spiteful nature.

But then Vidhya (under the pseudonym of Veena) had turned up in Nelliampathi – a small hill station in Kerala, India – and joined work as a cook at the resort where Sathi worked. She and Sathi had become fast friends and things had been going swimmingly until just a couple of days ago when Vidhya had run away without a trace.

All she'd left behind was a letter addressed to Sathi, claiming her innocence, and urging Sathi to find a diary that had allegedly belonged to her mother.

The address she'd left pointed them towards a dance school in a nearby town, but when they visited, they'd been told that the location of the school had shifted to Kochi, a district a few hours' drive south of Nelliampathi.

Nakul finally looked away from his daughter, conceding defeat. 'Fine. But be careful. And keep me updated.'

Sathi's lips twitched in response to his sulky tone. 'Deal.'

Ten minutes later, they were finally off. Sathi slumped against the seat and yawned, no doubt feeling the late night – well, early morning now. Sleep hadn't really been a priority for any of them since the revelation that Veena was actually Vidhya.

'Why don't you get some sleep?' Zakiy suggested.

'Nah. I would if I could, trust me. But every time I close my eyes...' She trailed off, shuddering.

Zakiy couldn't think of anything to say that would help. So, he decided a distraction was in order. 'I see there's trouble in father-daughter paradise,' he teased.

She rolled her eyes. 'He's just... a bit overprotective. Especially after... you know.'

He did know. Sathi and Nakul had lived like practical strangers for years in their house in London and had only recently been reconciled after Sathi found out that her mother had not died in childbirth as she'd originally believed. The shocking discovery had led her to India to uncover the truth. Nakul had gone into overdrive with worry about his daughter and had finally followed her to Nelliampathi after believing – mistakenly – that Zakiy had kidnapped her.

'It's okay,' he assured her. 'He's just worried about you.'

'Yeah, but I don't get why he still acts like you're some kind of criminal.'

He didn't reply, wondering whether there was a good reason for Nakul's hostility, despite Zakiy being cleared of all charges re: kidnapping. Maybe he sensed a different kind of threat from him.

Oh yeah, another one of those problems in his life?

Zakiy was in love with his best friend.

His feelings had crept up on him, finally tackling him out of left field when it looked like Sathi might return to London with her father. The astounding relief he felt when she decided to stay had made him realise that she was much more than a friend to him.

She was the one he wanted to spend the rest of his life with.

There was just one slight problem: Sathi was clueless about his radical change in perspective, and he had no idea how to enlighten her without getting punched in the face.

'Earth to Zakiy,' Sathi said, waving a hand in front of his face. She looked at him in concern. 'You okay?'

He glanced at her, and immediately became caught up in the deep pools of her eyes, which were the colour of dark chocolate and glistened with compassion. He didn't know how he'd been so blind about how he felt about her. But now that he'd clued in on his own heart, he could barely focus on anything except how much he wanted to take her into his arms and never let go.

'Look out!'

Sathi lunged over and jerked the steering wheel, narrowly avoiding the autorickshaw that had decided to overtake the Jeep from the left. Glaring at the driver who had sped away, Sathi sent an angry honk after him. 'Idiot!' she muttered.

Shifting her attention back to Zakiy, she touched his arm. 'Are you okay?' she asked again.

Railing angrily at himself, he forced himself to refocus on the road. 'I'm fine,' he said, mustering a breezy tone and staring straight ahead. 'Sorry about that, I'd better concentrate.' Doing his best to block out how it felt to have her warm fingers on his arm, he moved his hand away under the pretence of needing both hands on the wheel.

'It wasn't your fault,' she said automatically, but something in her tone made him think she had sensed a rebuff in his action and was hurt by it.

Zakiy felt despair cloud in on him. How on earth was he going to make this work?

'Nataraja Dance Academy?'

Sathi blinked up at the huge signboard above the gate and turned to him. 'This is where Amma's diary is?'

Zakiy kept his traitorous eyes on the board. 'This is the address Vidhya gave us.'

4

He parked Toothless in an empty spot near the gate and the two of them walked up the driveway to the entrance. When Sathi saw the palatial hall that greeted them at the ornate door, she let out a little gasp of delight. Zakiy smiled and trailed behind watching her as she floated further into the room, enraptured.

He could understand her joy; the hall was breathtakingly beautiful, the floor cream-coloured marble with veins of wine-red threading through it. An elaborate chandelier hung in the centre of the hall, a hundred dangling crystals catching the light and glittering like bejewelled flies. Large can lights fixed in corners of the floor projected light inwards and threw the centre of the hall into brilliant spotlight.

Zakiy's gaze was drawn to the most spectacular feature in the room; an enormous bronze statue stood at the head of the hall, at least seven feet tall, displaying the form of a man encased within a circle of fire. Because he'd already braced himself as soon as he found out that Madhu's diary was at a dance academy, he managed to contain the sudden emotions seeing the statue caused to bubble up within him. Struck simultaneously by awe and wistfulness, he edged closer until he was standing directly in front of the sculpture, the top of his head aligned with the god's shoulders.

Unconsciously, Zakiy's shoulders relaxed their tense pose as he took in those familiar features; the god stood with his left arm and left leg raised and extended to the left as he balanced in mid-air. His right foot rested on the head of the demon of ignorance, and his hair flew out like a fan to either side of him, waves undulating. Snakes extended from his body, their bodies slithering sensuously through the air.

He felt Sathi come up behind him, drawn by his absorbance with the statue.

'Who is that?' she asked in a hushed voice.

'Lord Nataraja,' he responded, glancing at her. She looked blank, so he explained, 'He's a manifestation of Lord Shiva, the god of Death; Nataraja is the god of dance and dramatic arts.'

'How are dance and death related? Is it like that saying, "dance with Death"?' she asked.

'Not exactly.' Zakiy grinned and then looked back at the Nataraja statue, unable to keep from gazing at the grace of the god's stance. 'Shiva is the god of rebirth as well as death and destruction, and when the universe is weary and weighed down with the sludge that is the result of corruption of any remaining goodness in the mortal soul, Shiva dances the Thandava, the dance of destruction. Then, once the universe has been destroyed along with the evil accumulated over the millennia, he allows himself to be lost in the dance of creation, the Lasya. Through it he creates a new universe, one filled with souls whose goodness had drawn them closer to the gods. Just like he prepares dead souls for rebirth, Shiva prepares a weary universe for fresh life. He only destroys so that he can recreate a better world.'

Sathi stared at the god's serene expression, a look of awe of her face. 'Wow. I never realised there was so much significance behind Shiva. I've never even heard about this dancing form of him.' She turned those expressive eyes towards him. 'Did your dad teach you?

Flushing, Zakiy took a sudden moronic interest in his shoes. Why had he opened his big mouth? While his father was undoubtedly an expert in all things related to Hindu mythology, Zakiy's obsession with Nataraja had an entirely different root. He couldn't tell her - it was too embarrassing.

Thankfully he was spared the necessity of replying when an extremely irate-looking man marched up to them. 'What are you doing here? This is a private property, not a museum!'

Sathi took an automatic step back from the statue, her eyes wide. 'Er, sorry. We got distracted by this sculpture of Lord Shiva - it's so beautiful.' She offered a shy smile that faltered when the man's stony expression didn't change.

6

'That is a statue of Nataraja, the great cosmic dancer.'

She blinked. 'Right. Yeah. Um... Well, we're actually here to, um, ask about Vidhya Raman.'

'Who?'

Heart sinking, Zakiy repeated, 'Vidhya Raman? She told us that she left something, a diary, here that we need to find.'

The man's impatience was palpable now. 'This is a dance academy,' he enunciated clearly, as though he thought their brains were addled. 'We teach dance here. We do not provide locker service!'

Sathi's face slowly darkened with embarrassment, a sight that enraged Zakiy. 'Look, there's no need to be rude. If you don't know who Vidhya is, then do you know anyone who would know?'

'As I have explained to you once before, this is a dance academy,' the man repeated. 'Unless you have any sort of interest in dance, I suggest you remove yourselves from these premises- Hey, what are you doing?' the man demanded, staring at Zakiy as he removed his shoes and socks. He picked up his phone and found the music he wanted. He pressed play and set the phone back on the floor near his shoes.

'You said this was a dance academy, right?' Zakiy asked casually as he bent to touch the ground in blessing and touched the same hand to his forehead. 'So, let's dance.'

Closing his eyes, he assumed the exact posture of the Nataraja statue behind him. The beat of drums infiltrated his every cell. His eyes opened, and he threw himself into a Rudra Thandava, the dance of destruction. His hands and feet flew with grace, his feet slapping against the ground in rage and his expression reflecting the austere detachment needed to demolish the universe for the purpose of rebuilding it anew. He squatted and lunged, his hands painting intricate gestures through the air. He channelled all his anger and the despair of his unexpressed feelings towards Sathi into his dance. Finally, breathing heavily, he drew his dance to a close in time with the music and came to a stop with his head bowed in front of Nataraja, who seemed to be smiling at him in approval.

Slow, solitary applause rang through the sudden silence left in the wake of Zakiy's Thandava. Pulse pounding loudly in his temples, he glanced up in surprise. The man who descended the ornate staircase off to the side of the hall exuded power; his head was clean-shaven (seriously, the only hair came from his eyebrows) and he was dressed simply in loose yoga pants and a tank shirt. Typical dance clothes, clothes that Zakiy – sweating in his heavy jeans - would have preferred during his little impromptu performance.

Still applauding, the man came to stand directly in front of Zakiy. Smiling slightly, the guy nodded to him. 'That was an exceptional demonstration of the Thandava. Such passion, such fury... it rivals the Thandava the Lord himself danced at the loss of his Sathi.'

Sathi's head jerked at the sound of her namesake. 'Huh?'

Zakiy, still flushed from the dance, felt his face heat up even more. He could see from his peripheral vision that Sathi was gaping at him with her mouth hanging open.

The man turned to Sathi. 'Sathi was Shiva's first consort, and true love. They were blissfully happy together, but her father did not approve of their marriage. He insulted Shiva in front of Sathi and she, overcome with anger and humiliation that her beloved Lord had been slighted by her father, called on the god of fire to consume her. When Shiva heard of her death, he lost all control and ordered that her father and all those supporting him be beheaded. The Thandava he danced at her loss nearly destroyed the world before its time.'

Sathi seemed struck speechless, and gazed at him wordlessly while the guy enthused, 'I've never seen the Thandava performed with such passion. Young man, who is your Master?'

Why, Zakiy groaned to himself, had he opened up this can of worms? Trying to speak without actually using his vocal cords, he whispered, 'I don't actually have a Master.'

Surprise flickered across the guy's expression, gouging a deep V on his forehead. 'But then how did you learn the dance?'

Zakiy didn't know where to look. 'I, er, kind of taught myself.' The guy's eyes widened even further, so Zakiy rushed to forestall further questions by going on the offensive. 'Sir, please can we speak to the dance master here? It's very important that we speak with him about an old dance student, Vidhya Raman.'

'Vidhya Raman?' The guy surprised him by breaking into laughter. 'An old dance student? My dear boy, she is the most talented dancer I've had the opportunity of teaching.'

'Wait.' Sathi stepped forward. 'You're the dance master?'

The master turned his attention to her, eyes twinkling. 'Yes, child. I'm sure you expected a wrinkled prune of a guy with more hair than anyone should be allowed to have. I'm sorry to disappoint,' he added, winking and tapping his shaved dome.

'Um...'

Trying desperately to avoid eye contact with Sathi, Zakiy asked, 'So you knew Vidhya Raman?'

'Of course. She began to study the art of dance with me when she was six years old, and she was well on her way to being awarded a kalathilakam when she suddenly stopped coming to lessons.' The master shrugged. 'Her brother had just died, and she was moving to the city with her mother and younger siblings so she could find a job to support them.'

'Did she give you anything before she left?' Sathi sounded like she hardly dared to breathe. 'Like a book, or a... diary?'

The master's eyebrows rose, and he seemed to size her up. 'Why are you asking about Vidhya?' he asked.

Sathi hesitated. 'She and my mother were friends, and she left that diary for me. She told me to come here.'

The master gasped. 'That's why you look so familiar!' he exclaimed. 'You're Madhu's daughter.'

'You know Amma?' Sathi sounded stunned.

He chuckled. 'You have no idea how many times I've had to throw that cheeky monkey out because she was distracting everyone. She was a menace.' His fond smile softened the criticism. His expression sobered as he took in the mingled joy and pain on Sathi's face. 'Madhu...?'

'She's dead,' Sathi bit out.

'I'm sorry. I know she and Vidhya were very close.' He paused, considering. 'Vidhya came to see me a long time after she quit lessons. She gave me a diary and made me promise not to tell anyone about it. She said she didn't trust anyone else, and that she was scared to keep it with her. But if she told you about it, then she must have wanted me to give it to you. Come with me.'

He turned and headed back up the ornate staircase. Zakiy was about to follow when he felt himself being tugged back by the elbow; he turned to find himself assaulted by the scent of jasmine and spice that was Sathi.

It wasn't perfume; he knew she didn't wear any. It was as though all that was good about India – all that he loved about his home country – had been infused into her skin to form the most intoxicating fragrance in the world.

Sathi – thankfully – didn't seem to notice the effect she was having on him. 'What's the story with your dancing back there?'

He felt the heat return to his face again. Scrambling for a distraction, he twisted out her grip and gestured to the dance master, who was almost at the top of the stairs. 'This probably isn't the right time. Besides, there's nothing to tell.'

She glanced up at the master and let go of Zakiy. 'Fine.'

But as he turned to climb up the stairs, she called out, 'Don't think I'm letting it go, though. I'm getting that story out of you, by hook or crook.'

Embarrassed as he was, Zakiy couldn't help the grin that crept onto his face. She would, as well.

The dance master led them into a room that Zakiy presumed was his office. He went straight to his desk and rummaged around in a drawer before pulling out a very old, very battered notebook.

Sathi gasped. She reached out a hand as though to touch the book, even though it was a few feet away. To touch what could very possibly be her mother's diary.

She walked forwards a few steps like she was in a trance, her expression unreadable, her hand still reached out, her stare intent on the diary. The dance master handed it to her wordlessly, seeming to sense the gravity of the drama afoot.

'Vidhya seemed very out of sorts when she came to see me that day, like a cornered animal.' He heaved a sigh and looked up at them. 'I never saw her again.

Chapter Two

The Diary

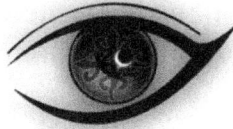

2^{th December 1979}

Merry Christmas!

I just got this book and I've decided I'm going to make it my diary. I'm going to write in it every day!

Today was Christmas so Santa Claus (well, Uncle, because you know, Santa Claus doesn't exist) left me lots of presents under the tree. I got lots more than Girish, even though he said I wouldn't get any this year, so there! Aunt said it was because he'd been a bad boy this year, and I'd been a very good girl.

I'm not so sure about that. But who am I to argue with Santa Claus?

26th December 1979

Today I went to a workshop with Uncle, at our school. Uncle said all the kids from the school were going to make a painting and he said

I should do one too. I was very excited. I took ages to decide what to paint – then I decided to paint a horse.

I really liked one this other girl painted – she'd drawn a monkey with its paw caught in a cookie jar. It made me laugh, though Uncle got annoyed and said she should have done something more original. I don't know what he meant, but I caught her eye and smiled when Uncle wasn't looking.

I really wanted to talk to her afterwards, but I didn't get a chance because Uncle wanted to go home straightaway.

9th March 1982

This book made me laugh – I got it for Christmas ages ago and resolved to write it in every day. 2 whole days I managed to keep it up for! That's typical me, anyway – I really don't have the patience to write a diary entry every day.

It's so funny, I just read the last thing I wrote in here, and it's about Vidhya. That was the day after I first met her, and now we've been best friends for 3 years!

She's calling me now. We're entering this art competition and we're thinking of doing some appliqué work. Not sure what our subject will be, but we need to figure it out, fast!

5th April 1982

We won the competition! I can't believe it – they're hanging our work in the school library. They took photos and everything and one came printed in today's newspaper! There's an article as well, all about Vidhya and me. I'm going to cut it out and stick it right here.

(Hey, I just had an idea. Since I'm not going to write in here every day I'll only write on special occasions – like today.)

I showed Aunt and Uncle the newspaper article and they were pleased – but they also got a bit annoyed with me and said I should have concentrated on my studies rather than getting involved in frivolous things. I was a bit upset, but then Vidhya cheered me up by saying I'd get straight As even if I didn't go to school for a year. That girl is crazy, but I adore her!

9th April 1982

unniuttotnajnedocnahtuhzeuhcinamureehturoyraiduhtannukkevah tallimaravivunannemayraknajnmuhzoppemukkirahcivanihtnemuk kravallemanaakannuttapliyihteermahtnawslanosreplagnayraakihtu hzeuhtannukkevudnokuhtaetneedocukkinelihtaudnumanamihbaeh skaploppiukkineaylavallumahsehsivmunnomayrakallinahtihzeudno kuhtaoaic

Sathi stared at her mother's diary entry from April 1982 in blank shock. Were her eyes playing tricks on her, or had she suddenly and inexplicably lost the ability to read the English language?

She refused to entertain a different possibility as her eyes roamed over and over the stream of nonsense that her beloved Amma's words had abruptly become. Then she turned to the next page. And the next. And the next.

'Sathi? What's wrong?' Zakiy asked.

She shook her head and started frantically flipping through the thick pages, almost tearing them in her haste. She kept going until she reached the blank pages at the back, at the very end, where her mother's words ran out and there was nothing more of the woman Sathi ached to know.

She let the diary drop, limp, into her lap and stared bleakly out of the windscreen. 'Code. She wrote the diary in code.'

"No results found for your search."

The words mocked Sathi from where they glared out from the computer screen.

She didn't understand; how was it possible for a language that used the English alphabet to be totally alien to Google? She'd run comparisons to Spanish, French, Latin, German, Italian and a hundred other languages and had found no match for her mother's writing.

God, she was exhausted. She'd spent the whole journey back to Nelliampathi trying to decipher the code. When they got back to Zakiy's parents' big mansion, she'd shut herself in one of the guestrooms.

Wearily, Sathi's eyes found Amma's beautiful face in the old photo she'd placed beside her on the bed.

Why did you have to make it so difficult? she silently asked her serene mother.

And yet through her frustration Sathi couldn't help admiring her Amma – this spirited young girl who had developed such a complex code during her teens. She obviously had secrets she was determined no one should learn.

No one who was unworthy of uncovering them, anyway.

Did that mean she, Sathi, was unworthy of learning her mother's secrets?

Pushing aside that unwelcome thought, she examined again the first coded entry, trying to find some weakness she could use to crack the code and unlock Amma's story. There was nothing, no capitalisation, no punctuation, just the dates and the incomprehensible stream of letters. She concentrated on the dates, wondering if the numerical values had some deeper meaning.

After an hour of calculating and recalculating she gave up. If Amma was trying to give a clue through the numbers, then she had been wasting her time. Next Sathi tried sounding out the "words", hoping that they would make sense phonetically. When that too failed, she ignored possible meaning and tried looking for patterns instead. Another fruitless attempt, as it turned out.

'Gah!' she groaned, falling back on the bed and blinking up at the ceiling. 'This is impossible.'

Sathi turned her head to look at the wall clock. Fifteen hours. That's how long she'd spent on her mother's diary since they reached Zakiy's house. It seemed like her Amma hadn't meant her diary as something she would pass onto her daughter, to guide her, to give her something to remember her by.

The tears that began to prickle at her eyes were halted by the hesitant knock at the door. Zakiy's voice called out, 'Everything okay in there?'

Sathi thought about lying and saying yes, but what came out instead was a sullen, 'No.'

The door opened and her best friend poked his head into the room. For some weird reason, he had a brightly striped apron tied around his waist and a huge white chef's hat wedged tight over his brown curls.

Sathi lifted her head to stare at him for a moment, and then flopped back down. 'I'm not even going to ask,' she said, glowering at the ceiling again.

'But I'm going to tell you regardless.' The bed sagged under his weight as he sat down in a tiny corner of free mattress by her elbow. She could have moved to give him more space, but she just couldn't make the effort.

Zakiy poked her in the arm, and irritated, she snapped, 'What?'

'You're offending my sensitive artistic sensibilities by not paying attention. Do you know what I learned to cook today?'

'What?'

'I can't just spoil the suspense like that. I must build up to the story.'

She groaned again, but he paid no attention to her. 'So, first, Dattu and I locked Abdullah up in the outdoor shed. You know otherwise he'd just "supervise" us with his stupid pinched nose in the air and lips pursed up like he's sucking on lobster.'

Amused despite herself, the corners of Sathi's mouth twitched. Zakiy continued, 'Then Dattu and I cornered Manish and made him share his world-famous banana fritter recipe.'

Manish was a friend of theirs, an ancient guy who ran a tea stall on the edge of town. He was usually quite territorial about his recipes. He was also a big softie, especially when it came to Sathi.

'That's pretty impressive,' Sathi said, unconscious that her voice was a monotone.

He sighed. 'Okay, what's wrong?'

When he received no response, he glanced at the diary lying on the bed next to her. He picked it up, weighing it in his hands with a thoughtful expression. 'You haven't been able to crack the code?'

She shook her head.

'You'll figure it out. It's only a matter of time, you know that.'

Sathi gave a hollow laugh. 'If it was a matter of time, I would've figured it out already.' She paused and stared broodingly at the diary. 'She never meant for anyone to read it, and I just don't think I'm going to be able to decode it.'

'Don't give up now, Sathi. I mean, look how far you've come already. You found your mum's diary – that itself is a miracle. You can do this.'

She didn't respond, misery and hopelessness twisting together into a hard lump in her heart.

'Come on, Sathi,' Zakiy urged. 'This is just a small setback; you can do it!'

Irritation sparked in her. 'Could you just stop spouting platitudes? It's seriously getting on my nerves.'

He was silent for so long that she found herself unable to peek at his reaction. Then he stood up without a word and left the room.

Remorse instantly flooded her; she'd unfairly taken out her frustration on him, just as she'd been doing since her wonderful grandparents turned out to be possibly the worst examples of human beings alive, and their horrible black magic turned her into an unstable mess of churning emotions.

Her friendship with Zakiy had nearly disintegrated because of her issues, and only recently had they managed to work through her weird mood swings and rebuild their trust in each other. And now she was making the same mistakes over and over again, and hurting Zakiy when he was doing all he could to help her.

She'd just gotten to her feet and opened the door to go after him when Zakiy suddenly appeared in the doorway; he wordlessly passed her his phone and walked away before she could say anything.

Caught off guard, she glanced between his retreating back and the phone in her hand. She put it to her ear. 'Hello?'

'Hello, Sathi. How are you, sweetheart?'

'Maira!' she exclaimed, delighted. 'Oh, you have no idea how glad I am to hear your voice right now!'

She could hear the smile in Zakiy's mother's voice when she replied. 'I missed you too, Sathi.' Maira hesitated. 'Zakiy told me that you found your mother's diary.'

Sathi's smile faded. 'Yeah. She didn't write every day, so it goes right up until around the time... around the time she died. But after the first few entries it's all in code.'

'And you haven't been able to decode it so far.'

It hadn't been a question, but she answered anyway. 'No.'

'Why do you think that is?'

'Because it's too hard!' Sathi burst out. 'I've done everything I can think of, and nothing has worked. I don't think she wanted anyone to be able to read it. Not even me,' she added softly.

A beat of time passed before Maira replied. 'Sathi, do you mind if I'm frank with you?'

Sathi's throat closed in with apprehension. 'Go on.'

18

'From what I know about you, you're not the type of person to back down from a challenge. I've seen you wrestle with the impossible until you get what you want from the situation. So now if you feel like you can't do something because it's too hard, then there's some other reason for it.'

A hot trail of resentment burned through her chest like acid reflux, and she wanted to demand why she wasn't allowed to give up occasionally. Recognising the vile turbulence of her emotions, Sathi forced herself to clamp her mouth shut and take a deep breath.

Instead of snapping at Maira like she had at Zakiy moments ago, she made herself consider the older woman's words calmly.

She's right, she realised eventually. Sathi stared at her mother's diary, stroking the faded black cover. I never give up. So why am I so tempted to now?

Maira kept quiet, allowing her to think.

Sathi closed her eyes and tried to shut out everything but the diary in her mind's eye; she relived her reaction when the dance master held it out to her – fascination mingled with apprehension.

She'd wanted nothing more than to open it and discover the truth of what happened to her mother, once and for all. But at the same time, she'd wanted to run out of the room and never look back.

Her eyes sprang open in shock. 'Fear,' she blurted, almost forgetting the phone clutched to her ear. 'I'm afraid of the truth.'

Maira's voice was gentle. 'That's a perfectly natural reaction.'

'But I don't want to be a coward!' Sathi's voice was frantic, panicked. Her heart thudded loudly in her chest, almost drowning out Maira's next words.

'Then you have no option but to overcome your fear.'

'How?'

'Well, the first step is to figure out what it is that scares you about the truth.' Maira's voice was so calm, so matter of fact, that it forced Sathi to follow her example.

'Okay,' she breathed, trying to get herself under control. I'm stronger than this, she told herself fiercely.

Miraculously, her body seemed to respond to her mind's show of power and quietened down enough for her to think about what Maira had said. Okay, she repeated in her head. What am I so damn scared of?

Was it the thought of finding out who'd killed her mother?

Okay, yes, that scared her, but she was more than ready to find out. It had been a mystery that had been eating away at her for almost a year, and she was sure she was strong enough now to face that truth. After thinking that Vidhya had been the culprit, she didn't think anything would faze her.

Sathi scanned over the first few entries, the ones not in code, and an unconscious smile formed on her face as she imagined this spunky teenager. Someone who didn't sound anything like Sathi.

Her smile dimmed. Is that what was bugging her – the fear that she wouldn't measure up to her mother?

Or was she afraid that the Amma in the diary – the real Amma – wouldn't measure up to the Amma she'd imagined?

A quiet gasp left her lips as realisation punched her in the throat. 'Sathi?'

'I think I know what I'm so scared of,' she said numbly. 'Once I read her diary, that's it - I can't imagine what she was like anymore, I can't fantasise anymore, because I'll know. And as much as I want to know her, I'm scared the reality won't live up to the Amma in my imagination.'

Maira didn't reply for a heartbeat, and Sathi wondered whether Maira was going to tell her how ridiculous she sounded.

'Sathi, I'm going to tell you what Zakiy told me about you just after you two first met. He told me that when you found out that your mum was killed by someone in India, you came out here all alone with no support whatsoever. He said that you were the bravest person he'd ever met.'

A rush of gratitude warmed her heart, even as guilt twisted her stomach over how badly she'd treated someone who had such a high opinion of her. 'That wasn't bravery,' she mumbled. 'I had no other choice.'

'Of course you had another choice. You left your whole life behind to get justice for your mother. You could've forgotten about it all and decided to go on with your life. You could've waited until you could persuade your father to come with you.' Maira paused. 'Don't you see, Sathi? The choices you made aren't about the options that were available to you. They're about who you are - about what you're willing to live with.'

Sathi bit her lip. She'd never thought of it that way.

Maira continued, 'Then there's the bravest thing I've ever seen anyone do - your decision to confront your grandparents after-' she stuttered a little, 'after what they did to Aman.'

Sathi stiffened. Not only were her mother's adoptive parents the worst possible grandparents in the world, but she'd also found out that they'd been responsible for the debilitating mental illness that had affected Maira's eldest child and Zakiy's big brother. All because of a vendetta Sathi's Great-uncle had against Zakiy's father.

To take revenge, Bhaskar and Sathi's gem of a Great-aunt had concocted some kind of disgusting potion of black magic that they'd then given to 10-year-old Aman. He had collapsed and subsequently developed schizophrenia.

That discovery was what had finally given Sathi the strength to fight back against the evil that were her grandparents.

Recovering her composure, Maira said, 'Even when you realised your grandparents' part in Aman's illness, you had the decency to tell us everything. I think you underestimate how much courage you have, sweetheart. If you can do all those things, then you can do this too.' Her voice softened. 'And remember - your mother might not have been the perfect person she is in your imagination, but she must have been pretty special to give birth to such a wonderful daughter.'

Tears filled Sathi's eyes at how highly Maira viewed her. The unconscious tension that had been suffocating her lifted, leaving her feeling oddly light.

'You're right,' she choked out through a swollen throat. 'I'm being an idiot. I'm over-analysing things as usual. Of course I can read her diary. I can crack this code.'

There was pride in Maira's voice when she next spoke. 'That's my girl.'

'You've put things into perspective for me. I can't believe I was being such an idiot,' she said again, marvelling over how easily she'd spiralled into darkness and cynicism.

'Don't beat yourself up about that now,' Maira warned.

Sathi chuckled. 'I won't, I promise. Thank you.'

'You're very welcome, Sathi. Anytime you need things put in perspective, just pick up the phone and call me, okay?'

'Okay. Love you.'

'Love you, too.'

She was about to hang up when Maira said, 'Sathi?'

'Yeah?'

'I know you tend to try and deal with problems on your own. But there's nothing wrong with accepting help from the people who love you.'

'I know,' Sathi said, confused. 'I will call you next time, I promise.'

'And so you should. But I was talking about Zakiy.'

'Oh.'

'He would do anything to help you, sweetheart. All you need to do is ask.'

Clutching Amma's diary to her chest, Sathi made herself walk further into the living room until she stood behind the sofa where Zakiy was sitting. Taking a deep breath for courage, she cleared her throat.

Zakiy turned, and the wary look that came into his eyes when he saw her made her stomach clench. After a pause, he held out his hand, palm up, and she glanced from it to his face, confused.

'My phone,' he said.

'Oh.'

Sathi put the phone in his hand, and then grabbed his wrist when he started to pull back. He stopped, looking up at her with a questioning look.

'I'm sorry.'

Slowly, one side of his mouth quirked up, and she was relieved to see the wariness fade from his eyes. 'What was that cheesy movie dialogue – in such big, big towns such small, small things happen, señorita.' Zakiy frowned. 'That really didn't translate well. What I mean is, you're forgiven.'

Sathi gave a half-sob in relief and flew at him, throwing her arms - diary and all - around his neck. He stiffened for an instant before relaxing and hugging her back. Then he put his hands on her shoulders and pulled back to look at her. 'You okay?'

'Yeah. Thank you for calling Maira for me.'

'I had a feeling you would be able to open up to her.'

'You were right.'

The flicker of hurt that Zakiy tried to keep out of his eyes made her want to cut her tongue out. 'No, I didn't mean it like that - of course I need to open up to you as well.' She stopped and forced herself to think before she spoke. 'First of all, I was being an idiot. I understand that now. Your mum made me understand why I was feeling so... so... dejected.' She told him about her realisation, explaining what Maira had said.

Zakiy didn't look up when she fell quiet, and she was terrified that she'd caused irreparable damage. She felt like she'd do anything to recover that easy smile she relied on.

Then he glanced at her, and she saw that, instead of being unhappy over her insensitive words, he was grinning.

'What?' she demanded, pretending indignation even though she could barely keep her own grin from forming.

'Nothing. I just can't believe you nearly gave yourself an aneurysm over this.' He paused to shake his head at her. 'On the other hand, I can believe it. But next time do me a favour - when you're freaking out, tell me and I'll slap you out of it.'

'Thanks a lot,' Sathi said scathingly.

'You're welcome.'

She took a deep breath and met his eyes. 'I know your mum said I have the courage to do this, but I'm still scared. I need help. I need your help.'

His face lit up with genuine joy, though he kept his trademark grin in place. 'What good is Sir Galahad if he can't even do such a small thing to help his Lady?'

Ever since Zakiy (or Sir Galahad as he called himself) had agreed to help her decipher Amma's diary, she'd felt like her shoulders had shed at least a kilo of weight. As they sprawled out on the floor of his living room, Sathi marvelled again at her fortune in finding such a friend. She sent up a fervent Thank you! to her goddess.

Speaking of Devi: Sathi reached into her ratty backpack that had - literally - travelled across the world with her and pulled out two photographs she always carried with her. One was a shot of her mother, showing a beautiful woman with smiling lips and a head of curly black hair. As usual, Sathi's eyes lingered on Amma's face with longing and her chest seemed somehow simultaneously hollow and bursting with emotion.

She resolutely put the photo down and turned her attention to the next one, a beautiful depiction of the supreme goddess in the Hindu pantheon, the Divine Mother and ultimate personification of nature.

Sathi had started believing in and loving this benevolent goddess not just because of the hope she'd inspired in Sathi at times when she felt tempted to give up her impossible quest, but also because Amma had loved Devi, too.

Filled with more peace than she had since the whole Vidhya/Veena fiasco had erupted, Sathi refocused on the riddle that was her mother's diary:

unniuttotnajnedocnahtuhzeuhcinamureehturoyraiduhtannukkevah tallimaravivunannemayraknajnmuhzoppemukkirahcivanihtnemuk kravallemanaakannuttapliyihteermahtnawslanosreplagnayraakihtu hzeuhtannukkevudnokuhtaetneedocukkinelihtaudnumanamihbaeh skaploppiukkineaylavallumahsehsivmunnomayrakallinahtihzeudno kuhtaoaic

Zakiy reached down and tapped the beginning of the first line. 'You know, "unni" is a Malayalam word for "son". It's an old-fashioned term, though, and is only used nowadays as a name, usually for a Hindu guy. Do you know if your mum knew anyone called Unni?'

Sathi wracked her brain. 'No. No one I can think of, anyway.' She suddenly grew excited at the implication. 'Wait, so do you think this is Malayalam written in English?' She scanned over the passage again, trying to translate as she went, but there was no meaning she could glean. She glanced at Zakiy hopefully. After all, he had a better grasp of their mother tongue than she did. Surely, he'd be able to decode it.

He was still scrutinising the sentences, and she could see him mouth some of them. She kept quiet, watching him avidly. After several minutes, he turned over a page and tried doing the same with a different, random passage.

'No,' he said finally. 'That's the only discernibly Malayalam word I can find. The only other one that comes close is "yraid" which could be a really weird spelling for the Muslim name "Raheed".' He paused, releasing a frustrated breath. 'But I don't think so.'

'Maybe they're all old-fashioned terms?' Sathi asked plaintively, knowing she was grasping at straws.

The sympathetic look Zakiy gave her was enough of an answer. Then his trademark grin made a re-appearance. 'Even if the Malayalam thing was a dead end, I did notice something else. Two words are repeated a lot: "najn" and "edoc". The first one's there in other entries too. They're probably words like "the" and "is" in English, so if we can crack them then we'll be able to decode the rest.'

She could only stare at him in astonishment.

'What?' he asked self-consciously.

'That was kind of awesome. I didn't realise I was dealing with a decoding guru.'

Instead of crowing over the praise like she'd expected him to, Zakiy flushed and ducked his head. 'Anyway, let's write out these two words in big letters and see if they make more sense that way.'

Once they'd done just that, they got comfortable and prepared to invest some serious time getting intimate with their chosen word. After half an hour of staring at "najn" with no progress, Sathi sat up. 'That's it. Let's swap – unless you've managed to come up with something?'

At some point Zakiy had managed to suspend himself upside down from the sofa. His hair brushed the floor as he craned his neck to look at her. 'Nope. Unless you think it could be "e-doc" – as in "electronic document"?'

Sathi grimaced. 'Probably not.'

'Ah well,' he sighed, righting himself and climbing to his feet. He held out his paper, and she tried to hand him hers, but he shook his head. 'That's the best I can do on an empty stomach. I'll see if I can scourge some of those fritters for us.'

She waved him off and stretched, trying to work out the kinks in her own body. In the process she ended up with her feet over the cushions of the sofa, so that she was horizontal from head to waist and vertical the rest of the way.

Ouch. Wincing, she took a leaf out of Zakiy's book and twisted so her head dangled over the floor and allowed the paper with edoc written on it to flop over her face and block out the glare of the bright overhead light. Huh. This position was surprisingly comfortable.

As she stared at the word, half-asleep, it hit her. 'Zakiy!' she yelled. Her voice was slightly strangled because of the strange angle she had twisted her neck into.

He appeared at the door, mouth stuffed with fried fruit. 'What? I didn't do it!'

Sathi filed his guilty conscience away for later perusal – she had more pressing matters to deal with. 'It's code!'

Zakiy frowned. 'Well yeah,' he said slowly, as though worried that blood flow to her brain had ceased. 'I thought we'd established that.'

'No, no,' she said impatiently, waving the paper at him. 'It's the word "code" written right to left!'

He stared at her blankly for a moment, then gasped and snatched the other paper. 'Njan!' he yelled triumphantly. 'The Malayalam word for "I" or "me".'

Sathi lunged for her mother's diary, turning the pages to the first entry that was written in code. Reading from right to left, the Malayalam words written in English made perfect sense:

Ive decided Im going to write in code from now on I always thought keeping a diary was stupid I mean why would you willingly write down all your personal thoughts for everyone to see and so my code Im quite proud of it actually only I havent got anything special to write about today so ciao

Eyes shining, Sathi looked up to see Zakiy grinning down at her. 'You did it,' he said, voice bursting with pride.

'We did it,' she corrected, hugging her mother's diary – now open to her with its secrets – to her chest. 'You're the best best friend in the world.'

A shadow passed through his eyes, and he walked forward to rest a hand on her shoulder. 'Always,' he promised as he held her gaze.

Chapter Three

Truth at Last

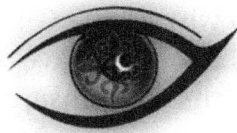

3rd January 1995

3   I don't know what to do. I feel like I'm trapped in a nightmare from which I can never wake up. Devi, what am I going to do?

I need to calm down. There's no one I can tell; no one I can trust, not anymore. Vidhya's the only one... but how can I possibly tell her? No! I can't tell, not her, not anyone. All I can do it write it all down, maybe then I'll know what to do. But I need to start from the beginning. It's the only way.

Okay. Okay. Today I went over to Vidhya's house to ask her if she had my green shawl, because I couldn't find it anywhere and wanted to pack it before going back to Thiruvananthapuram tomorrow. But when I got there the door to her house was open, and no one seemed to be around.

I walked in and was about to call out Vidhya's name when Girish suddenly rushed out from the kitchen. I called out to him in surprise, but he didn't seem to hear or see me as he ran past me and out of the house, tucking something into his pocket.

Wondering what was up with him, I followed him outside, but by then he'd climbed onto his bike and was halfway up the street. There was no way I could catch up with him now. Puzzled, I went back in the house and into the kitchen. It was empty except for an almost drained cup of tea.

I heard Vidhya's brother then, whistling as the shower turned on, and realised that Vijay must have made Girish a cup of tea before going for a shower. Though why hadn't Girish seen or heard me as he left? That was weird. I was about to leave, thinking I'd see if Vidhya was with Jay (those love birds were inseparable nowadays), when I suddenly heard Vijay cry out in pain and something clattering to the floor.

I rushed to the bathroom. 'Vijay, are you okay?' I shouted through the door, my hand hesitating on the handle.

'Help!' he rasped from inside, and that was all the invitation I needed. I threw open the door, and just managed to catch Vijay as the death grip he had on the edge of the sink failed. I lowered him gently onto the floor. He groaned, clutching his chest. He didn't seem to be bleeding, and I realised the pain had to be internal.

'Hang on,' I told him, pushing down my panic, and ran out to the landing and phoned for an ambulance. Then I called Jay's number, mentally crossing my fingers, and thank Devi, Vidhya answered. 'Vidhya! It's Madhu. Come home quickly, I think Vijay's having a heart attack.'

Then it was just a matter of waiting and trying to soothe Vijay until the ambulance came. Vidhya and Jay rushed up just as they were carrying Vijay into the ambulance, and the three of us climbed in after him. Vidhya's mum and little sisters met us at the hospital as Vijay was rushed inside.

The next few hours were horrible. I couldn't seem to make my limbs work, and Vidhya sat silent and unmoving as her sisters sobbed in her lap. When it seemed like we would be staying the night at the hospital, I said I would get something to eat for the family and collect a change of clothes.

Jay stood up and offered to come with me, but I waved him away, knowing Vidhya would feel better with him around. I wanted to be alone, anyway.

I went back to Vidhya's house and, refusing pointedly to look at the gaping bathroom door, started methodically putting together a bag of clothes. I packed some toiletries as well and I was headed to the door when the landline rang.

Dropping everything, I ran into the kitchen and pressed the receiver to my ear. 'Hello?' I said breathlessly.

My best friend's voice sounded like a stranger's when she spoke. 'He's gone.'

I dropped the phone in shock, and it rammed into the kitchen counter as I pressed a hand to my mouth. A sob exploded from my chest as I thought of Vijay, who'd always said he had four sisters, not three, because he included me in that count. His unshakeable patience and comforting presence had been a constant fixture in my life for as long as I could remember. He couldn't be gone... someone so uniquely kind could not have been taken by something as common as a heart attack.

Tears overflowed from my eyes, and I dropped into a chair before my knees gave out. As I did, my hand touched something cold. It was the teacup I had seen earlier when Girish had rushed out...

The breath hitched in my throat as I suddenly remembered that Girish was supposed to be in Nemmara today. Aunt had told me yesterday that he had to attend a training session and would leave early in the morning.

So, what had he been doing in Vidhya's house?

Now that I'd started thinking, I couldn't seem to stop. I remembered how Girish had left without seeing or hearing me - or pretending not to have seen or heard me. I remembered Vijay leaving our house yesterday looking upset about something. I remembered the raised voices I'd heard from the living room between Aunt and Uncle and Vijay. I remembered the menacing look Girish had given Vijay when he stormed out after the argument...

My eyes flicked to the teacup again. I remembered how Girish had rushed out earlier, tucking something into his pocket... Vijay had only gone to have a shower after I'd seen Girish run out.

It was possible that while I was outside Vijay had gone into the kitchen to drink his tea. I knew he liked to drink it in one long pull once it was almost stone-cold. I'd thought Vijay had made the tea for Girish and then gone to have a shower. But what if he'd made it for himself and then left it in the kitchen to cool while he got ready for his shower?

What if Girish hadn't been drinking the tea, but putting something in it before Vijay drank it...?

No, no, no! I pushed my hands into my hair, shaking my head back and forth; what was I thinking? Just a heart attack, I told myself. It was just a heart attack. No one could've known. Nothing could've been done.

But no matter how I tried to convince myself, my gaze kept getting drawn to the remaining dregs of tea in the cup. My mind flashed back to one of my lectures, where I'd learnt that certain plants and minerals could be both toxic and medicinal.

Specifically, I remembered that the medication given to heart patients could themselves cause heart attacks if given in a high enough dose.

I got up on shaky legs and got a small plastic bottle from a cupboard. Then I poured the dregs in the cup into the vial, screwing the lid on tight. I clutched it in my hand, determination filling me. Even if I was reading into nothing, even if I was making a mountain out of a molehill, I had to find out for sure. For Vijay's sake.

10th January 1995

I haven't told Vidhya anything about my suspicions. I didn't tell her even when she said she was dropping out of college to get a job. Her mother couldn't afford to pay for her master's degree now, and someone needed to look after her younger sisters. They were still at school after all. They're going to sell up the house in Nelliampathi and move to Palakkad, where Vidhya and her mother would try and find jobs to keep the family afloat. I thought maybe Uncle would offer Vijay's old job to Vidhya but he didn't. I couldn't bring myself to ask him why not.

I managed to keep my emotions under control while we said goodbye, though all I wanted to do was burst into tears and beg her not to go. If only Nakul wasn't so far away! Now I'm back at college, studying for finals. The only way I can help Vidhya and her family is to figure out what's in that vial, and I know just the way to do it - I'm going to sneak into the chemistry labs at night until I find out.

20th May 1995

I was right. God, how I wish I wasn't, but I was right. It took me months to figure it out, but the tea Vijay drank just before he died had traces of nightshade in it – a lethal plant. I've done every test I can think of, and even got my professor to confirm it. (He was curious about why I was looking at it, but I fobbed him off with some nonsense about a side project.)

I can deny it no longer. Girish killed Vijay... murdered him. I just can't believe it. Why would he do something so coldblooded? How could he?

The argument I overheard between Vijay and my aunt and uncle keeps going through my head, relentless. I haven't even been able to bring myself to go home since Vijay died. I made excuses to stay during weekends and holidays, claiming extra coursework or that I felt too tired to travel with baby he-she on the way. I'd invested that time into finding out the truth about Vijay's death.

But now I know what and who had killed him; but not why. And though it fills me with dread to think of it, I know there's only one sure way to find out the answers to my questions.

I need to talk to my aunt and uncle.

24rd May 1995

As I psyched myself up to ring the doorbell, I rested a hand on my swollen belly and imagined that my little sweetheart was lending me strength.

He-she had been doing that a lot lately; what with Nakul in London and Vidhya gone, my only comfort has been the thought that no matter what happened I could never be truly alone – not with he-she inside my womb. I could face anything as long as my baby was with me.

Determinedly, I reached out and pressed the bell. Uncle opened the door, and his face broke into a smile as soon as he saw me. He held out his arms. Making myself smile back, I stepped into his embrace briefly but couldn't let myself be comforted as I normally would – not when I was about to turn his and Aunt's world upside down. I pulled back to see Aunt walk in; she smiled in greeting but didn't make any move to hug me – she'd never really been the touchy-feely type.

I was relieved to note that they were alone in the house; Girish wasn't there, thank God. After we all sat down and exchanged the necessary small talk, I took the plunge and asked about Girish.

'He's fine, enjoying himself at medical school. He said he will come home on Friday.' Uncle paused. 'We weren't expecting you so early in the week, molé. Though of course we're happy to see you!'

He laughed, but for some reason it sounded off to me, forced, as though he had some inkling of why I had turned up unexpectedly in the middle of the week. But it seemed he didn't want to tip his hand too early. The idea chilled me, but I forced myself to push forward into the real reason for my visit. 'I took permission to come home early because I wanted to talk to the two of you in private.'

A flash of something – trepidation? – passed through Aunt's eyes, and she looked to Uncle for guidance. He didn't look at her, schooling his expression into polite concern as he waited for me to continue. 'Did you know Girish was here in Nelliampathi when he should have been at that training thing in Nemmara a few months ago?' I asked.

'What?' Aunt asked. 'Of course he wasn't!'

'He was,' I insisted. 'I saw him.'

'Where did you see him, Madhu?' Uncle asked quietly, cutting across Aunt, who'd clearly been about to argue further.

I swallowed. 'I saw him leaving Vijay's house – the day Vijay died.'

'So? Maybe he had to come back for something, and then left to go to Nemmara.'

I shook my head. 'You don't understand. Girish... he put something in Vijay's tea. That's what caused the heart attack. That's why he died.'

Aunt rushed to her feet. 'Madhu, what rubbish!' she shouted. 'How dare you say such things? How dare you accuse Girish of something like that?'

'I'm not accusing anyone. I'm just telling you what I saw.'

Uncle fixed me with a shrewd gaze. 'But did you actually see Girish putting something in Vijay's tea?'

I hesitated. 'I... no, not really.'

Aunt scoffed.

'But I saw Girish run out of the house and he acted like he didn't see me when I called out to him. I went in the kitchen and there was a cup of tea there and when I tested it in the lab I found nightshade in it. That's what caused Vijay's heart attack, I'm sure of it!'

Uncle's expression had not changed. 'But molé, why would Girish do something like this? He had no reason to wish harm on Vijay.'

'What about that argument you had with Vijay a week before his death?'

For the first time Uncle looked wrong-footed, almost panicked. But he recovered his composure almost instantly. 'Oh that. That was nothing, molé – just a simple disagreement.'

I shook my head stiffly. 'It was more than that. I saw Vijay leave – he was nearly in tears, and Girish almost seemed like he was threatening him.'

'What nonsense!' Aunt spat out. 'The devil has obviously gotten into you, otherwise you wouldn't say things like this.'

'Whether that's true or not, you'll have to tell the police why you and Vijay fought when they come to take your statement,' I said calmly.

'The police?' Aunt repeated, her anger suddenly draining into numb disbelief.

'Yes. That's why I came here today. I wanted to let you both know before I go to the police and tell them what I know.'

'You ungrateful little worm! After all we've done for you, after we took you in when your insolent parents snuffed themselves... After we fed and clothed you for all these years, is this how you pay us back? By getting our son arrested?'

Tears sprang to my eyes, and my voice broke as I answered her. 'I never wanted to hurt either of you, you know that. I love you both, and I love Girish too. But if he did this, if he killed Vijay, then he needs to be held accountable for his actions.'

36

'You worthless cow! How dare you? How dare you say such things about my son?' Aunt looked like she was going to lunge towards me, but Uncle held her back with a sharp look.

'Molé, I'm sorry,' he said, sadness breaking out over his expression. 'We should have told you the truth from the beginning. We didn't want to worry you unnecessarily, and anyway we never thought for a wild moment that things would turn out like this.'

I took a deep breath. 'What happened?'

Uncle fixed his sorrowful eyes on me. 'We asked Vijay to come speak to us before he joined work that day because we heard he had got involved with some girl from his village, who then committed suicide. We wanted him to clear his side, but he just got angry when we pressed him on the subject and refused to say anything about it. He even started shouting and threatening us – that's when Girish became angry. You know how he is – he won't hear a word against either of us.'

That was true. There had been many cases of broken noses when Girish was growing up, and all those fights had started because someone insulted Aunt or Uncle. Girish had always been extremely protective when it came to them.

'Finally, we had no choice but fire Vijay. That only made him more abusive, and Girish had to almost bodily throw him out in the end. That was the last we saw of him until we heard that he'd died.' Uncle hung his head. 'We thought it was just a heart attack. We didn't dream that Girish would...'

My head was spinning. So, this was why Girish had taken matters into his own hands. He had felt like Vijay was a threat to his parents. But what Uncle had said about Vijay being involved with a girl and then threatening Uncle and Aunt seemed impossible to me – it didn't make sense when I thought of what I'd known of his character. Yet why else would Girish do such a thing?

'Why didn't you say something earlier? Why didn't you stop him?' I demanded, wishing I'd known, wishing I'd been able to stop Girish before he did something so horrible, so unforgivable.

Uncle didn't meet my eyes. 'I'm sorry. We didn't know. We couldn't have even guessed...'

I forced myself to regain control. There was no point in casting blame. And now that I knew the reason for Girish's actions, it seemed even more important that I go to the police. Girish needed help; he needed to understand he couldn't go around hurting people who said things he didn't like. He had to be stopped.

I stood. 'Thank you for telling me this,' I told Uncle. Aunt was still glaring at me balefully, but I made myself give them both a weak smile. 'I'll tell the police everything, and hopefully they'll be more understanding. They'll understand that he didn't mean to do it.'

Even as I said it, though, doubts plagued me. If Girish hadn't meant it, would he have lied in wait to pour poison into Vijay's cup? I shook off the thought – that was for the police to decide, not me.

'You mean you are still going to the police?' Uncle's stunned voice cut through my thoughts.

I looked up at him. 'Of course. He needs help, Uncle. He can't go around killing everyone who insults you or Aunt.'

'You would have him locked away? Your own cousin?'

'No one has the right to take a life!' I burst out, my heart breaking at the expression on Uncle's face. A face that could have belonged to a stranger at the moment. 'No one.'

'His life would be ruined. His career as a doctor would be over.'

'How can he become a doctor after what he's done? What he's done goes against every principle of that profession!'

Uncle's voice was suddenly as cold and hard as his expression. 'Your mind is made up?'

I wanted to sob. I pressed my hand against my stomach, against my baby. Everything will be fine, I thought, half to myself and half to little he-she. Everything will be fine as long as I have you.

38

I willed the words to be true.

'Yes,' I told Uncle. 'I can't have this on my conscience. I'm going to report Girish, whether you like it or not – and if you truly want what's best for him, you'll cooperate with the police.'

With those words I turned and left, walking so quickly that I was only one step away from running. When I reached the end of the driveway, though, I had to slow down because a splitting headache suddenly burst from the middle of my forehead. I stopped and clamped my hands over my eyes, willing my head to stop spinning. When I opened my eyes, everything was blurred, the green of the trees merging sickeningly with the sandy mud. On top of the headache, a sharp pain stabbed below my ribs, and I hunched over, gasping.

This wasn't just a migraine – this was serious. Panic-stricken, I stumbled forward out into the road just as a couple got out of an idling autorickshaw. Gratefully, I collapsed into the empty seat and begged the driver to take me to a hospital.

Pre-eclampsia. Apparently, that's what it was. The doctor said something about "high blood pressure" and "common in first pregnancy" but I was too out of it to care too much about the details. At least he-she was fine. I don't want to think about what might have happened if the autorickshaw driver hadn't got me to the hospital as quickly as he had.

Nakul was worried sick, of course, and said he would get on a flight immediately, but I managed to convince him not to come yet – I'd rather he saved his leave for when he-she is due. But that's not the problem; the doctor is saying that I have to stay in hospital until delivery because of the pre-eclampsia – it's risky for the baby otherwise. But that means I won't be able to go to the police about Girish for another few months. How can I keep quiet about Vijay's murder for that long?

At the same time, how can I do anything that might hurt my baby – my little he-she, who was completely dependent on me for life?

No matter how much I wanted justice for Vijay, I know I will have to put he-she first on my list of priorities. At least until my baby is strong enough to survive without me.

6th June 1995

I can't believe I lived with Aunt and Uncle for so many years – for most of my life – without realising how cruel they are. They came today under the pretence of making sure I was okay, but all they wanted to do was argue Girish's case and try to persuade me against going to the police.

When they first came the two of them acted all contrite, but their colours changed quickly – or perhaps they just showed their colours more quickly this time now that I've seen what they're really like. It makes me ashamed to call them my family.

I can't help feeling a bit unsettled, though, to think of how they smiled when I finally asked them to leave. They gave up too quickly – like they're planning something, though I have no idea what. I felt so uneasy that I succumbed to temptation and sent Nakul a letter asking him to come back early. It's not just because of Aunt and Uncle. I feel like he-she is going to come early, no matter what the doctor says. And I want Nakul to be here – I don't want to go through this alone. He needs to be here with me, with us.

I did something else I vowed never to do; I contacted Vidhya and asked her to visit me. I know how dangerous it would be for her to come here, to this hospital, where she might run into one of my relatives at any time. Anika is here almost constantly, because she is the one who helps me to shower, and Karan brings food for us every day. But something inside me is telling me I need to see Vidhya – and

40

give her this diary. I don't know why, but I can only assume it is Devi guiding my thoughts.

This is my last diary entry. I have an idea that will make it safe for Vidhya to come here undetected, and once I see her, I know I will feel better. I'll give her the diary, but I won't tell her about Girish and Vijay until I'm sure I can get justice for her brother.

Until then, there's no one I trust more to keep this diary safe.

Chapter Four

Missing Link

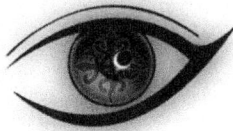

S athi looked up from her mother's parting words, her heart feeling like it had metamorphosed into stone. She let the papers that were the decoded diary entries float to the floor and clenched her fists in her lap, trying to block out the pain. How could what felt like a piece of granite cause such agony in the middle of her chest?

A warm hand closed around hers, forcing her fists to loosen. Zakiy's fingers threaded though hers, and it was like the cold pain encasing her heart softened and fissured apart, and tears began to course down her cheeks.

Zakiy slid closer to her, and she turned her face into his shoulder, sobbing now. He let her cry without saying anything, just holding her and making sure she knew she wasn't alone.

That was the point at which her father burst into the room.

The two of them glanced up into his fuming, almost manic expression as he stared down at them. Glared might be a better description, and it wasn't difficult to figure out what held his attention. Zakiy quickly withdrew his hand from Sathi's, and she shuffled a few inches away from him.

'Hi Dad,' she muttered sheepishly, trying to dry her tears inconspicuously.

Dad took a double take at her puffy eyes, and if possible, became even more enraged. He turned on Zakiy. 'What have you done?' he thundered. 'If you hurt my daughter, I swear to God I'll–'

'Dad!' she interrupted, mortified. 'Zakiy didn't make me cry.'

He paused and glanced at her. 'Then? Why are you–' He went as still as stone as his gaze caught on the small black book on the floor in front of her. 'That's... Is that...?'

'It's Amma's diary,' Sathi confirmed in a voice thick with tears.

His face blank with shock, her father dropped to his knees and gathered the diary in his hands. 'I thought I'd lost it,' he whispered, his voice breaking. Tears were running down his cheeks now.

Sathi moved closer and put her arms around his shaking shoulders, and he held on to her like he would drown if he let go. It felt strange to be reassuring him like this; she'd always been intimidated by her father, partly because she'd thought he hated her for being the cause of his wife's death.

Now she knew that his hatred had been directed inward, but it was hard to shake the memory of how her dad's anger used to make her crumble on the inside. Now she was the one holding him up.

Sathi glanced up and caught sight of Zakiy; his expression was very soft as he gazed at the two of them. Then he saw her looking and beamed at her, his joy on her behalf obvious. The hard lump in her chest seemed to melt a little.

Her father eventually regained control over himself and sat up, seeming embarrassed at his show of emotion. He swiped a hand over his eyes and gave her a watery smile. 'You decoded it?'

'We did,' Sathi corrected, indicating herself and Zakiy. She hesitated. 'That's not all...' They filled him on the heart-breaking truths her mother had uncovered before her death.

As they spoke, the truth sunk into her. Her mother's death had been at the hands of her own family. Her Amma's aunt and uncle had killed her to protect their own son, a teenager who had committed murder out of misguided love.

When Zakiy explained about Vidhya's brother, her father jumped up, eyes wild. 'You mean Vijay? Girish killed Vijay?'

Not waiting for an answer, he grabbed the translated pages out of Sathi's hands and pored over his wife's words. 'No, no, this makes no sense.'

'What? What is it?' Sathi asked,

'Vijay wasn't involved with that girl, the girl who committed suicide. He was a bachelor; he wanted to devote his life to the temple. That girl... I think she was his friend. Madhu said Vijay and her parents fought because of her death. We need to find out more about her.'

Sathi bit her lip; he was right. This girl was the key, but how to find out more about her? If Vidhya had stuck around, they could've asked her, but they had no way of contacting her.

'We could check newspapers?' Zakiy suggested. 'Revisit the Stick-insect?' She shot him a smile at the reference to the local librarian.

'Newspaper...' her father echoed. 'Of course!'

'Dad?'

He ignored her and looked at Zakiy. 'You have a car?'

Zakiy looked half-petrified and half-indignant. 'Yes, sir. Well, I have my Jeep.'

'Come on, then.'

Without waiting for either of them, he marched out. Exchanging perplexed looks, they scampered after him to see that he had got into the front seat of Zakiy's Jeep and was waiting impatiently.

44

As Zakiy started the engine, Sathi leaned forward into the space between the seats to get her father's attention. 'Dad, what's going on?'

'Madhu gave me some papers before she left to come to India after you were born. She wouldn't tell me why, but she made me promise to always keep them safe. I brought them with me. Maybe they hold the answers to your questions.'

That was all he'd say until they reached the treehouse-slash-cottage her mother had designed. Dad got out of the Jeep without a word and rushed up the stairs, unlocking the door and leaving it open for them as Zakiy hastily parked. When they found him in his bedroom, her father had his suitcase open on the middle of the floor and was haphazardly throwing things out as he searched.

Zakiy ducked to avoid an UFO just as her father yanked out a thick blue folder. He took out some yellowed sheets that were obviously from old newspapers; Sathi craned her neck to try and see the year, but Dad was feverishly looking through the papers and she couldn't make it out. She met Zakiy's puzzled look with a shrug of her own.

'There!' Dad exclaimed, thrusting the paper into her hand, and pointing to a small section. She barely registered Zakiy moving close so he could read over her shoulder as she scanned the short article. Confused, she looked up at her father. 'This is an obituary... it says a girl called Meera Ramesh committed suicide...'

She trailed off as she saw the date and realised the significance. 'This is the girl. Vijay's friend.'

Dad nodded. 'Exactly. Now I understand why your mother gave me this. On its own it's not significant but-'

'When you combine it with her diary it starts to make sense,' Sathi finished.

'But why didn't she give me the diary? I looked for it everywhere after-' Dad broke off, his eyes welling with tears for the second time.

She moved to slip her arm around his waist and squeezed. Again, she felt the odd sense of role reversal as she comforted him. 'I think she was trying to protect you,' she told him, following her gut. 'She didn't want you to get hurt, so she made sure you only had part of the story.'

As she spoke the words, another truth occurred to her. Her eyes met Zakiy's again as he echoed her thoughts. 'She also made sure Vidhya only had part of the story. Actually, she had less than that because Vidhya didn't know her code. She was protecting both of you.'

'She was telling the truth. Vidhya didn't kill Amma.' The staggering relief Sathi felt was mingled with sorrow that she would probably never see her friend again. She wished for the hundredth time that Vidhya had tried to convince her of the truth instead of leaving her with nothing but a letter and more questions.

'We need to talk to someone who knew this girl,' Zakiy was saying, leafing through the newspaper. 'This says she committed suicide, just like the diary, but it doesn't say why-' he broke off. 'Sathi, look at this,' he said urgently.

She quickly read through the article he was pointing at, which described a community wedding in which a hundred couples were married at the same time. The costs of the wedding had been borne by a charity – the charity owned by her great-uncle.

'This can't be a coincidence,' she said, looking up.

'It's not,' Zakiy said. 'This article isn't even part of the same newspaper. Your mum took them from different days and put them together.'

'Why?' Dad asked.

Sathi felt the sick feeling in her stomach intensify. 'Because Meera's suicide is linked to Bhaskar somehow. That's why Vijay was killed. He knew the truth behind her death.'

The man who answered the door was obviously surprised at the late-night visitors. 'Yes? Can I help you?'

46

Sathi stepped forward. 'We're really sorry to disturb you so late, but we need to speak with your wife urgently.'

He frowned. 'My wife?'

'Yes sir,' Zakiy said, giving the man his most charming smile. 'Could we come in? We'll be very quick.'

When he still didn't move, Sathi added, 'Please. We just need to ask her some questions.' She took a deep breath. 'It's about her sister.'

'What about my sister?' asked a voice from behind the door, and it opened further to reveal a woman who bore such a striking resemblance to the picture of Meera Ramesh in the obituary that Sathi knew she must be her younger sister, Meena.

'Ma'am, could we come in?' Zakiy asked. 'We just need to talk to you for a few minutes and then we'll be gone.'

Meena's dark eyes regarded them silently for a moment before she nodded and laid a hand on her husband's arm. He reluctantly moved back to let them in.

Once they were seated in the couple's living room with coffee and snacks (uninvited guests or not, Indians took hospitality seriously), Meena asked, 'Why do you want to know about my sister?'

Sathi took a deep breath. 'This is going to sound really strange, but your sister was a friend of a friend of ours.' She had actually been a friend of a friend's brother, but this situation was bizarre enough without adding in that confusing detail. 'We wanted to ask you about her death.'

Meena's husband (who had introduced himself as Babu) frowned. 'She committed suicide.'

Sathi didn't look away from Meena's eyes as she spoke. 'Why?'

'I really don't want to talk about this,' Meena said in a low voice, a tear rolling down her cheek.

Babu moved to put a hand around her shoulders. 'Then you don't have to,' he told her. Still holding her against him, he turned to face them. 'This is a very painful subject for my wife. Please understand.'

'I do understand,' Sathi said softly. 'I lost my mother to the same monsters who took your sister from this world.'

Meena's head jerked up. 'What? No... she killed herself.'

'Maybe, but they're the reason she killed herself.' Zakiy took the newspaper article about the community marriage and put it on the coffee table in front of the couple.

Meena picked it up, looking like she'd seen a ghost. 'No,' she repeated. Tears started pouring down her cheeks, stronger than before.

'Enough. You two need to leave now,' Babu said firmly, trying to take the paper from his wife's hands.

'No!' Meena yelled, yanking it back and crumpling it in her hands. Shocked, Babu stared at his wife. 'Meena?'

'It was my fault!' she sobbed. 'I'm the reason Meera killed herself.'

For a moment there was stunned silence as Meena's shoulders heaved with grief and, Sathi realised, guilt. This woman had carried around guilt about her sister's death for years, and guilt had a way of leaching all the joy out of the world.

Sathi should know; she'd blamed herself bitterly for her mother's death for years before she'd found out that she had been murdered, and not killed in childbirth as she'd been led to believe. Sathi moved to sit on Meena's other side. Hesitantly, she laid a hand on the woman's shoulder. 'You can't blame yourself for her death. It was her choice.'

Meena shook her head. 'You don't understand. She didn't have any choice. She died to protect my father and me. Otherwise, they would've killed all of us.' She took a great shuddering breath and looked at her husband. 'I'm sorry. I should have told you, but I was scared.'

Babu kissed her forehead. 'I know Meera's death hurts you, that's why I didn't ask you anything. But I had no idea that you were blaming yourself.'

48

Meena shut her eyes for a moment, and her lips moved silently as though in prayer. Then she opened them, and her gaze sought out Sathi. 'You said before that they killed your mother. Is that true?'

Her throat suddenly closed off with emotion, Sathi could only nod.

Meena nodded. 'Then I can tell you. You deserve to know the truth.' She clenched her fists in her lap as she spoke. 'Meera and I were always close, especially after our mum left us.' At Sathi's startled look, she smiled sardonically and clarified, 'She's not dead. She left our dad when we were young, and we haven't seen her since.'

'As we grew up, though, our father became more and more worried. He didn't know how he was going to afford to marry us both off.'

Zakiy leaned closer her to explain, 'In India it's the bride's family who have to bear the costs for the wedding. Especially when it's an arranged marriage, and there's dowry involved.'

Not that different to old upper class Western families, Sathi thought, thinking of Father of the Bride.

Meena continued, 'Meera's marriage had really been weighing on my father when he heard that this charity was arranging community weddings for girls in our village.' Seeing Sathi's puzzled expression, she smiled and elaborated, 'The charity receives donations from people, and uses that money to fund a hundred weddings at the same time, usually at a nearby temple. The grooms may also be from poor families, and they weren't allowed to ask for dowry.'

Meena scoffed. 'Of course, we only realised later than they had other ways to extract dowry from the bride's family, except that money wasn't going to the groom.'

'Hold on,' Sathi interrupted, holding her hand up. 'You mean the charity was taking money from the bride's families?'

'Not just money. They told us to write the deed to our house in their name if we wanted Meera's marriage to take place as planned.'

Sathi was speechless. She thought she'd lost the ability to be shocked by the horrible things her mother's family did, but the surprises just kept on coming.

'My father begged them for mercy. If he lost the house, he and I would've had to live on the streets. They didn't care about that, though. They just told us to sign over the documents, otherwise they'd make sure Meera never got married.'

Sathi didn't want to think about how they would accomplish that; virginity was a big concept in India and losing it – whether by choice or force – out of wedlock was a sure way to blackmark a girl and label her as "tainted". She didn't know how much things had changed in the modern day, but it definitely would've been an issue twenty years ago.

'Did you go to the police?' Zakiy asked.

Meena shook her head. 'They threatened us. They said that if we mentioned this to anyone, they would...' She took a shuddering breath. 'They said they would take me away and my father and Meera would never see me again. That's why Meera killed herself that night. Either they would take the house, or me. She didn't see any other choice.' Meena buried her head in her hands, shoulders heaving.

Sathi met Zakiy's eyes, and his expression reflected the same sick feeling in her stomach.

Babu looked between them and his wife in confusion. 'But who are you talking about? Who was threatening you with all this?'

Silence met his question, only interrupted by Meena's occasional sniffs.

'Bhaskar, my great-uncle,' Sathi said finally. She looked to Zakiy for support, and he nodded. She took a deep breath and added, 'My mother saw Meera's friend, Vijay, fighting with Bhaskar. I think it was about Meera, because he suspected that her death had something to do with Bhaskar. He confronted Bhaskar, and that's why Girish killed Vijay.'

'Wait.' Meena looked up. 'Girish? You mean Bhaskar's son?'

50

'Yes.'

'Why?' Babu asked Meena. 'Do you know him?'

'He came with Bhaskar that day, but Bhaskar was the one to do all the threatening. Girish was more like... like a bodyguard.'

'A bodyguard?' Sathi repeated.

'Yes... but he barely seemed like he knew what was going on. I remember my father tried to appeal to him for mercy, but he didn't react at all. It was almost like he'd been drugged.

Chapter Five

Culpabilities

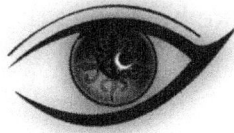

'I still can't believe Girish could kill someone,' Sathi said once they were back in the privacy of the Jeep.

Zakiy frowned. 'But what about your mum's diary? She actually saw Girish in Vijay's house minutes before his death.'

'I know... Girish is very protective of Bhaskar and Goudhamy, though. Maybe they manipulated him into believing that Vijay was a threat.'

He slowly blew out a breath. 'Regardless, what do we do now?'

She chewed on her lip, thinking. 'I have an idea,' she said finally. She glanced at him. 'You're not going to like it, though.'

Sathi waited outside the hospital until she spied him disappearing into his office through the glass doors. She forced herself to count to five before slipping inside and navigating her way through the busy reception area to the office door. She knocked once and took a deep breath before opening the door.

The man standing behind the desk glanced up from some papers and then took a double take as he recognised her. 'Sathi?' he said, staring in shock.

She gave him a small smile, though her eyes hid sorrow. 'Hello, Uncle Girish.'

'What... where did you disappear off to? You didn't say anything to us - you just left!'

She thought back to that horrible night months ago, the night she'd finally realised the truth about her great-aunt and great-uncle. The night she'd seen her aunt – Girish's wife – walk into Great-Uncle's room like a zombie, under the trance of Great-aunt's black magic. If Sathi hadn't seen her, if she hadn't screamed and woken Girish up... Sathi didn't even want to think about what might have happened. No, what would have happened.

Instead, she met Girish's gaze and delivered her prepared explanation. 'I'm sorry about that. I had to leave because a friend of mine needed my help. I ended up going to Mysore for a few days after that.'

Her uncle looked confused, but instead of questioning her further he seemed to accept her words at face value. Sathi's heart sank; his lack of reaction was only cementing her suspicions.

'Right. Erm... well, how are you, Sathi?'

'I'm good. How are you? And Aunt Maya?'

'We're both well, thank you.'

A long awkward silence. 'Can I...' she trailed off and pointed to the chair in front of his desk.

'Oh! Yes, of course, sit down.' He waited until she sat to follow his own advice. He sat fiddling with the papers, avoiding her gaze. In fact, now that they'd covered the basics, he didn't seem to know what to do with himself, or what to say to his long-estranged niece.

Time chuntered along relentlessly. She was trying to figure out how to break the silence again when her uncle unexpectedly blurted, 'You look so much like her.'

Startled, her eyes flicked to his. She was thrown by the unusual level of emotion there. Then she remembered that she wasn't the only one who had lost someone she cared about. Her mother had also been Girish's cousin – his sister.

Holding his gaze steadily, Sathi found the courage to speak. 'Yes, I do. But I never got to meet her.'

Girish's hands began to fiddle with the papers on his desk again. 'Oh... well... Yes, of course... of course you haven't met her. You'd just been born when she...' he trailed off, dropping his eyes from hers.

'When she died, yeah.' For once her throat didn't clog up with pain at those words. 'Do you know how she died?'

'Well... yes. She died giving birth to... I mean, she died in childbirth.'

'No!' Sathi paused to bring her emotions under control. 'No. That's not how she died.'

'What?'

'I said, that's not how my mother died. She was killed by someone trying to cover up a crime.'

She had her uncle's full attention now. 'What? Who?'

'Do you remember Vijay, the servant boy who worked for your father?' she asked instead of answering him.

'Yes, I remember him. He and his little sister worked for us, doing odd jobs around the house and temple.'

'Do you know what happened to them?'

Girish frowned. 'I'm not sure. I think they moved away from Nelliampathi years ago. I was still in school at the time.'

'Vijay didn't move away. He died.'

'What?'

Sathi studied him intently, looking for any sign that her uncle was deceiving her, putting on an utterly believable yet indisputably fake act - like the ones his parents were experts in putting on. But his eyes were guileless, his expression almost blank, like he truly couldn't comprehend the things she was saying.

It was as though the memory of what happened to Vijay was hidden out of reach in the recesses of his mind, and he had no way of accessing it. She hadn't really expected anything else, but the truth still filled her stomach with lead.

She stood up abruptly. 'Nothing. I have to go.'

Her uncle just stared up at her wordlessly. He didn't react as she crossed to the door and slipped through it. Her vision was blurred through the film of tears that covered her eyes, so she didn't immediately recognise the person walking towards her where she stood next to her uncle's office. When she did, she moved quickly, sliding into a nearby alcove just as Aunt Maya reached the door to the office.

As Sathi watched her aunt walk past, she was stunned by how different she looked. Her eyes were fixed ahead with no expression, sunk into her cheeks with deep circles underneath. Her skin was coarser somehow, darker than it used to be, and she walked with her shoulders hunched, stooped like an old woman.

She was pregnant, yet she didn't look like any of the pregnant women Sathi had seen before. Those women had always seemed to glow with happiness, and their soft, rounded bellies only served to enhance their beauty. She'd often watched them greedily, avid with envy and longing as she thought of her own mother.

Maya was different, though. There was no happiness on her once beautiful face, no trace of that vivacious young bride Sathi had known; no sign of the joy of a mother bringing new life into the world. She just looked exhausted, depleted of all energy - like the child growing in her womb was leeching off her own life.

Not caring anymore whether her aunt saw her, Sathi fled to the hospital exit and climbed into the passenger seat of the Jeep idling outside in the ambulance bay. She turned her face to the window, a single tear tracing slowly down her cheek.

When they got back to Zakiy's house, her father was waiting for them at the front door.

Sathi squared her shoulders before getting out of the Jeep, bracing for a lecture. It caught her off guard when they got closer and saw his expression was more apprehensive than angry.

She frowned. 'Dad? What's wrong?'

He glanced at Zakiy before returning his gaze to her. 'Vidhya is back. She wants to talk to you.'

Sathi stared at Dad, disbelieving. She'd thought she had lost the capacity to be shocked by now, but apparently not. When she glanced at Zakiy, he just shrugged, equally surprised.

She let out the breath she'd been holding. 'Alright. Let's go see what she has to say.'

The five of them – Jayaram was there too – ended up in Zakiy's massive dining room, around the huge granite-topped table. Despite sitting facing each other, no one seemed to be able to look at each other.

When the silence was beginning to become unbearable, Vidhya finally looked up. 'Sathi, I'm sorry.'

Sathi kept her face expressionless. 'What for?'

Vidhya clasped her hands on the table in front of her. 'I shouldn't have left the way I did... I should have told you who I was from the beginning, I should've explained...' she trailed off, her voice fading out.

There was a beat of silence. 'Is that why you came back?' she asked, her tone neutral. 'To explain?'

Vidhya looked stricken, as though Sathi had hit her.

Jayaram opened his mouth angrily, but Vidhya silenced him with a shake of her head. 'No, Jay. I deserved that.' She took a deep breath before lifting her eyes to Sathi again. 'No. I came back because I never should have left in the first place. Jay is the one who helped me

56

realise that. I want to help you bring Vijay and Madhu's killer to justice. Girish has gotten away with it for far too long.'

That broke through Sathi's composure. 'You know about Girish?'

'I filled them in while we were waiting for you,' Dad explained.

Sathi exhaled. 'Well, you're wrong about Girish. He didn't kill anyone.'

'What?' Dad twisted in his seat to stare at her. 'Madhu saw him put nightshade in Vijay's drink!'

'I know, but Zakiy and I just went to see him.'

Zakiy shot her a look, but he didn't contradict her.

'You did WHAT?'

Sathi winced. 'I needed to see him, Dad. He doesn't even remember that day.'

'He could've been pretending,' Jayaram said.

She shook her head, frustrated. 'He wasn't, okay? He was like Meena said – like he'd been drugged.'

'Who's Meena?'

Zakiy filled them in while Sathi recalled what she knew of Girish. It was Bhaskar and Goudhamy's black magic controlling Girish's actions, she was sure of it.

Jayaram leaned forward. 'You think its Bhaskar and his wife who are behind all this.'

It wasn't a question, but Sathi nodded.

'What are you going to do?'

Sathi thought over all that those two had done. They'd extorted money and property from people who couldn't afford to get their children married. They'd caused the death of a girl who had committed suicide because she didn't want her dad and little sister to lose their home.

Then there were the more personal grievances. Her eyes rested on Vidhya, who had lost her brother to their evil. Next to her was Jayaram, looking at her with his eyebrows raised as he waited for an answer. He had lost his best friend and the girl he loved – something

57

he'd never really recovered from, judging by his general bitterness towards life.

Then there was her father... Amma had been everything to him, and her death had punched a hole in his heart that not even his own daughter could fill. A daughter who had lost both her parents – one to death, and the other to grief.

Finally, her eyes rested on Zakiy. As far as she was concerned, his loss had been the most severe. His entire life had been shadowed by his brother's illness, an illness brought about by spite and small-mindedness.

Five people. Five people whose lives had been ruined, all because of greed and envy, lust and pride.

'I'm going to kill them,' she vowed.

Jayaram scoffed. 'Great idea. Then you can go to jail and be labelled as the lunatic who murdered her own grandparents.'

'They're not my grandparents,' she gritted out through clenched teeth.

Jayaram ignored her. 'Is that what you want? To rot in jail for the rest of your life, while they're named martyrs?'

She glared at him, fists clenched. 'I don't care! They killed my mum. They killed your best friend.'

'Exactly! Death is too light a punishment for people like them. They need to suffer first.'

Her heart thudded in her chest, thinking of the torture chamber she'd planned to build for her mother's killers. 'What makes you think I won't make them suffer first?' she asked in a cold, emotionless voice.

She could feel more than one shocked set of eyes on her, but she kept her gaze focused on Jayaram. His opinion of her was the one that mattered least.

Jayaram gave a mirthless smile. 'Now you're back to lunatic land. I didn't mean that kind of suffering.'

'Well, what do you suggest?' she demanded, throwing her hands up. 'Ask them nicely not to do it again?'

Jayaram grinned, and the effect was like a light going on behind a Halloween mask; disturbing to say the least. He really needed to lose the whole homeless bearded man appearance. 'Actually, I suggest the opposite.'

He pulled out a stack of newspapers from his bag and threw them on the table. Sathi immediately recognised them as old articles about Bhaskar.

'Everyone thinks they're such good people – they make sure they don't leave behind any evidence of their evil. We need to rip away their masks and show the public what they really are. Then you can torture and kill them, if that's what you want. But I guarantee you, this is a more fitting punishment for them.'

Jayaram's declaration left behind a stunned silence.

Unexpectedly, it was her father who broke it. 'We're going to make the snake that bit us extract its own venom from the wound.' Seeing her confused expression, he explained, 'It means we're going to make sure they're responsible for their own downfall.'

Jayaram nodded. 'Exactly. We're going to hit them where it hurts the most. Their pride.'

PART TWO

Chapter Six

Unmasked

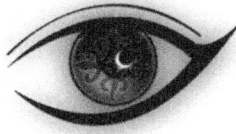

A re you sure this is a good idea?' Sathi murmured to Vidhya.
Vidhya gently pulled Sathi's fingers away from where they
were picking at a scab on her knee.

'Relax. Jay knows what he's doing.' She reconsidered. 'Most of the
time, anyway.'

Sathi chuckled, but it was a nervous sound. 'That doesn't really –'
She broke off and lunged for the TV remote. 'This is it!'

Sathi turned up the volume so they could hear the new reporter as
she was saying, 'Breaking news. Dowry scam exposed as famous
philanthropist caught red-handed on camera. Investigative
journalist Susan Roy used hidden cameras to film Bhaskar
Pushkaran, founding member of local NGO Ashraya, threatening the
bride's family for money just days before the annual community
marriage ceremony. Ashraya is renowned for conducting marriages
for free, but today's shocking revelation suggests that its founder is

not so altruistic as he seems. We have Susan Roy here with us to tell us more. Welcome, Susan.'

The camera panned to show a woman with a pixie cut and glasses, wearing a dark grey churidar. 'Thank you, Preethi.'

'So, can you tell us more about this dowry scandal?'

'Of course. I've been investigating these kinds of scams that can unfortunately go disguised as charity, and I received a tip that Bhaskar may be involved in something nefarious. One of the girls who was supposed to get married in the community wedding on Thursday contacted me and told me she was being threatened by Bhaskar. I immediately went over to her house and set up hidden cameras and microphones to record the negotiation.'

The reporter picked up a USB. 'This is a copy of the recording that you kindly provided us with. It is a conversation between Bhaskar and the girl who contacted you, correct?'

'Yes, that's right.'

'Good.' Preethi turned to face the camera. 'Now we will play a clip of the recording that Susan acquired.'

The screen went completely black for a second before Bhaskar's calculating expression appeared. 'So, do you have the money ready?'

A girl's voice sounded off-screen. 'Sir, please, I beg you. We don't have that kind of money.'

'Well, I'm sure we can figure something out, molé, don't worry.'

Sathi cringed at hearing that smothering endearment again, nausea rising at the slippery, snake-like quality of his voice.

Bhaskar looked around appreciatively. 'What about this house? You won't need it once you're married, will you? Write the deed in my name, and I will make sure your marriage goes ahead as planned. Otherwise...' he trailed off, and the screen froze on his menacing expression.

Sathi switched off the TV. Despite the sick feeling induced by seeing Bhaskar, she felt her lips spread in a wide grin.

She tuned to face Vidhya. 'Jayaram did it. He actually did it!'

Vidhya's eyes were shining. 'I can't believe it. Bhaskar is finally starting to pay for what his crimes.'

Sathi was about to respond when they heard a car screeching to a halt outside. Moments later, her father, Zakiy and Jayaram piled into the room, beaming.

'You did it!' Sathi exclaimed, not knowing who to hug first. She settled for squeezing in between Dad and Zakiy and giving them both half hugs simultaneously. She even grinned at Jayaram, who had gone straight to Vidhya's side and stood so that their arms touched.

'All thanks to Jay here,' Dad replied, affectionately squeezing her back.

Jayaram looked pleased at the appreciation. 'That journalist, Susan Roy, was my college classmate. She's the one who set everything up.'

'But you're the one who talked her into it,' Zakiy countered, walking over to clap him on the back. 'You also talked the news channel into running this story today, even though the Great-Villain has a lot of political clout and would be extremely pissed off at them.'

Sathi met Jayaram's eyes. 'Thank you,' she said quietly. She looked around so that her gaze included everyone in. 'All of you. You have no idea what your support means to me.'

Her father rubbed her back. 'That's what family is for. And now our family has expanded.'

She smiled and nodded, her eyes filling with happy tears for once.

'Plus,' Jayaram interjected, 'I'm only just getting started.'

Sathi agreed completely; yes, this was a good start, but it was in no way enough punishment for those who'd destroyed the lives of so many people.

'So, what's our next step?' Zakiy asked.

There was a pause.

'I'm not sure,' Sathi admitted. 'It's one thing to expose his greed; how do we expose what he's done to Aman? Or Vijay and Amma's murders? We don't know what Amma did with those chemicals she was testing. You're sure she didn't give it to you, right?' she asked Vidhya again.

'I'm sorry, no.' Vidhya shook her head sadly. 'She only gave me the diary.'

Unfortunately, that made sense; her mother had wanted to protect Vidhya and giving her the key evidence that proved her family's guilt would have put Vidhya in a lot of danger.

'Where did she leave it?' Sathi wondered aloud.

Her father cleared his throat. 'She might not have left it.'

Sathi frowned at him, confused. 'She might not have had the chance to save it,' he added gently, his eyes filling with pain.

With a jolt, she understood. Amma had probably died because of that crucial evidence; it's destruction had necessitated her death as well.

Sathi rolled her shoulders as she walked, trying to relieve the tension that always found its way between her shoulder blades. Her shift at the resort had been hectic, with barely a moment to rest all day, and she was knackered.

She had managed to convince her father to let her spend the night at the campsite. She missed building a campfire and drinking cocoa with Zakiy. She'd also missed hanging out with just him; it felt like ages since they'd really spent time together alone.

She could soon see the glow of the campfire Zakiy had got ready for her, and her steps quickened. As she got closer, she saw Zakiy sitting in front of the fire with a book in one hand and a cup of cocoa in the other. There was another cup on the ground next to him.

Sighing in happiness, Sathi plopped down next to him. She picked up her cocoa and leaned her head against his shoulder. Zakiy stiffened for a moment before relaxing. He shut the book and half turned towards her. 'Hello. I didn't hear you coming.'

'That's because you're deaf,' she retorted sleepily, eyes closed as she sipped her drink. She smiled. As usual, it was perfect.

'You're welcome.'

'Huh?' She opened one eye to see him smirking down at her.

'Well, I assume you meant to thank me for making you cocoa instead of being rude.'

'Yeah, yeah, whatever. It's not even that good,' she lied, hiding a grin. For a while Zakiy had been acting kind of weird with her, and it was a relief to have things back to normal again.

'What are you reading?' she asked before he could think of a comeback.

'A book of fairy tales.' Sathi was about to ask him if he wasn't a bit too old for that when he added, 'Your dad threw it at me.'

'Huh?' She turned to stare at him.

He shrugged. 'That day when he was looking for the newspaper articles your mother gave him – he was throwing things out of his suitcase, remember?'

She took the book from him and turned it over to see the title. 'Oh yeah... but how did this get in his suitcase? I'm pretty sure it was on my bookshelf in London with all my other books.'

'Your dad probably packed it by accident.'

'I guess,' she said, though she still thought it was weird.

'What is it?' Zakiy asked. 'There's something about this book that bothers you.'

Buying time, Sathi opened the book to the page that marked the beginning of the short Cherokee story named "Wolves Within".

An old Cherokee told his grandson, 'My son, there is a fierce battle between two great wolves within us all. One is Evil; he is anger, envy, sorrow, regret, greed, arrogance, self-pity, guilt, resentment, inferiority, lies, false pride, superiority and ego. The other wolf is Good; he is joy, peace, love, hope, serenity, humility, kindness, benevolence, empathy, generosity, truth, compassion and faith.'

The boy thought about what his grandfather had said for a moment, and then asked innocently, 'Grandfather, which wolf wins?'

The old man smiled and replied quietly, 'The one you nurture.'

'Unbelievable,' she muttered.

'What?' Zakiy asked, his tone worried now.

'Look at this,' she commanded, pushing the book at him.

He quickly scanned the page and then looked back up at her. 'What about it?'

'I dreamt about this book when I stayed at the G-Vs house, the night I left that place. The wording of the story was a bit different in my dream, though.'

'Different how?'

'It had the seven deadly sins listed as the attributes of the evil wolf. You know, anger, greed, pride, gluttony, lust, envy and... and...'

'Sloth,' he supplied.

'Yeah, sloth exactly. But none of the versions I looked at online have that. They have something similar to what's in this book. I thought the reason I dreamt the seven sins version is because that's what was in my book, but I guess I was wrong.'

Zakiy turned the book over in his hands. 'Maybe you're misremembering your dream?'

She shook her head emphatically. 'No, I'm sure I remember it right. I think this is a message from Devi.' Sathi sighed. 'But I don't know what we're meant to do with that information.'

'It must be linked to the G-Vs,' Zakiy said. He rifled through his backpack and located a pencil. 'Do you mind?' he asked, indicating the book.

Sathi shook her head, and he pulled it into his lap so he could write the seven words from her dream in the margin next to the story. He looked up and grinned. 'I thought it might help to have them written down.'

She smiled back, and then something occurred to her. 'What were you doing with this book anyway?' She paused as she recalled his earlier explanation. 'I refuse to believe Dad threw it at you.'

Zakiy shifted uncomfortably. 'Well, he threw it in my direction. And I picked it up.'

'Why?'

Was he blushing? Sathi waited as he huffed out a resigned sigh and finally met her eyes. 'I was curious about what baby Sathi liked to read,' he admitted.

She didn't know what to say. His admission had done something strange to her insides, and she couldn't seem to look away from his intense gaze. Her cheeks heated, and now she was the one blushing.

'Um, uh, is there any more cocoa?' she stuttered, blurting out the first thing she could think of.

Zakiy didn't respond for a moment; his dark eyes seemed to be searching for something in her face. Finally, he broke that unshakeable gaze, and she could breathe again. 'Cocoa. Yes, here.' He poured the rest of the contents of the small saucepan into her cup and abruptly stood up. 'I'm going to bed. Goodnight.'

'Yes, me too, goodnight!' she said quickly, her voice high-pitched enough to make her wince.

As Zakiy disappeared into his tent, she quickly finished her lukewarm cocoa and hurried into her own tent. She mechanically got ready for bed and snuggled into her sleeping bag. She closed her eyes, refused to think, and fell asleep immediately.

She was in a beautiful, familiar meadow. Long grass brushed her ankles, and the sweet breeze played with her hair, blowing it back like a rippling black curtain. She was smiling and had just turned her face up to soak in the warm sunlight when a loud roar shattered the tranquillity of the meadow.

Sathi moved towards the sound and stopped in shock when she saw the dragon that had been haunting her dreams for several months. Except this time, it was in the meadow and full-sized, rather an indistinct shadow inside flames. It had seven heads undulating like individual serpents, except their tails all merged into one thick

68

trunk, which widened into a body covered in scales and ended in taloned feet.

Sathi flinched as the dragon let out another ear-splitting roar, and then she was blinded by a flash of light. When she could see again, a woman had appeared in front of the dragon.

She was beautiful and wore a white sari with a pink blouse. She had white flowers woven into her hair, and a garland of pink lotuses was strung around her neck. A golden crown sat on top of her head, with more golden jewellery strewn around her neck, arms, and dangling from her ears. She had four hands, and in them were a rosary, an ornate pot, something rectangular, like a book but half the width, and a musical instrument that vaguely recalled a cello.

A moment later, a man appeared next to the woman. Sathi stared: the man had four heads, one facing forward, backward and to each side. He also had a crown on each head, and a garland of lotuses around his neck. The woman smiled at him, and they began to walk forward.

As they moved, a peacock materialised at the goddess's feet; it strutted along, tail feathers spread out in a gorgeous fan. Then Sathi blinked, and the peacock turned into a snow-white swan that swam in the water that suddenly lapped against the woman's feet. Then the water disappeared, and the swan shifted back into the peacock; the form of the bird shifted back and forth several times a minute.

The woman stopped directly in front of the dragon. She closed her eyes, and her four hands became two, now holding a bow and arrow. The peacock-swan gave a low cry, and the woman's body glowed with light. She opened her eyes and took aim, and with a snick, the arrow flew from the bow and pierced one of the dragon's heads, severing it from the body.

There was another flash of light, and all three – the woman, the four-headed man, and the peacock-swan – disappeared, leaving behind the dragon roaring in pain.

Sathi was alone in their campsite when she woke up. She lay still, trying to process her dream. What did it mean? Was the woman Devi?

Bleary-eyed, she sat up with her teeth chattering; it was significantly colder this morning. Her hands touched something soft and warm, and she realised that a hoodie had been neatly folded up and left next to her. It was her favourite one, the green one she'd stolen from Zakiy ages ago.

Smiling, she pulled it on. She vaguely remembered Zakiy coming into her tent earlier in the morning and saying something about having to go to college. She'd obviously been too sleepy to really pay attention.

Unlike that tension-filled moment the night before. She shivered. She was going to have to do some thinking about her best friend and the unwelcome way she was starting to feel about him.

Later, she decided. She couldn't deal with it right now. Too many things had changed in her life recently, and she needed her friendship with Zakiy to stay the same. She couldn't lose that to some new feeling.

Resolutely, she pushed back those unwanted thoughts, as well as the troubling feelings about her dream, and stood up to clean up their campsite. She saw that that Zakiy had already washed up their cups and saucepan from the night before, so she grabbed both her and Zakiy's laundry bags and headed back to the resort. She'd have coffee, then she'd start the laundry and shower and change before another shift. She hoped Vidhya was working.

Due to her lie-in this morning, she didn't have time to visit Manish for his incredible tea, something she'd fallen in love with the day she arrived in Nelliampathi. Luckily for her, the coffee Vidhya brewed was almost as amazing. Sathi took a moment to appreciate just how thoroughly spoiled she was by the people in her life.

Humming, she meandered through the beautiful forest until she reached the edge of it. The beautiful architecture of the huts designed by the resort lifted her mood even further, and she bounced into the kitchen. 'Good morning, Vidhya-'

She broke off as she looked around the empty kitchen. No Vidhya. Shoulders slumped in resignation, she headed to the washing machine in the corner and dumped the clothes inside before starting the wash cycle.

Then she abandoned the kitchen to head to her room and dug around in her suitcase until she found the small electric kettle she'd hidden in there. She filled it with water and plugged it in guiltily; she was pretty sure she wasn't allowed to have a kettle in here.

She didn't feel like talking to anyone else before she had her coffee and making it in the kitchen would be a sure way to attract other people with whom she'd then have to share her coffee with. Nope. Not happening.

While the kettle boiled, she took out her small bottle of instant coffee and sugar, and figured she'd have to go steal some milk from the kitchen. She might make some more of her macadamia nut and white chocolate cookies later... Zakiy loved them, and he'd cleaned out her current stash already. They were one of her favourites as well, but she enjoyed surprising him with them even more than she liked eating them herself; she loved the way his eyes lit up when he realised she was baking them.

She was trying to remember whether she was out of macadamia nuts when she heard a noise outside. She froze when the door to her room opened, and her great-uncle stepped inside. He locked the door and smiled. 'Hello, molé.'

The bottle of coffee slipped from her fingers as she backed away, horrified.

Bhaskar sauntered forward, like he had all the time in the world. 'I know you were behind that journalist bitch. How dare you mess with me?'

Sathi's breath was stuck in her throat, and she couldn't even scream for help. She felt around in her pocket for her phone, but it wasn't there. She groaned mentally when she remembered she'd put it down on the kitchen counter while loading the washing machine.

'You're just like your mother. She stuck in her nose where it didn't belong, and look where it got her,' he sneered. 'You should have known better.'

Sathi looked frantically around for something she could use as a weapon. She edged around the table, trying to keep as far away from him as possible.

'I always wanted her, you know.'

Shocked, her eyes flew to Bhaskar. Bile filled her throat as he continued, 'She was beautiful, just like you. Or, I should say, you're just like her. I couldn't have her, so I'll have you instead.'

Sathi reached the counter on the other side of the room and groped blindly behind her back.

'I was going to get you that night you left. Then I thought my new daughter-in-law was more deserving of my personal attention that night.' He laughed, and her skin crawled. 'I could have you any day I wanted.'

His words shot steel into her spine, and her hands closed around the handle. 'See, that was your mistake,' she told him calmly. 'You can never have me.'

Bhaskar stalked towards her, his eyes cold as the grave. 'You little bitch –'

Sathi swung the kettle in his direction, and scalding hot water splashed over his face. With a cry, he fell, cradling his face as angry burns blossomed across it.

Kettle in hand, she started inching around him towards the door. He must have sensed the movement because he growled and reached for her blindly.

In one smooth arc, she poured the rest of the water down between his legs. Once his yowls of agony subsided, she met his eyes, letting him see every ounce of her disgust. 'That was for all the women you've raped.'

She ripped off the sheet from her bed and used it to tie his hands together, and then tied the other end to one of the bars on her window.

She shut and locked the door from the outside and walked to the kitchen to retrieve her phone.

She Googled the number for the local police station and made the call.

Chapter Seven

An Offer

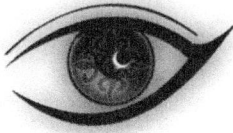

H er father arrived before the police did.
   He rushed up to her and pulled her into a hug. 'Oh God, my baby girl, are you OK?'

Sathi smiled at him, but it seemed wooden even to her. 'I'm fine.'

Dad looked at her for a long moment. 'Where is he? Where is that bastard?' he yelled.

She flinched even though she knew his anger wasn't directed at her. 'He's locked up in my room, Dad, don't worry. I'm safe. Let the police deal with him.'

'Where is the damn police, anyway?' he asked, taking out his own phone.

Sathi left him to it and sat down at the kitchen table, laying her face against the cool surface. She must have dozed off because the next thing she knew her father was shaking her awake gently.

'Ma'am?' The khaki-clad policeman stared down at her. 'Are you Sathi Varma?'

She quickly sat up. 'Yes.'

'You called us here to report that a man called Bhaskar Pushkaran tried to assault you. Is that correct?'

'Yes.'

'You also told us that he was injured while you defended yourself and that you've secured him in your room. Can you take us to him?'

'Of course,' she said, standing and leading the policeman to her room and unlocking it. She stood back so he could go inside first.

'Constable Ramesh.' Another man in police uniform strode up to them, and the first policeman immediately stood to attention and saluted him. 'Report,' the new guy ordered.

'Sir, I came here after getting a call from Ms. Sathi Varma.' The constable gestured to her. 'She reported that a man had tried to assault her and that she had managed to escape and then secure him in her room.'

The new guy turned to her. 'I'm Circle-Inspector Hari Prakash, I believe your father requested a more senior officer to be present.'

Sathi grimaced. 'I'm sorry, I didn't know he was going to do that,' she said, glaring at her father.

Dad was staring at the CI. 'I don't know that I requested anything,' he began, but was cut short by the sound of shouting.

'That little bitch! Sir, arrest her, she attacked me,' Bhaskar shouted from inside her room.

The CI took in the scene, first looking at Bhaskar, hands still tied up and ugly burns decorating his face, then at the kettle that lay empty on the floor. Then his gaze landed on Sathi. 'Hot water?' he asked her.

She shrugged. 'I was making coffee.'

The faint trace of a grin appeared on the CI's lips, which disappeared as he turned back to the constable. 'Arrest him.'

'Yes, sir.'

Bhaskar started shouting again, and the CI motioned for them to follow him. They walked back to the kitchen, where it was quieter. In a low voice, he said, 'I should warn you, that man has a lot of political influence.'

'I know,' Sathi replied. 'I'm his niece's daughter.'

The CI's brows rose. 'I see. Well, this may not surprise you, but this isn't the first time he's been accused of rape.'

'Then why is he still free?' Dad asked incredulously.

'Because the girls always end up withdrawing their complaints.'

Sathi's voice hardened. 'Well, that's not going to happen with me.'

The CI looked at her intently. 'Are you willing to testify against him in court?'

'Yes,' she nearly shouted, exasperated.

'Good.' The CI smiled in satisfaction.

She blinked. 'What?'

'I've been itching to take that bastard down for years,' he admitted. 'He always hid behind politics, but now I've got proof, from his own family. He can't get this case thrown out like he did the others.'

Sathi smiled slowly. It looked like she'd gained another ally.

It was late in the afternoon when Constable Ramesh finally finished taking her statement and left. Sathi had been disappointed to learn that Bhaskar was being taken to a hospital first to treat his burns, but the CI had assured her that he would be in police custody the whole time. He'd given her his number before he left and promised to keep her updated on the case.

Sathi's boss had turned up a while ago, startled to find police officers on the premises. Once she'd been filled in on what had happened, Nidhi immediately gave Sathi the rest of the day off. Sathi's protests fell on deaf ears, and her father insisted that she return to the treehouse with him.

Sathi leafed idly through an old magazine that had been left on the coffee table, wishing that she was working. It would have given her something to do and helped time pass more quickly.

Dad had forgotten about a Skype meeting he'd had scheduled with his colleagues back in London, and she'd told him to go ahead with it. He was having enough problems with work after taking an extended leave to come after her; she didn't want to make the situation worse for him.

Someone knocked on the front door, and she jerked upright. Her heart started racing, and her breath came in short bursts. She couldn't make herself get up to open the door; what if someone else in her family had heard about the arrest and come to take revenge?

Logically Sathi knew her father was just a room away, and that he would never let anyone hurt her. Her fear was a powerful force, though, and it held her in its insidious grasp. Tears of shame were filling her eyes when the knocking suddenly stopped.

Sathi strained to hear what was happening outside. She had just worked up the courage to stand up when her phone shrieked out its ringtone, startling her. She rummaged among the sofa cushions until she found it and sighed in relief when she saw it was Zakiy calling.

'Hey,' she said weakly into the phone.

'Are you OK?' The worry in his voice was obvious; he'd been stuck at college all day, and he'd obviously just seen her message from earlier and freaked out.

'I'm fine,' she told him. 'Where are you?' she asked, suddenly overwhelmed with the desire to see him.

'I'm outside your treehouse. I knocked but no one answered. Did you go somewhere else?'

Sathi didn't answer; she just flung the door open, and there he was. They stared at each other for a moment.

She rushed forward and threw herself in his arms. The knot of pain and grief and fear that had fused itself into her heart poured out of her, and she knew she was trembling.

Zakiy stumbled, then one-handedly deposited his backpack and phone on the floor by the door while he held onto her with his other hand. Once he had freed his arms, he wrapped them around her and rubbed soothing circles on her back, making shushing noises as he held her to her chest.

She wasn't sure how long they stood there, her cheek against his shirt, her arms around his waist, before her heart rate calmed down, and she began to notice something weird.

She'd hugged Zakiy many times during their friendship, but this was the first time that wherever they touched burned like naked skin exposed to the scorching midday sun.

Her cheeks flushed as the heat worked its way through her body; she kept her eyes tightly shut, but Zakiy's sharp intake of breath and sudden racing heartbeat told her that he felt it as well.

Slowly, she pulled back to look at his face, still resting within the circle of his arms. His eyes were open and gazing down at her with an expression that was both vulnerable and knowing.

She thought about how weird he'd been acting lately and realised that maybe he'd already figured out something that she was only just starting to piece together. Embarrassment and pleasure mixed to form a heady brew, and she found she couldn't meet his gaze anymore.

'Sathi,' he started softly, but was immediately interrupted by his phone's ringtone.

Zakiy cursed as she broke away from him, using the excuse of searching for his phone to hide her face. She found it, thrust it at him, and then escaped outside to lean against the railing of the little balcony.

The fresh mountain air felt icy against her flushed cheeks, and she gulped in air.

All she could think was, Oh shit.

'What is it, Abdullah?' Zakiy growled into his phone, torn between irritation at being interrupted by his parents' caretaker, and elation at what had just passed unspoken between Sathi and him. He couldn't tear his eyes away from where she stood with her back to him; her long, raven-coloured hair glistened in the sunlight.

As always, Abdullah spoke as though he had something stuck way up his butt. 'Master Zakiy, I have a message to pass onto Miss Sathi.'

Zakiy frowned. 'What? What message could you possibly have for Sathi?'

At his words, Sathi turned around to face him. Her expression was unreadable.

'Master Zakiy, a woman came to the house today asking to speak to Miss Sathi,' Abdullah said.

'What woman?'

'She said her name is Anika.'

His eyes widened. 'Is she still there?'

'Yes, Master Zakiy.'

'Okay, tell her to wait. We're on our way.' He ended the call, then picked up his bag and joined Sathi outside. He made sure to leave a healthy distance between them.

'What was all that about?' she asked, her eyes searching his face.

He took a deep breath. 'Do you remember Anika?'

Her eyebrows rose in surprise. 'Uncle Karan's wife? Girish's sister-in-law?'

'Yup. She's come to the house, asking to talk to you.' He paused. 'She came to see me today.'

'What? When?'

'She was waiting for me at the college gate. That's why I took so long to get here.'

'Why would she want to talk to me?' she wondered.

He shrugged. 'She wouldn't tell me. She just said she needed to talk to you and asked if it would be okay to come by the house today. I meant to tell you but—'

Zakiy broke off, and the reason he'd become distracted lingered between them like a mirage. He took a step forward. 'Sathi, we should —'

'No!' The word exploded from her. 'No,' she repeated, but this time it was a broken sound.

The pain in that single syllable stopped his protest in his throat. She looked up at him, and her eyes were as fractured as her voice.

'I just can't,' she murmured, her expression pleading with him to understand. 'Not right now.'

He swallowed back his disappointment and anguish. It was obvious that something was holding her back from him. He wasn't going to push her into something she didn't want, no matter how much he wanted it. At the same time, he couldn't quite squash the hope that she'd change her mind. Maybe not today, but someday.

'Okay,' he said, trying to mask his pain with a cheerful expression. He wasn't sure how successful he'd been, especially when he noted the mingled relief and sorrow in Sathi's expression. She knew him too well not to understand how much her rejection had hurt.

Trying to distract himself, he retrieved his keys from his pocket. 'Let's go see what Anika has to say.'

Sathi couldn't believe it. The woman sitting opposite her sipping coffee was her other aunt, married to Girish's elder brother Karan. She had met Anika, Karan, and their small son during her stay at the G-Vs' house but had never really expected to see them again.

Anika looked up, a wry smile on her lips. 'I guess I was the last person you were expecting to see,' she said, weirdly echoing Sathi's thoughts.

Sathi hesitated, then decided honesty was best. 'Pretty much.'

'I heard about what Bhaskar did. Are you okay?'

Sathi shrugged with false bravado. 'He didn't get to finish what he started. I didn't let him.'

Anika simply nodded. 'You were in control. Sometimes they take that control away from you.' Her eyes locked with Sathi's, and she understood clearly what Anika was leaving unsaid. Anika sighed, breaking the pregnant silence. 'I came today because there are some things you need to be aware of. You may have exposed Bhaskar's true self, but you have only scratched the surface of the evil hidden in that family.'

Anika paused, and her eyes flicked to Zakiy before returning to Sathi. 'What I tell you now must stay between the three of us.'

Sathi started to speak, but Anika cut her off. 'Give me your word! Otherwise, I leave now.'

'I promise,' Sathi said.

Zakiy nodded in agreement. 'Of course. We won't tell anyone else.'

Anika seemed to be assessing how sincere they were. 'Okay.' She dropped her gaze, focusing on her hands folded neatly on her lap. 'You know that I am married to your Uncle Karan. Well, what you don't know is that I was trapped into that marriage.'

Sathi and Zakiy exchanged shocked glances, unnoticed by Anika as she continued. 'When I was sixteen my parents told me they couldn't afford to send me to school anymore and that I should start earning my keep. They sent me to work for your grandparents as their maid. Initially they were very caring; they took pity on me and offered to pay for my continued education.'

Anika's lips twisted in a wry smile. 'I was thrilled, of course. My dreams about going to college were within my grasp again... or so I thought. What I didn't realise was that Bhaskar and Goudhamy weren't helping me out of the goodness of their hearts; they were making me indebted to them so I would keep quiet about what they had planned for me next.'

Anika took in a deep, shuddering breath. 'I don't know when I first noticed the way Karan looked at me. I was still working in their house when he came home from university. He would always be watching me when I cleaned, or cooked. He would never say anything, but I still remember how his gaze made me feel. I was too scared to say anything, though, in case I offended his parents.'

'Then one day his parents went out and asked me to stay behind to receive a package they were expecting to be delivered. They told me that no one else would be home, but about ten minutes after they left Karan showed up. He told me that his parents had lied to me and had left the house so that he could be alone with me. I was scared and I tried to run away from him, but he had locked all the doors. I tried to scream, but he grabbed me and clamped his hand over my mouth. He slapped me and then dragged me to his bedroom, where he—'

Anika broke off as she glanced up at their horrified expressions. She blinked, as though forcing herself to shake off the shackles of her memories. 'Well. I'll stop there. I'm sure you can guess what happened next. Afterwards, I ran home to my parents to tell them what happened.'

She chuckled once, a humourless sound. 'I guess I was hoping that they would march back to Karan and beat him up, or something like that. Instead, they told me to pack my things and go back to Karan's house. I found out later that his parents had paid them off... basically sold me to them, to sate their son's lust for me. They moved into a bigger house in another town not long after that, and I never saw them again.

'I became pregnant when I was seventeen, after being raped continuously by Karan for more than a year. When I turned eighteen his parents told me that unless I wanted to be labelled as a whore by the whole town, I should marry Karan. At least I would have a father for my child, instead of him being named a bastard. By this point I had already lost everything; my parents, my education, my will to fight... so I traded my losses for the status of a wife and mother, something that would at least give me a measure of respect in the society I was forced to live in.'

Anika closed her eyes, tears running silently down her cheeks now. Sathi moved to sit beside her, laying a hand over the older woman's.

Anika gripped Sathi's hand as her gaze found hers again. 'The reason I'm telling you all this is because for the first time in years I'm seeing someone stand up to their evil – and winning. I want to join your fight. I want to see that family torn down.'

Sathi had to wait a moment before she was able to speak. 'Anika, I'm so sorry that you had to go through something so... so... awful. I would welcome your help, but please understand that you don't have to help us.' Her voice hardened. 'There's no way I'm resting until I see them ruined, and hearing your story has only increased my determination. I know Zakiy feels the same way.' She could see Zakiy nodding in agreement in her peripheral vision. 'So, you don't owe us anything,' she added gently.

'I understand. I want to help you anyway,' Anika said earnestly, wiping away her tears.

Zakiy leaned forward. 'Help us how, exactly?'

'Karan is a criminal lawyer, and as I speak, he is preparing his defence against Sathi in Bhaskar's upcoming trial for attempted rape. He will claim that you're a liar, and that you falsely accused Bhaskar.'

'Why would I falsely accuse someone of rape?' Sathi exclaimed.

Anika smiled. 'You probably wouldn't, but the truth is that many women have done it – for financial gain, or for revenge. In India, the tendency is to believe the woman's story in such cases, and unfortunately many women have taken advantage of that.'

Sathi digested that in silence. 'So, what do you propose we do?'

'I will testify against Bhaskar. I will tell them the truth about his character, on how he preys on women. My testimony will be enough to convince the judge to rule in your favour.'

Chapter Eight

Counterattack

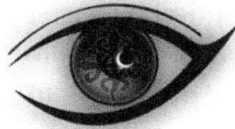

After Anika left, Sathi and Zakiy slowly made their way back to the treehouse, knowing her dad would panic if he found Sathi missing after his Skype meeting. Sathi kept mulling over everything Anika had told them, but she couldn't focus fully on the puzzle she presented. She was too distracted by Zakiy and the unnatural silence between them.

She couldn't believe how aware she was of him! Even though they were walking further apart than they usually did, she could feel the heat radiating off him. She peeked at him sideways, and guilt shot through her veins at his subdued expression. Sathi knew she was being selfish; he had opened his heart to her, and she'd rejected him. She could see what her reaction had done to him, yet she couldn't find the words to fix things.

Sathi could no longer lie to herself and knew her feelings towards her best friend were more than just friendly. Yet she knew relationships did not come with an attached warranty; once you change the dynamics from friendship to romance there was no way to change it back. Just the thought of losing Zakiy as a friend made her feel like she couldn't breathe properly – she wasn't willing to risk that for the elusive possibility of love.

Peeking at him again, she realised that she may not have a choice; her rejection may have already caused irreparable damage to their friendship. The thought was enough to make her chest start cramping with pain.

When they reached the treehouse Sathi was so relieved to escape the awful awkward tension between her and Zakiy that she didn't register the bike parked next to Zakiy's Jeep. It was only when they let themselves in that she realised Vidhya and Jayaram had come to visit.

'Hi,' Sathi said in surprise. 'What are you guys doing here?'

Jayaram opened his mouth to speak, but Vidhya silenced him with a hand on his wrist. Sathi wished that trick would work with her. 'We heard about Bhaskar,' Vidhya said, her dark eyes full of concern. 'Are you okay?'

'I'm fine. They took him to hospital under police custody to treat his burns. The CI told me he would call me to file the... the FIR?'

Jayaram nodded. 'The First Information Report. It's basically the first step in registering a criminal case against Bhaskar.'

'Good,' Sathi said fiercely. 'It's time for him to face the consequences of his actions, rather than hiding behind black magic.'

Jayaram winced. 'Funny you should mention consequences...'

She stared at him. 'What's that supposed to mean?'

'Susan Roy was arrested today.'

'What?' she exclaimed, looking at Vidhya, who nodded sadly. 'Why?'

'It's a goddamn set-up,' Jayaram fumed, pacing. 'Payback for exposing Bhaskar as a fraud. One of the girls in her newspaper office is claiming that Susan was forcing her to sleep with a politician to garner favour. They're saying that Susan is a Madam.'

At Sathi's confused expression, Vidhya quickly explained, 'A Madam is what they call someone who runs a brothel.'

'That's ridiculous,' Zakiy said. 'Do they have any proof?'

'I don't know all the details,' Jayaram admitted in frustration. 'Susan's mother called me and told me she was arrested last night. I'm waiting for a friend of mine to get together the bail application paperwork, and then we're heading over there to try and get her released on bail.'

'This is my fault,' Sathi whispered, sick to her stomach. 'Bhaskar made up this false case against Susan in revenge for exposing him.'

Vidhya put her arm around Sathi's shoulders. 'Don't blame yourself. Think about what you suffered. You were nearly raped today, Sathi!'

'If anyone's to blame, it's me,' Jayaram said grimly. 'I'm the one who got Susan involved.'

'Don't you start,' Vidhya retorted, shaking her head at him. 'Why don't we put the blame where it belongs – at the hands of that horrible man? He's the one who attacked Sathi, and he's the one who brought these false charges against Susan. If we focus on guilt and self-blame, we're letting people like him win.'

'Hear hear,' Zakiy interjected, offering Vidhya a high-five. She slapped his palm with hers, smiling despite herself.

'As usual you're right, my love,' Jayaram said, kissing her cheek. She blushed and looked at her feet. He checked his watch. 'I'm going to head over to the police station,' he told Vidhya. 'I don't want Susan to be locked up a moment longer than she needs to be.'

'I'll come with you,' Zakiy said quickly, not looking at Sathi. Out of the corner of her eye she could see Vidya glancing between Zakiy and Sathi with growing concern.

Thankfully, as soon as Jayaram and Zakiy left, her father finished with his work and came to join Sathi and Vidhya in the living room. Sathi jumped at the chance to fill them in on Anika's offer to help them – carefully editing out the part about her being raped by her husband.

'So, Karan is going to be defending Bhaskar,' her dad said thoughtfully when she finished.

'Yup. Apparently, he's ruthless.'

'That much is true,' Vidhya added. 'Madhu and I used to go watch him in the courtroom whenever we could, because Madhu wanted to support her brother. But we've both been shocked to see the lengths to which Karan would go when trying to win a case. He and Madhu used to argue about it all the time, until he finally forbade us to go to court.'

Worry shadowed her dad's eyes as he gazed at Sathi. 'So, you need to be careful.'

Her stomach clenched, but she made herself smile at her dad. 'Don't worry. We have the truth on our side.'

I just hope that's enough, she added silently.

Jayaram stayed at the local police station all night and most of the next morning, trying to get Susan out on bail. When he finally walked into the Zakiy's living room just before noon, Sathi was sure he had been successful. One look at his face, however, squandered that hope. 'They wouldn't give her bail?' she asked in disbelief.

Jayaram shook his head wearily, looking like he was a heartbeat away from falling asleep standing. Vidhya silently got up and returned with a cup of coffee, which he accepted gratefully. 'They're claiming that it's a non-bailable offence, but when I ask them to explain how they keep bullshitting and fobbing me off.' He paused to take a long gulp of coffee. He clutched the cup close to his chest and focused his gaze on Sathi. 'Now I have even worse news.' Jayaram glanced at Vidhya for fortification before announcing, 'Bhaskar has been granted bail.'

'What?!' Sathi and Zakiy shouted at the same time. Jayaram winced and held up his hand to nip their outrage in the bud. 'He's still in hospital being treated for his wounds–' Here he allowed himself a grin before continuing, 'But he's no longer under police custody.'

'How is that possible?' Sathi demanded, feeling like the little solid ground beneath her feet was dissolving like quicksand.

Jayaram shrugged. 'He has powerful friends, both politicians and senior police officers. He must have called in a favour.' He paused to take another sip of coffee. 'The CI has called you in to give a statement tomorrow.'

Sathi frowned. 'I've already given my statement,' she reminded him.

He shook his head. 'That's just a preliminary one, they usually call you down to the station to take a more detailed one.' He hesitated, then added, 'Don't worry. I'll make some calls and try to figure out what's going on with Susan and Bhaskar. For now just focus on giving as clear a statement as you can to the police. After all, you haven't done anything wrong.'

She nodded, but couldn't help thinking: Neither did Susan, but that didn't stop her getting wrongfully imprisoned.

The next day, Sathi and her father waited inside the local police station, watching as a police Sub-inspector and his assistant searched for her original statement, the one she'd given on the day Bhaskar tried to rape her. She sat in disbelief as the two of them dug through hundreds of dusty piles of files, scattered across the various desks dotted around the room.

Finally, after at least half an hour of searching, they found her file. It took them another ten minutes to acquire a blank piece of legal-sized paper. They placed a sheet of carbon paper underneath it and sandwiched it with another piece of paper. The assistant meticulously folded the edge of the paper to act as a margin and uncapped his pen before looking up at the SI expectantly.

The SI started dictating to the assistant in Malayalam, taking another half an hour just to cover basic details like her name, address and relationship to Bhaskar.

'When did you arrive in India?' the SI asked, addressing her for the first time but not making eye contact. She was about to about to check her phone to look up her flight details when her father answered immediately with the exact date.

'Did you come with her?' the SI pounced immediately, and she watched her father's skin darken with shame.

Anger shot through her. 'No, he couldn't travel on that day because of work, so he came a few days later,' Sathi lied blithely, refusing to discuss their dysfunctional relationship with this policeman who couldn't even find a file in a reasonable amount of time. Plus, she couldn't understand how it was relevant to her case against Bhaskar.

'Did you meet your grandparents as soon as your arrived in Nelliampathi?'

'No, they were out of town for a wedding. I only met them a few months later.'

'What happened when you met them?'

Sathi shifted uncomfortably. She didn't want to discuss the months she'd spent with her grandparents, but that was the whole point of her being here, wasn't it? To get justice, for herself and for all the people her grandparents had hurt.

She took a deep breath and explained how Bhaskar and Goudhamy had felt the need to control everyone and everything, how badly they had treated their daughter-in-law, Maya, and the rifts they'd tried to create between Maya and their son. When it came to the night she had finally left the house, she hesitated. Giving any more details would affect her aunt, and she didn't want to go there if she didn't have to.

The SI looked up. 'Yes? Is that why you left the house? Because you felt they were controlling?'

'Yeah. I just couldn't live there anymore.'

'Did you have an argument with your grandparents before you left?'

'No. I just left quietly, without telling anyone.'

The SI peered at her over his glasses. 'There must have been some reason why you left, some argument or other.'

She stiffened. 'As I said, there was no argument.'

'Why did you leave that night then?'

Her dad leaned forward. 'Why is that so important?' he demanded. 'The issue here is about her being assaulted a few days ago, not the time she spent with them several months ago.'

'Sir, we need to ask these questions,' the SI responded condescendingly. 'Please let us do our job.'

Dad opened his mouth to retort, but Sathi laid a restraining hand on his arm and subtly shook her head. This wasn't like choosing not to disclose her relationship to her dad. What happened to Maya was crucial to the case, and there was no point in hiding it from the police. It may even end up helping Maya.

'I left the house that night because I witnessed something horrible,' she admitted. 'I saw Maya, their son Girish's wife, going into Bhaskar's room after everyone else was asleep.'

The SI raised his eyebrows. 'She was having an affair with her own father-in-law?'

'No, no!' Sathi pressed her hands against her temples in frustration. 'It was against her will! It was like she was in a trance or something. She didn't know what she was doing.'

The SI looked sceptical. Sathi decided to take the plunge. 'Bhaskar and his wife practice black magic,' she blurted. 'They gave her a glass of milk a few hours before this happened. I think that's what made her go into Bhaskar's room.'

The SI and his assistant stared at her. 'Black magic?' the SI asked finally. He chuckled, and his assistant started grinning as well.

Her fists clenched, and she resisted the urge to knock their heads together.

90

'Well, Miss Sathi, I have to inform you that Maya has not come forward with any accusations of sexual assault, and unfortunately, we cannot put down "black magic" as evidence in a police statement.' His assistant snorted at that, and the SI smiled in response.

Sathi spoke through gritted teeth. 'I only told you that because you asked me why I left their house so abruptly that night. I can't help it if you refuse to believe me.'

The SI shook his head. 'Yes, well, you'll find that not many people will believe that story of yours. Anyway, let's forget all that. So, after you left your grandparents' house, did you ever contact them? Or did they contact you?'

She tried to swallow her irritation and embarrassment. Obviously, mentioning the black magic had been a bad move. 'No, I never contacted them again. I only saw Bhaskar again on the day he tried to rape me,' she said pointedly, trying to force the SI to focus on the real issue here.

'So, you didn't send him a message asking him to meet you that day?'

Sathi frowned. 'What? No, of course I didn't!'

The SI pierced her with his gaze. 'Did anyone see him attacking you?'

Still reeling from the comment about the message, she took a moment too long to respond. 'No, I was alone in my room. He came in and locked the door.' She pointed at the file in front of them. 'It's all in the original statement I gave,' she said, her voice almost a growl.

This time it was her father's turn to lay a cautioning hand on her arm. 'Inspector, is there something going on here that we don't know about?'

The SI ignored him as he abruptly changed tack. 'You're a student, aren't you?'

She nodded, confused.

'How could you afford your trip to India? Did your father pay for the tickets?'

'No, I used the money I saved from my part-time job in the UK.'

'You're starting university soon?'

She nodded again, not understanding what any of this had to do with the case.

'I hear it's quite expensive to study in the UK. How are you planning to pay your fees?'

'Like everyone else – with student loans.'

'Have you applied for a loan?'

'Of course, I have!' Sathi nearly yelled. 'How is this relevant to what Bhaskar did?'

The SI was unperturbed by her outburst. 'So you must have needed the money for something else,' he mused.

'What money?' she snapped. 'What the hell are you talking about?'

'I'm talking about the money you demanded from Bhaskar. When he refused, you made him meet you at a time when you knew you would be alone. You attacked him, and then you falsely accused him of trying to rape you.'

A fist banged against the desk, making Sathi jump. 'That is enough!' her dad shouted, a pulse jumping in his temple. 'I thought you brought my daughter here to help her get justice. I can see now that you're just helping Bhaskar. Where is your CI? We refuse to speak with you, we will only speak with him.'

'He is busy at the moment; you can't see him.'

'Bullshit,' her dad scoffed, standing. Sathi followed suit. 'He is the one who called us down here. You tell CI Hari Prakash that we want to see him right away. Let him decide if he is too busy to see us.'

'I'm afraid that won't be possible,' the SI sneered.

'Why the hell not?'

'Because we have a new CI here now. CI Hari Prakash has been transferred to Thiruvananthapuram. You'll have to go down there if you want to see him.

Chapter Nine

Divine Advice

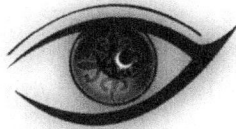

T hey were playing us from the beginning,' Jayaram ranted. 'If I'd known they were looking at you as a suspect, I would have come with you.'

Vidhya put a comforting arm on his shoulder. 'How were you supposed to know?' she asked reasonably. 'You were still trying to get bail for Susan. Even you can't be in two places at once, my love.'

'That must be why they denied her bail,' Zakiy guessed. 'To keep you distracted.'

Despite their words, Jayaram looked so dejected that Sathi felt compelled to add, 'They're right. It wasn't your fault. They won this time,' she added bitterly, shoulders slumping.

Zakiy leaned forward, catching her eye for the first time since... the incident. 'They may have won this battle, but the war is still on. And we will win,' he said fiercely.

Gratitude and guilt clogged her throat; she just nodded.

'Tell me exactly what questions the SI asked and how you replied,' Jayaram said. 'Word for word.' He reached for a pen and notepad and made notes as Sathi and Nakul repeated the story in as much detail as they could.

Once they finished, Jayaram tapped the pen against the pad thoughtfully. 'One thing confuses me,' he said finally. 'Usually, in India at least, the tendency is to believe the victim in cases of sexual assault – it's normally up to the offender to prove his innocence.'

When he saw her confusion, he explained, 'It's not innocent until proven guilty in such cases. It was a way to protect women, but unfortunately there have been too many instances where this unwritten rule has been abused by women for ulterior motives. Anyway, the reason I bring this up is because there must be some reason why the police are refusing to take your word for what happened.'

Nakul frowned. 'Isn't it simple? They've all been paid off! That much is clear from their attitude.'

'True,' Jayaram admitted. 'They also got CI Hari Prakash transferred because Karan knows he's incorruptible. They used their political clout to get a new CI assigned here – someone they can control.'

'Do we know that for sure?' Vidhya asked. 'I mean, what if the new CI is willing to help us? It doesn't hurt to try.'

Jayaram shook his head. 'No, I know him. He's on Karan's payroll. That's why he made sure he wasn't available today to see you.'

Sathi couldn't believe how corrupted the system was here; was money really everything? Did the law and justice mean nothing?

'What if we go to Thiruvananthapuram and talk to Hari Prakash?' Zakiy suggested. 'I could drive us down there.'

'There's no harm in talking to him, but now that he's been transferred there's not much he can do. All he can do is advise us.'

'He gave me his card,' Sathi remembered. She dug through her bag until she found the slightly bent business card. She scanned it quickly and held it out, confirming, 'His number is on there.'

Jayaram took it and carefully dialled the number into his phone. 'I'll call him now and see if he has some insights into how to proceed. I'll also call a contact I have at the police station and see if I can find out any more about what's going on.' He walked a few steps away, phone held to his ear.

Nakul and Vidhya resumed discussing the SI who had questioned Sathi, and Zakiy scooted his chair closer to hers. 'Are you okay?' he asked, concern obvious in his eyes.

That was it for her. His one kind question caused tears to well up and spill over her cheeks.

Zakiy stood. 'Come, on let's go to our campsite for a bit,' he suggested, tugging on her arm. Warmth tingled up from where his fingers gripped her, scattering her thoughts even further. 'But... Jayaram...' she spluttered.

'He'll call us when he's done,' Zakiy said calmly. 'You need a break from all this.'

He paused to meet Nakul's gaze, and her father nodded his permission, worry for his daughter evident in his face. 'Go vavé. I'll call you as soon as Jay's done with his phone calls,' he promised.

Sathi nodded absently and allowed Zakiy to lead her away. Lost in thought, she barely registered the drive to their campsite or Zakiy making a fire. He gently pushed a cup of cocoa into her hands before he sat down next to her.

'Drink it,' he urged. 'I swear, my cocoa-making skills have improved.'

Despite herself, she snort-laughed and took a sip. As warmth shot down her throat, the tight ball of tension she'd been carrying around since the police station seemed to unravel slightly.

'Want to talk?' he asked quietly.

She was silent for a heartbeat. 'I don't know what to think,' she admitted. 'Every time I think we're taking a step forward, it seems like we're being sucked ten steps back. First Susan, then that SI...' She shook her head. 'How can they accuse me of lying about something like this for money? Is this really how they treat the people who give a complaint?'

'Unfortunately, it's like someone very aptly said – in this country, you have to bribe government officials to do the job they are paid to do. The corruption level is off the charts.' Zakiy paused. 'Sorry. That wasn't exactly comforting, was it?'

She smiled. 'No, but it was honest. And that makes it comforting.'

He gave a low chuckle in response. 'Glad to be of service, m'lady.' His shoulder brushed hers accidentally, and she gave a shiver. She turned to meet his gaze, and tried to put everything she couldn't seem to say into her eyes.

His expression softened, and his shoulder brushed hers again, this time deliberately. 'I can wait, you know,' he said softly, holding her gaze. 'There's no rush. Just know that I'm here for you. No matter what.'

Sathi closed her eyes and laid her head against his shoulder, feeling warmth cascade into her body through his. 'Thank you,' she said simply.

They stayed like that, not talking, until Nakul called to tell them Jayaram was done with his phone calls.

'I spoke to CI Hari Prasad,' Jayaram told them with no ado as soon as they settled back in around Zakiy's dining room table. 'He's just as frustrated with this whole situation as we are, but again, there's not much he can do about it now that he's been transferred. However, he did advise us to speak to a senior officer and get them to put pressure on the local police to take the case more seriously.'

He paused to turn his notepad around, showing them a name and phone number. 'Hari Prasad said he will talk to the Assistant Commissioner of Police. ACP Vinayan was friends with Hari Prasad's father, who is a retired police officer. If the ACP agrees, he'll call us back with an appointment later today.'

Jayaram flipped to the next page in the notepad. 'That was the good news. Now for the bad. I reached out to my contact at Nelliampathi police station, and things are pretty much as bad as we feared. Karan was there a lot over the last couple of days, no doubt buying off the officers there to discredit Sathi and weaken the case against Bhaskar.'

'So is that it, then?' Zakiy demanded, his voice mirroring the same frustration that was reflected on all of their faces. 'Karan throws his money around, and they do whatever they want?'

Jayaram shrugged. 'You know how the system is – whoever holds the most power will get the desired results. Wait,' he said, holding up a hand to forestall Zakiy's protest. 'We do have another option at our disposal. If the meeting with the ACP doesn't pan out, we can go directly to the court to complain that the police are refusing to investigate. We can get the court to order them to take action. They won't be able to ignore a direct court order.'

Vidhya laid a hand on Jayaram's arm. 'Jay, that's brilliant!' She leaned it to kiss his cheek.

He looked embarrassed but pleased, at both the kiss and the murmurs of agreement that went around the group. He shrugged modestly. 'It's nothing, really. It's just a routine part of a lawyer's job.'

Nakul spoke up. 'Maybe that's true, but you're helping my daughter without accepting even a consulting fee. We're extremely grateful,' he added, voice thick with emotion.

Jayaram's skin took on a darker tint, although his words were typically brusque. 'I'm not doing this for the money. I'm doing this to get vengeance for Vijay, and helping Sathi is just a part of that.'

'Thank you,' Sathi told him quietly, but sincerely.

Vidhya eyes shone with pride and happiness. 'So, to sum up, right now we're waiting for CI Hari Prasad to call us back about a possible appointment with the ACP.' She paused. 'What about Susan? Can't we do anything to get those ridiculous charges dropped?'

Jayaram glanced at the clock. 'That's where I'm going now. The police have to present Susan at court by 5 pm today, and I should be able to bail her out once she's there.' He glanced at Sathi. 'I've given the CI your number as well, in case I'm in court when he calls.' He stood to leave, then paused to tell her almost gently, 'Don't worry. We'll fight this every inch, and we have several layers of strategy. Ultimately victory will be ours,' he promised.

Sathi nodded gratefully, and he turned abruptly to leave for court.

Vidhya also excused herself. 'I have a shift at the resort,' she said apologetically, before coming up next to Sathi and pressing a kiss to her forehead. She blushed and ducked her head. 'I'm so proud of you,' Vidhya told her. 'Stay strong.'

'I'm proud of you too,' Nakul said, eyes suspiciously bright.

'Thanks, guys.'

Nakul stood and stretched. 'Now, kiddo, are you coming to the treehouse with me, or is it the campsite tonight?'

'The campsite, please,' she responded absently.

Zakiy couldn't help the joy that her words evoked in him, though he tried to keep his face as expressionless as possible.

The small grin playing around Nakul's mouth suggested that he hadn't been too successful in hiding his reaction. 'Okay, then, good night.' Nakul's gaze slid to Zakiy, and all traces of humour suddenly disappeared. 'Be good,' he ordered.

Zakiy gulped and fought the urge to salute. 'Yes, sir.'

When Nakul finally left, he sighed in relief. He turned to Sathi. 'Shall we, m'lady?'

'Wait a sec,' she said, her gaze far away. 'Is your Tarot deck here or at the campsite?'

He blinked in surprise, then grinned. 'Here, I think. I'll get it. You haven't asked for a reading in a while,' he observed.

This time her eyes focused on his. 'I want some advice,' she admitted ruefully . 'Some divine advice.'

'Are you saying my advice isn't divine?' he demanded in mock-offence.

She chuckled, and he had to fight the urge to brush the hair out of her face and then cup her face with his hand.

'Only when you're reading Tarot,' she joked, pulling him out of his fantasy.

Zakiy went to collect his deck from his bedside table, and then they set out to their campsite again. Sathi said little, and he let her think uninterrupted until they had settled around the little campfire. Zakiy took out his cards and started shuffling. 'So. What kind of advice are you looking for?'

Her black eyes flickered with gold from the reflected flames. 'I had a dream right after Susan gave that interview about Bhaskar. I saw that seven-headed dragon again, roaring and spitting fire.'

His hands stilled. 'Like the one you've dreamt of before? In the fire?'

'No. Well, yes, but it was different this time. I didn't see the woman doing black magic like I usually do, and the dragon wasn't in the fire – it was in a meadow, but it was like it was made of fire.'

'But the dragon was the same?'

Sathi nodded. 'Yeah, and it had seven heads, like a hydra.' At his blank expression, she gave a reluctant grin and explained, 'Its heads were like snakes – writhing around independently of each other.'

He paled. 'Right. Freaky snake times seven. Got it.'

'Don't forget about the forked tongues and the breathing fire and the taloned feet.'

Zakiy swallowed. 'Nope, definitely shouldn't forget that.'

'Anyway, there was the dragon, then a woman and a man appeared; the man had four heads, facing each direction, and the woman had this musical instrument and something that looked like a book. They also had a peacock that kept changing into a swan and then back again. They walked towards the dragon and a bow and arrow appeared in the woman's hand. She sighted an arrow and cut off one of the heads of the dragon.'

Zakiy blinked. 'Wow.'

Her gaze found his. 'That woman was Devi, wasn't she?'

He nodded. He'd recognised her immediately from Sathi's description. 'She sounds like Saraswathi Devi, the goddess of wisdom.' He picked up his phone and quickly Googled a picture to show her. 'Here.'

Her eyes widened. 'That's her!' Then she frowned. 'Except she wasn't sitting on a lotus flower.' She grinned impishly. 'That must be why she was wearing a garland of lotuses instead.'

Zakiy chuckled. 'Kind of difficult to sit and walk at the same time.'

'Exactly.' She pointed at the phone screen. 'There's the rosary, the pot – is that for water?'

'Yeah, and the book-like things are the vedas, the ancient Hindu scriptures. The musical instrument is the veena, which is like the great-grandmother of the violin family. She holds that because she's also the goddess of the arts.'

'Like the Greek goddess Athena,' Sathi murmured, her fingers reverentially tracing the goddess's face. 'So who was the man?'

'Lord Brahma,' he replied, retrieving his phone from her and bringing up a picture of the four-headed god. 'He's the god of creation, and Saraswathi's husband. His heads represent the four vedas and point to the four cardinal directions.'

Sathi didn't respond, her gaze on the fire away.

He shifted closer and gently nudged her. 'Sathi?'

She blinked, and her eyes slowly focused on him. 'I think I know what the dreams mean. But I need you to ask the cards if I'm right.'

He nodded, and picked up his cards again. 'Okay. What's your theory?'

'Remember the book of fairy tales?'

'The one your dad threw at me? How could I forget?'

She rolled her eyes at his dramatics. 'Allegedly threw. Anyway, remember I told you about the seven deadly sins?'

'Yeah, and you figured out that it was a clue from Devi.'

'Yes! Now that I've had this dream, I think she's letting us know we're on the right track. The seven headed dragon represents the seven deadly sins.'

'One head for each sin,' Zakiy realised, eyes widening.

She nodded emphatically. 'Exactly. When we released that video about Bhaskar we somehow defeated one of the sins. That's why one of the heads was cut off in the dream.'

'So now we just need to figure which sin was represented by that head,' Zakiy mused.

'I think I know,' Sathi said surprisingly. 'I think it was pride. I mean, our aim was to expose Bhaskar as a fraud and get rid of that mask he wore in public. Because of the dowry scandal he lost his image as a benevolent philanthropist,' she finished with satisfaction.

'That makes sense,' Zakiy agreed. 'Especially since Saraswathi Devi was the one to cut off the head representing Pride.' At her questioning look, he continued, 'Pride equals ignorance; it makes you think you know best. True wisdom makes you humble, because the more you learn, the more you realise that there is so much more that you don't know.'

He glanced at Sathi and blushed at her slightly awed expression. He hurriedly continued, 'Anyway, who better to get rid of ignorance and false pride than the goddess of wisdom and knowledge?'

'You're brilliant,' Sathi told him, eyes shining.

He shrugged. He tried not to appear too pleased with himself (and probably failed miserably). 'Well, let's ask the cards if we're right.' Zakiy closed his eyes and started shuffling in earnest, concentration on their conversation and asking if their speculations were correct.

When he felt that the cards were ready, he gave the deck to Sathi to cut. She did and handed them back, and he drew seven cards from the deck and laid them out on the ground in front of them.

He ran his eyes over the cards, getting a feel for their general vibe, while listening within to his own intuition. He nodded to himself, and then grinned as he focused on the second card of the Major Arcana: Intuition.

'I would say that we are a hundred percent on the right track. Look at these two cards – Awareness and Intuition. They tell you to listen to your inner instincts. Then there's the Wisdom card – I guess that's self-explanatory, seeing as the goddess of wisdom herself turned up in your dream.'

Zakiy turned his attention to the next two cards: Obstacles & Challenges and Deception & Envy. 'I think these refer to our current situation. We're facing a lot of difficulties on our path, and I guess it's safe to say that we're being deceived – especially by the police.' They shared a commiserating look and sighed.

Sathi picked up the Deception & Envy card for a closer look; it showed a man in green robes in the process of either putting on or taking off a winged mask. His eyes were slanted down, with a greenish tint, and lime-green smoke billowed behind him.

'Envy' she said slowly. 'Is this another clue? Maybe this is the next head that needs to be cut off,' she mused.

'Maybe,' Zakiy said, taking the card from her and staring at it. 'Have you noticed whether Bhaskar and Goudhamy were envious of anything?'

Sathi thought about it. 'They never wanted Girish and Maya to spend time together, away from them, especially Goudhamy. It's like she always wanted Girish's undivided attention.' She paused. 'Does that count as envy, though?' she wondered, voice filled with doubt.

'Let me ask,' he responded, shuffling again. Almost immediately, a card flew out and landed face down in front of them. He flipped it over: Patience.

'Hmm... I would say that's a "no", or at least a "not yet". We should focus on the other sins for now.'

102

Sathi nodded while Zakiy turned his attention to the last two cards from the original seven-card spread. He started with the one that was easier for him to interpret. 'The Destiny card represents the Wheel of Fortune,' he explained. 'In this context, I think that represents a change in the status quo. The change itself could be positive or negative, but ultimately the message is that the wheel is turning – meaning that change is imminent.'

His eyes went to the last card, and he sighed. 'I'm not sure what to make of the Sacrifice card, to be honest.'

Sathi quietly picked it up and studied it intently. It showed a woman in a white dress standing waist-deep in water, her hands clasped in prayer above her head. Behind her, a brilliant rainbow shimmered against a backdrop of clouds shaped like flowers. Just looking at the woman gave Sathi goosebumps. 'It's Devi,' she whispered.

Zakiy stilled. 'I see. Well, then, I reckon this is her way of telling you that she's with you.'

She looked up at him. 'But the card says Sacrifice.'

'Sometimes certain cards can end up meaning something specific and unique to a certain person. That meaning often supersedes the original generic meaning of the card.'

Sathi's lips tilted up. 'So Devi is with us?'

'Of course she is. We're all in this together.'

Her eyes glistened with sudden tears. 'Good. We need all the help we can get.'

'So, m'lady, any other burning questions the great psychic-mystic Zakiy can answer for you?'

She raised an eyebrow. 'Psychic-Mystic?'

He shrugged. 'It sounds cool.'

'I'm not sure cool is the right word, but never mind that. No, I don't have any more questions, except...' She broke off, looking thoughtful.

'Yeah?' he prompted.

'Maybe we could ask about our next step. Pride was the first head to be cut off, so what should we focus on next?'

He started shuffling, and after several moments a card popped out. Movement, Choices, Decisions. It showed a man standing in front of four different coloured doorways.

Sathi chuckled. 'I guess that's classified information.'

He shook his head in resignation. 'I think that's all the information the gods are willing to share at the moment.'

She nodded in agreement. As he started putting the cards away, their phones buzzed. Sathi pulled hers out. 'It's a group text from Jayaram. He says we're meeting with the Palakkad ACP at 4 pm tomorrow. That's good, right?' she asked doubtfully.

Before he could answer, another message came through. 'Oh! Susan got bail!'

'Finally!' he exclaimed. He grinned at her. 'Let's take this as a good omen for the meeting tomorrow.'

Chapter Ten

Bribes, Blackmail & Betrayal

Zakiy and Sathi sat outside the ACP's office.

They'd been there for ten minutes already, and the ACP was running late. They were the only ones there; Nakul had a work meeting he couldn't miss, and although Sathi had wanted Jayaram to come with them, he'd said it was better not to have a lawyer involved straightaway – it might piss off the ACP and make him less inclined to help them.

Nevertheless, Jayaram had written up an official police complaint on her behalf, and it was tucked in the file that she nervously clutched in her hand.

When the ACP finally arrived another twenty minutes later, they stood up hopefully. He swept past them into his office. They sat back down, deflated, and waited for several more minutes until he finally called them in via his assistant.

'Good afternoon, sir,' Zakiy said as they entered his office.

The ACP looked up. 'Ah yes, good afternoon. Sit, sit,' he said, indicating the chairs in front of his desk. 'So, how can I help you?' he asked.

Sathi noticed that his gaze kept flicking to the TV in the corner, which was running a new channel. She cleared her throat to get his attention. 'Sir, my name is Sathi Varma. I'm here because my mother's uncle tried to rape me.'

At her words the ACP finally gave her his full attention. Encouraged, she continued, 'I filed a complaint at the local police station, but they're not taking me seriously. They're treating me more like a suspect than a victim.'

'The man who tried to rape you – what's his name?' the ACP asked, his eyes straying to someone waiting outside his office. He smiled and nodded, holding up five fingers, before turning back to Sathi.

She felt irritation shoot up inside her. 'Bhaskar. Bhaskar Pushkaran.'

'But he's local philanthropist, isn't he?' His eyes strayed to the TV again, and her jaw clenched. She wanted to get up and turn the TV off.

Probably realising that her fuse was about to blow, Zakiy quickly took the complaint Jayaram had written from her and handed it over to the ACP. 'If you read this, you'll understand that Bhaskar was only a philanthropist on paper. He was recently exposed in a dowry fraud, and in revenge he attacked Sathi. When she complained to the police, they accused her of making a false complaint against Bhaskar.'

The ACP took the complaint and leafed through it half-heartedly. 'Why would you give a false complaint?'

Sathi gave a mirthless laugh. 'That's what I want to know as well.'

'What reason did your local police give? They must have questioned Bhaskar about this incident.'

'Bhaskar told them I asked him to meet me at the resort where I work and blackmailed him for money.'

106

'Does he have any proof of that?' the ACP asked.

'No!' Sathi almost shouted. 'Because it's not true!'

'What about any witnesses who saw him trying to assault you?'

'No,' she admitted in a lower voice. 'No one was around at that time.'

'Then it's essentially a he-said she-said situation,' the ACP pointed out, shaking his head. 'Anyway, leave this with me,' he added, indicating the complaint. He beckoned to his assistant. 'Stamp this and give them a receipt,' he ordered.

His attention wandered to the TV again while the assistant was getting their receipt. 'I'll speak to Bhaskar as well,' he said, his eyes glued to the screen. His words were a clear dismissal.

'So that was a complete waste of time,' Zakiy muttered to her once they were outside the police building.

She nodded in agreement as she reached for her phone to update the others. Her eyes widened as she looked at her lock screen. 'Wow, five missed calls from Jayaram, Vidhya and Dad. Oh wait, there's a text from Jayaram as well – he wants us to call him immediately.' She clicked on his number and put the call on speaker. 'Hey, sorry, I had my phone on silent while we were–'

'Never mind that,' Jayaram interrupted urgently. 'You need to get back to Zakiy's house.'

'Why?'

'Karan's here and he's saying he wants to talk to you.'

Sathi glanced at Zakiy, whose eyes were wide. 'We'll be right there.'

Karan smiled silkily as they walked in. 'Ah, molé. How are you?'

Sathi cringed internally at the sickening endearment that Bhaskar and Goudhamy had constantly used to address her. She made sure that her expression reflected none of her discomfort, however. This man didn't get to see her emotions.

'I'm fine, thanks, Uncle. How are you?'

'Oh, I'm well, although I wish we were meeting under different circumstances, of course.' He gave a little laugh. He watched her expectantly for a reaction, but only received a polite smile. His eyes tightened, although his expression remained pleasant.

'Well, molé, there are some serious things I would like to discuss with you in private.' Karan looked pointedly at Vidhya, Nakul, Jayaram and Zakiy.

Jayaram stepped forward. 'I'm afraid you're not going to talk to Sathi without me present.'

'And who are you?' Karan asked, his tone sneering.

Jayaram straightened his shoulders. 'I'm her lawyer.'

'And I'm her father,' Nakul interjected. 'I'm not going anywhere either.'

Vidhya and Zakiy didn't say anything, but their defiant expressions spoke volumes.

Karan tapped his fingers against the table. 'Alright then. It's a party!' He gave another humourless chuckle. 'Molé, you've probably heard that I'm representing my father in the case you've filed against him. I came here today to beseech you to withdraw your complaint.'

Sathi shook her head tightly. 'I can't do that.'

'Molé, do you think what you are doing is right? You are giving false complaints about a harmless old man.'

She gave a sarcastic snort. 'That harmless old man told me to my face that he's been wanting to rape me since the time I stayed at his house. He also admitted that he tried to rape your sister-in-law, Maya. I guess you don't care about that, either.'

Karan shook his head sadly. 'It's very distressing to hear you say such things. What satisfaction does it give you to spread these lies?'

'They're not lies! You're the ones lying, you and your disgusting parents. You're all in this together.'

'I came here to try and reason with you to do the right thing. I can see that your mind is made up. So. What do you want?'

Sathi blinked. 'What do you mean?'

Karan leaned forward. 'Do you want money? Or property?'

'I don't want any of those things!' Sathi practically screeched. 'I just want that horrible man put away in jail where he won't be able to hurt anyone else.'

Karan smiled indulgently. 'Well, we can't always get what we want, can we? So, we may have to settle for something that would make both our lives easier. What about a nice sum to put towards your college fees?'

'I told you, I don't want your money,' she repeated through gritted teeth. 'If you think you can bribe me into withdrawing the case, you'll be sorely disappointed.'

Karan's smile didn't waver. 'Alright then. Let's move on, shall we?' He pulled out a file. 'Say you go forward with this case. Do you have any proof that my father tried to rape you?'

Sathi didn't answer, and his smile grew. 'I see. And yet I have proof that you lured my father to your place and then assaulted him when he wouldn't give in to your blackmail.'

Her mouth dropped. She stared at him, speechless.

'What proof?' Jayaram demanded.

'Ah, I'm so glad you asked.' Karan took out a piece of paper from the file and lay it on the table in front of them. 'This is a copy of a text message your client sent to my client on the day of the alleged rape and assault.'

Jayaram read out the short message. '"Meet me at the resort in room 06. We need to talk."' He shoved the paper back at Karan. 'Sathi didn't send this! Anyone could have written that.'

Karan carefully smoothened the paper. 'Well, if you follow the proper chain of evidence, you will find that this text message was sent from your client's phone, on the morning of the incident. When my client went there in order to talk to his granddaughter, your client demanded an obscene sum of money from him. Angered by his refusal, she brutally assaulted him and then falsely accused him of trying to rape her.'

'This is bullshit,' Dad burst out. 'You and your police friends have cooked up this false evidence.'

Karan didn't bat an eyelid. 'That's an interesting, but untrue, claim. This evidence has been verified by the cyber police. Now, this text message, coupled with the photographs of my client's injuries and this signed statement from Susan Roy, gives us all the proof we need.' With a sly smile, he pulled out another sheet of paper and put it on the table.

Jayaram snatched it and scanned through it. All the blood drained out of his face.

Vidhya came forward to stand next to him. 'What? What is it?'

Karan was the one to answer. 'It's a statement that Susan Roy gave to the police while in custody, stating that she was part of a conspiracy led by your client to frame my client in a dowry scam.'

Shocked silence met his words. Karan carefully placed all the papers back into the file and then fixed Sathi with a paternal smile. 'Molé, all this evidence against you is more than enough to prosecute you on charges of assault, extortion, and cheating. So, I ask you again: are you willing to withdraw your complaint against my client?'

As she met his cold, reptilian gaze, Sathi felt her numbness being replaced with calm understanding. 'So, this is how you win your cases, huh, Uncle? First bribery, then threats. Well, let me tell you something. No matter what false evidence you fabricate, no matter how you threaten me, I won't withdraw my complaint.'

Karan's eyes narrowed in his first true show of irritation. 'I see that you have inherited your mother's obstinacy. Just make sure you don't meet the same end she did.'

Rage wrapped around Sathi. 'Thank you for your advice,' she replied icily. 'Please convey the same sentiment to your father.'

Karan snorted. 'I guess I'll see you in court then.'

'I look forward to it.'

After Karan left, all her strength seemed to drain out of her. She sank onto the sofa while Zakiy silently motioned for Abdullah to bring them tea. Only after they were all sipping from fragrant mugs did Dad break the silence. 'Did Susan really sign that statement?'

Jayaram seemed exhausted. 'I'm afraid so. They must have threatened her pretty badly. I'm not defending her,' he hurried to add at Dad's look of outrage. 'She was behaving strangely yesterday, she wouldn't really meet my eyes. And she hasn't answered any of my phone calls since. This must be why they finally granted her bail, because she agreed to give this false statement against Sathi.'

'Well, no matter the reason, she stabbed us in the back,' Vidhya said, her eyes flint.

'I'm sorry.' Jayaram hung his head. 'I thought we could trust her.'

'It's not your fault,' Sathi said woodenly. 'She must have had her reasons. They framed her pretty badly, just like they're framing me now.'

Vidhya rubbed his back. 'She's right, my love. You blaming yourself doesn't help anyone. It's only in times of adversity that you find out who your true friends are.'

'And it's better to know now than later,' Zakiy put in. 'The question is, what's our next step? The police are no help to us – it's clear where their loyalties lie, and the meeting with the ACP only augmented that.' He brought the others up to speed on the ACP's total disinterest.

'Well, let's move onto Plan B in that case,' Jayaram decided. 'We'll approach the court directly and force the police to properly investigate Sathi's case. What I'm worried about, though, is this text message. Karan seems very confident that he can prove Sathi sent it.'

'I didn't text him!' Sathi burst out, her emotions flaring out of control as usual. She paused and took a deep breath, trying to get her anger under control. 'Sorry. I know you know I didn't send it. I have no idea how they would be able to prove that.'

Jayaram looked thoughtful. 'Did you have your phone with you all day? On that day, I mean?'

She shook her head wearily. 'I left my phone in the kitchen. My hands were full of laundry, so I put my phone down on the kitchen counter while I loaded the washing machine. Then I forgot it there when I went to my room. That's why I couldn't call for help when Bhaskar forced his way into my room.'

'Someone must have taken it from the kitchen,' Jayaram mused.

Nakul leaned forward. 'Isn't your phone locked though?'

She nodded. 'Yeah. With face lock.'

'Is your phone Android or Apple?' Jayaram asked.

'Android.'

Jayaram winced. 'Then someone could have used a picture of you to unlock it. The face recognition on Android phones isn't that sophisticated.'

'So someone stole her phone to send that message to Bhaskar, and then put it back?' Zakiy asked, frowning.

'Yeah, it was there when I went to find it to call the police.'

'Check to see if that message is still on your phone,' Jayaram ordered.

Sathi pulled out her phone and scrolled back to her messages from that day. 'No. They must have deleted it after they sent it.'

Jayaram sighed. 'So this was a well-organised plan. Bhaskar had a plan to get out of both the rape and the dowry case, all by discrediting you.'

'Karan is the mastermind behind this,' Sathi told them, remembering what Anika had said. 'His criminal intelligence is Bhaskar's get-out-of-jail-free card.'

'So we need to figure out a way to counter his intelligence,' Jayaram stated. 'The problem is that we don't have proof, whereas they've created this mountain of false evidence to support their version of events.' He paused, thinking. 'Will Maya testify against Bhaskar?' he asked suddenly.

Zakiy shook his head. 'She doesn't even know what happened to her. Sathi said it was like she was in a trance, right?'

Sathi absently agreed, her mind a thousand miles away. Jayaram had identified the main hurdle in their path; they needed proof, and the best way to get it was to persuade another victim to testify. However, Maya wasn't the one they needed – they needed Anika to testify.

Once Jayaram had left for his office to draft the complaint to the magistrate, Zakiy dropped off Nakul and Vidhya at their respective homes.

As soon as they were alone, Sathi brought Zakiy up to speed on her idea to get Anika to give a statement on their behalf. He agreed that it was their best course of action, and Sathi tried to call Anika, but the line was busy. After five minutes of getting the same busy signal, Sathi looked up the address Anika had given them in case they needed to meet her.

Soon they were drawing up to a terraced house at the edge of the tea estate. They strolled up to the door and knocked, but there was no response. 'Try calling again,' Zakiy said, knocking for the third time.

Sathi shook her head after a few minutes. 'Still on another call,' she said, putting her phone back into her pocket. She peered around. 'Let's go around the back, maybe there's a window we can find that's open.'

'Are you planning to pry the window bars apart and climb in?' Zakiy enquired as he followed her.

'No, smart-aleck, I thought we could call out her name through an open window.'

'Damn. I thought I was going to see some secret ninja skills you've been hiding from me. I'm disappointed now,' he whined.

Sathi rolled her eyes. As they turned the corner of the house, she spotted Anika standing in her backyard. She was about to call out her name when a low, sultry laugh stopped her in her tracks.

'I got your package,' Anika said, her voice husky. 'I can't wait to try it out.' She paused while the other person responded, and she laughed again. 'Well, it's not like I need it when you're around.' She sighed. 'I know, baby. I miss you too. We'll be together soon,' she promised, hanging up and turning around.

Anika's hand flew up to her mouth as she gasped. 'Oh!'

'Sorry!' Sathi blurted. 'We didn't mean to overhear; we were just trying to contact you. Your phone was engaged,' she ended awkwardly, squarely putting her foot back into her mouth.

Zakiy nodded frantically. 'Yeah, so Sathi wanted to find an open window so we could get in.' He flinched as Sathi groaned. 'Wait. That came out wrong...'

Anika lowered her hand and giggled. 'Do I need to file a police complaint against you two?' she teased.

Sathi exhaled. 'Funny you should say that... Let's go inside, I feel like this will be a long story.'

'Of course.' She ushered them into the sitting room. A box sat on one of the chairs, and as Zakiy reached out to move it so they all had space to sit, Anika snatched the box away, flushing. 'Excuse me,' she murmured as she hurried away.

Sathi glanced at Zakiy questioningly, but his expression was a bit shell-shocked.

Before she could ask what was wrong, Anika was back. 'So,' she said with forced breeziness. 'What brings you here?'

Between them, Sathi and Zakiy managed to update Anika on everything that had happened since they last saw her. 'So, we really need you to give a statement to the police about what happened,' Sathi concluded. 'We desperately need your help.'

Anika didn't speak for a few moments. 'You said your friend Susan Roy gave a statement against you?'

The reminder of Susan's betrayal stung. 'Yeah. We think that's how she got bail, because she gave a false statement saying that the whole dowry exposure was a set-up to trap Bhaskar, with me as the mastermind behind it all.'

'I see. Well, yes, of course I will testify on your behalf, Sathi.' She paused. 'However, I do ask for your understanding. This is all happening a bit faster than I anticipated. I need more time.'

At their disappointed expressions, Anika hastened to add, 'I have to think of my son and make sure his future is secure. Karan and Bhaskar will disown me as soon as I publicly go against them. And I shudder to think what else they might do. I need some more time to get my affairs in order. Please understand,' she entreated, looking between the two of them.

Sathi was the first to break the pregnant silence. 'Yes, of course we understand. I don't want what happened to Susan to happen to you,' she admitted, although her stomach felt like lead as she considered how to take their police case forward without Anika's help.

Zakiy didn't speak.

'Thank you,' Anika said, eyes glistening. Discomfort crossed her expression. 'About that phone call... Well, he's the reason I'm fighting so hard to escape this horrible half-life with Karan. Jacob loves me and he treats Arjun like his own son. All he wants is for me to be happy, and I want a life with him. He is also in the process of getting a divorce from his wife, so I just need to wait a little longer before he will be able to bring me and Arjun to his home.'

Sathi forced a smile. 'That's great, I'm happy for you. I hope everything works out with you and Jacob.'

Anika took a deep breath. 'There's something else I wanted to tell you about Karan. As you probably realised, he is very intelligent, and shows single-minded ruthlessness to get things done. But criminal intelligence is not the only weapon in his arsenal. As you know, his

115

family is deeply involved in black magic; I've heard that Karan has a source of power somewhere that makes him so successful. If you want to defeat him, you will need to find and destroy that power first.'

Chapter Eleven

The Call

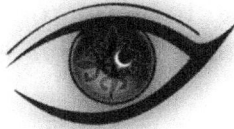

Lost in her own depressing thoughts, it wasn't until they were back at the campsite and sipping cocoa that Sathi realised Zakiy was uncharacteristically quiet. She glanced at him and realised that he was staring into their campfire with an unfocused expression. 'Hey,' she said softly, not wanting to startle him. 'What's wrong?'

He shook his head, like he was trying to clear it. 'Hmm? Nothing.'

'You've been like since we went to Anika's house,' she persisted. 'Are you upset that she can't testify right away?'

'No,' he said slowly. 'It's not just that. I mean, yes of course I'm disappointed, but I feel like something's off. It's like we're doing things half blind... no, at least eighty percent blind. Even with so many honest people to help us, we're drowning in lies and deceit.' As he spoke the Tarot card from yesterday floated across her mind: Deception and Envy.

'We need more guidance,' he said decisively.

'We could look at Tarot again,' she suggested.

'Nah, we need expert guidance. Not my amateur reading.' She wanted to protest that his readings weren't amateur, but he was already taking his phone out and dialling. 'Hello, Amma? Yeah, we're fine. Listen, Amma, there's been some issues here. I want to take Sathi to an astrologer to get some guidance. Do you still have the number of the guy you used to go to. You do? Yes, please send it to me. Sathi? Hold on.' He put the call on speaker and put in on the ground between them.

'Hi Maira,' Sathi said.

'Hi sweetheart! How are you?' Maira asked, her sweet voice bringing a lump to Sathi's throat.

She cleared her throat. 'I'm fine,' she managed. 'Maira, why does your son think I need to go see an astrologer?'

Maira's soft laughter floated across the air, and Sathi smiled in response. 'So typical of my boy, to not explain to you first before calling me for the number.'

'I'm right here, you know,' Zakiy interjected.

Both women ignored him. 'Sweetheart, an astrologer can help us by interpreting the actions of the various stars and planets on our life and give us some guidance in facing certain difficulties that we may be experiencing. It's a complex science, and one that's often dismissed as superstition by the Western world. The guy I always go to has an additional gift, because he has additional knowledge given to him by his ancestors about the person asking for guidance.' Maira paused. 'I assume that Zakiy has some reason why he feels it's necessary for you to visit this astrologer. Anyway, it couldn't hurt. You can also go with specific questions you want answers to.'

'I see. I guess that makes sense,' she said, though she felt doubtful. She'd been to an astrologer once before and had received vague advice that she hadn't found particularly helpful. Or maybe she just hadn't wanted to accept the guidance given to her then. Maybe she should give it another chance, especially since Zakiy seemed insistent.

Perhaps sensing her preoccupation, Maira said goodbye soon after. She turned to Zakiy. 'We could ask the astrologer about what Anika said, about finding Karan's source of power.'

He nodded absently. 'Yeah, we should ask about that.' Zakiy seemed lost in thought again, and Sathi felt unnaturally tired. She soon said goodnight and retired into her tent, falling into unconsciousness with relief.

Zakiy stared at Sathi's tent for a long time after she'd left, trying to make sense of the uneasiness he felt. He felt like they were surrounded by enemies on all sides, and the enemies were winning. They were missing something, and that missing piece would be the deciding factor in who ultimately won this war – good or evil.

His thoughts shifted to Anika. Something about her seemed off to him, although he couldn't quite put his feelings into words yet. That was another reason why he wanted to talk to an astrologer. He wanted to know whether his feelings were just paranoia, or if his intuition was trying to warn him.

He hadn't been able to bring himself to tell Sathi yet, but the delivery box that Anika has hastily removed from the sitting room had been a vibrator.

Zakiy understood that Anika had been a victim of repeated rape, and he wanted to be happy for the fact that she'd found a better man who seemed to love her for herself. But he couldn't help but wonder what sort of man would send a gift like that to a house with a small child in it.

Sternly, he told himself to stop being so judgemental. It wasn't like she was using the vibrator in front of her son! Just because she was a mother didn't mean she didn't have the needs and desires of a woman.

Of course, that didn't erase the irritation he felt at her going back on her word to help Sathi. Right now everyone was treating Sathi as the villain, while Bhaskar was the harmless old man who was being blackmailed. All the evidence was against Sathi, and Anika's testimony would be all that was necessary to restore Sathi's credibility.

Or maybe he was being too harsh. Anika obviously didn't have any financial stability and couldn't take a hasty decision that may put her or her son at risk.

Zakiy sighed and ran a hand over his face. He felt... dirty. Grimy. Like the evil around them had tainted his perspective, and now he felt like he had to second-guess all his thoughts. That was why he needed some outside guidance. When he couldn't trust his own judgement, his Tarot readings would also be skewed.

Tomorrow he and Sathi would go to see that astrologer. That had to help.

In the morning, Sathi left early for her shift at the resort – her first time back at work since the incident. Everyone, including Zakiy, had tried to persuade her to take it easy for a while, but she said she needed to get back into a routine. It would help to keep her sane, especially now that her case against Bhaskar seemed at a standstill.

When she finished her shift, Zakiy was waiting for her. 'I made an appointment with the astrologer. Let's go?'

Sathi shrugged. 'Sure.'

As they walked, she kept looking around.

When she frowned, he bumped her shoulder with his. 'What's up?'

'I feel like this road is familiar. Wait. Are we going to Srinivasan Panickar?' she demanded.

Zakiy stopped in surprise. 'You know him?

Her scowl deepened. 'I'm not going to him! I went to see him once, before I met you. He was useless.'

120

He blinked. 'Are you sure? My family's been going to him for years, and he's the one Amma calls whenever she needs guidance. He's very intuitive.' When Sathi didn't respond, he took a deep breath. 'Is it possible that maybe you weren't ready to hear what he told you?' he asked gently.

When he was met with stony silence, he figured he was onto something. 'What did he say?'

'He said I won't get justice for what happened to my mother on my own. He said I would need help from someone who has just as much right to justice as I do,' she replied grudgingly.

He didn't say anything, letting her process her own words. Finally, she sighed, and her anger seemed to ebb away. 'I guess he was right. I have you and Jayaram and Vidhya to help me now, as well my dad.'

Her face clouded over. 'I was angry at the time because I thought the astrologer meant my dad, and I was feeling too hurt and raw about our fight to accept that. I felt like my dad should have come out here to avenge my mother sooner, and I didn't like being told that I needed his help.'

'That's understandable. So, it seems the astrologer was mostly right,' Zakiy said delicately.

'Yeah. Except I kind of shouted at him and stormed out,' she admitted, her shoulders hunching. She peeked up at him to check his reaction.

He burst out laughing, more at her guilty expression than at her admission.

Sathi glared at him, but he could tell she was trying not to smile.

Zakiy held out his arm. 'C'mon, m'lady. Let's go and find out our future.'

If Srinivasan Panickar remembered Sathi and her outburst, he didn't show any sign of it. He simply asked for their names and birth stars and started to spin the shells against the desk with the palm of his hand, chanting too quickly for Zakiy to fully understand what he was saying. He did understand that he was asking for the truth to be revealed, with help from the planets.

'It is Makaram raashi,' Sreenivasan said once he had finished spinning and separated the shells into groups of threes. 'With this raashi, the planets stand as follows: in the second house there is Saturn, third empty, Uranus and Jupiter in the fourth, fifth empty, the Moon in the sixth, the Sun and Venus in the seventh, Mercury and Mars in the eighth, ninth empty, Neptune in the tenth and eleven and twelve empty.'

Sreenivasan pushed his glasses up. 'Jupiter in the fourth house means you have the blessings of the gods, and they are with you in force. The Moon is hidden in the sixth house, which is not so good. You feel extremely tired in the things you do; you feel bodily fatigue and find it difficult to finish things as you need to. I can also see that there is a lot of deception and lies surrounding you like a web. It is difficult for you to tell what is true and what is a lie. Gulikan is in the eighth house, so you have a lot of enemies who want to see you destroyed in any way possible.

'But Jupiter also has a direct view of the eighth house, and Jupiter has the power to destroy ten million spokes of evil. So don't worry, you will be able to overcome any obstacle that's in your path. According to your birth star, there will be positive changes starting from the next month in the Malayalam calendar.

'Saturn in the second house says you have enemies both from your mother's side of the family and from people you consider as friends or allies. Venus in the seventh house indicates there's a woman acting against you, and the Sun suggests that there is an enemy in male form as well. They are either your parents or people who are like parents to you, for example siblings of your parents. They want to see you defeated; your destruction is their goal.'

Sathi leaned forward. 'Right now, we are facing a powerful enemy, who is very intelligent. Can you tell us if there is anything we can do to overcome him? His name is Karan, we don't know his star.'

He nodded, spinning the shells again as he repeated the question to the gods. Once he was done, he examined the planetary positions once more. 'As you say, he is extremely intelligent, and dangerous too. He would do anything to achieve his goals, be wary of him.'

'Does he have some secret source of power?' Zakiy asked, wanting to verify the truth of Anika's words.

Sreenivasan thought for a moment. 'Yes, and some kind of protection as well. That's what makes him such a formidable enemy. The source of his power and his protection are deeply tied to his family; especially to his mother.' He shook his head. 'I'm unable to get any more information about that. He's too well protected.'

'What about the female who is an enemy?' Sathi asked.

'She is someone whom you consider your ally but is actually working with the enemy to betray you. She is wrapped in deception and envy, and she is feeding an ancestral evil.'

Zakiy gulped. 'Ancestral evil?'

'Yes. I can see that this evil has destroyed multiple generations of your family and will destroy you as well unless you defeat it. Let me check what we can do to help you.' He started spinning the shells again, this time asking for ways to circumvent the difficulties that lay before them.

'You need to go to Mookambika,' he said finally. 'Pray to the Devi there for strength and wisdom. Present her with a silk sari and thali and ask for her blessing in this righteous fight.' He thought for a moment and added, 'Go to Guruvayur as well and see the Lord. Light ghee lamps and offer milk pudding to him. You need their blessings in order to succeed.'

Zakiy nodded, trying to take in all that they'd been told. Sreenivasan wrote down the different offering they were supposed to give the gods and handed them the paper.

As they thanked him and stood to leave, he stopped Sathi. 'That paper has my phone number on it at the top. You can call me any time if you need guidance,' he told her, eyes kind. In that moment

Zakiy knew that he remembered Sathi from before, and that he understood her earlier outburst had simply been a reflection of her pain.

From the way Sathi's eyes started to glisten, she must have realised it too. She smiled at Sreenivasan. 'I will. Thank you.'

As they strolled back to their campsite, Zakiy crowed, 'Now aren't you glad I forced you to see him?'

He thought she would throw something at him, so he was caught completely off guard when she threw her hands around his neck. From the muffled sounds, it sounded like she was sobbing.

Shocked, he hesitantly wrapped his arms around her, waiting for her to withdraw from him like usual. Instead, she just tightened her hold on him. Slowly, he raised a hand to her head and stroked her hair, not saying anything, just letting her release the emotions she must have been bottling up.

It took several moments for her sobs to quieten, and even then, she didn't let go of him. He felt so incredibly touched that she trusted him with her emotions. When she finally pulled back, she didn't immediately move out of his arms. She gazed up at him. 'Sorry about that,' she said.

'Anytime, m'lady. Although you may have to buy me a new shirt.' He pointedly looked down at where her tears had drenched the material covering his chest.

She blushed and moved back, letting her hair fall forward to cover her face. 'I'll write you an IOU.'

'How do I know I can trust you?' he teased as they started walking again.

Sathi turned and speared him with an intense gaze. 'You can trust me.'

The air rushed out of his lungs. Those eyes...

She giggled at his stunned expression and spun away ahead of him.

124

His own cheeks feeling a bit warmer than usual, he followed Sathi. His Siren.

When they reached the resort, they decided to see if Vidhya was around to feed them. They were in luck, because they found her pottering around the kitchen, cleaning up after the dinner rush.

A delicious aroma floated across the air towards them, making Zakiy sniff the air like a hunting dog. 'You made chicken curry,' he exulted, hugging Vidhya with such force that he nearly toppled her over.

Sathi just shook her head and went in search for some bread. Nothing was better than Vidhya's spicy curry balanced by the sweetness of Indian bread. She returned to the table with two loaves and a plastic container that she set in the middle of the table.

Zakiy's head snapped up as his gaze zeroed in on the container. 'You didn't.'

She smirked. 'I did. This is my IOU, paid in full.'

Vidhya laughed. 'Let me guess. You made him macadamia nut and white chocolate chip cookies.'

'Also known as ambrosia,' Zakiy groaned with his mouth full of cookie.

When he went in for another one, Vidhya yanked the box out of his hands. He looked at her like he was a puppy she'd just spanked.

'You can have it back after dinner,' she promised, eyes full of mirth.

'Fair enough,' he agreed mournfully. Still, he cheered up as they dug into their dinner with gusto.

When they were reaching for second helpings, Vidhya cleared her throat. 'I spoke to Jay, and he asked me to give you an update since he's been busy with court all day. He said he's still gathering information on how to proceed with the case, and he's trying to find out if you can give a statement to the magistrate directly. He said he'll have the relevant facts by tomorrow, so he wants us to have a meeting to discuss our options.'

Sathi swallowed her bite and nodded. 'Thank you, and please give Jayaram my thanks too. I really appreciate everything you guys are doing for me.'

Vidhya smiled. 'You don't need to thank us, it's what family does. And we are a family now,' she said fiercely.

'I couldn't agree more,' Zakiy mumbled around his full mouth.

'Anyway, I'm going to head over to court and make Jay eat something,' Vidhya said, standing. 'I'll pack some of this for him.'

'Oh, so you made all this for him. Not for us,' Zakiy said, sniffing while cramming more bread into his mouth. The boy could definitely multitask. Then he ducked as Vidhya swatted his head and continued to ladle some of the chicken curry into a container. As she grabbed a fresh loaf of bread, Sathi offered, 'Take some cookies as well, for dessert.'

'No! Not my cookies,' Zakiy wailed dramatically.

Sathi and Vidhya just rolled their eyes at each other, and Sathi went to wash and dry her hands. Then she transferred a few cookies into a smaller container. 'Don't be a baby,' she told Zakiy as she pushed the rest of the stash towards him.

'I will be a baby when it comes to your cookies. Tell Jay he owes me.' He peered into the box, making sure his stock hadn't been depleted too badly.

'Will do,' Vidhya replied with barely controlled laughter. She waved and left, the food containers stacked in her hands and the bread tucked under one arm.

Sathi stared at Zakiy, who was sitting there looking very much like a squirrel hoarding his nuts. 'You're crazy,' she informed him.

He raised an eyebrow. 'You're only just realising this now?' He grinned and popped another cookie in his mouth. 'Want one?'

'How generous of you to offer me one of the cookies that *I* spent the morning baking for you,' she said, reaching for a cookie and

126

breaking it in half. She popped one half in her mouth and sighed. Macadamia nut and white chocolate had always been one of her favourites as well.

'You baked them for me?' he asked, his tone suddenly shy.

She held his gaze and nodded.

He silently pushed the cookies closer to her.

Chapter Twelve

Guruvayurappan

‘I have a confession to make,’ Sathi announced as they lounged around their campsite later.

‘Oh?’ Zakiy looked up from his Tarot. The Deception and Envy card had flown from the deck as soon as he took the cards out of the box. He’d been holding it in his hand, staring at it.

She glanced from the card to him and back again, obviously feeling bad for interrupting.

He put the cards back and gave her his full attention. ‘The cards will still be there later,’ he said gently, moving closer to her. ‘What did you want to confess?’

Her expression was embarrassed. ‘I didn’t understand most of what Srinivasan Panickar told us.’

He blinked in surprise and then wanted to slap himself. Of course, she hadn’t understood; a lot of what Srinivasan had said had been in Sanskrit, and even the Malayalam had been quite technical. Zakiy was a bit more used to it, but still there was stuff he'd missed as well. 'I should have thought of that. It must be very difficult for you to follow him. How did you manage last time?' he wondered aloud.

'I still didn't understand a lot of what he said, and I think that's partly why I got so pissed off at the little I did understand,' she admitted.

'Well, don't worry. Let's do a group call with my parents. They're the best at interpreting Srinivasan's words. I always record the readings, so I'll just send the recording to them. I'll ask them to listen and then call us when they're done.' As he spoke, he sent the message to his mother and got a response within seconds. 'She's on it,' he said in satisfaction.

They didn't have long to wait until his phone lit up with an incoming call. He answered and put the call on speaker. 'Good evening, Parents.'

His mother chuckled in response, and he swore he could hear his father's exasperated sigh from miles away. 'Hello, son. Is Sathi there?'

'Yes, I am, Uncle. I miss you,' Sathi added, leaning closer to the phone.

Her familiar vanilla-and-spice scent washed over Zakiy, and he closed his eyes briefly.

'I miss you too, Sathi,' his dad said, his voice suspiciously thick.

'What about me?' Zakiy demanded, eyes snapping open.

Silence.

'Wow. Thanks, Dad. Nice to know you care,' he grouched.

'Erm, it's not that, darling. Your father had to step away for a second. He needed a tissue.' Amma's voice was rich with suppressed laughter. 'Okay, he's back now.'

Sathi giggled as Zakiy pinched the bridge of his nose. 'So what did you guys think of the recording?'

His dad's voice was all business now. 'It seems like you're fighting a formidable battle, and you'll need all the help you can get from the gods.'

'Wait, Dad,' Zakiy interrupted. 'Can you first give Sathi a summary of how astrology works? This is all new to her, and I tried to explain but you know so much more than I do,' he said in a rare show of deference to his father.

Only a brief silence reflected his dad's surprise. He quickly recovered. 'Well, Sathi, an astrologer interprets the positions of the planets in relation to each other and how they affect a person's life. At the start, what he does is figure out the positions of the planets and which house they are in at that moment of a person's life. There are twelve houses and seven planets, plus the moon and the sun. Some of the houses are negative, like the sixth and eight, and if a planet is in a negative house, it can either dampen the positive effects of a planet or amp up the inherent negativity of another one. Jupiter is the most positive planet of all, and usually if it is in a positive or neutral house it means the gods are supporting you. Does that make sense so far?'

Sathi was nodding along. 'Yes, Uncle, it does. So today Srinivasan said Jupiter was in a good house and so it was negating the bad effects of another planet.'

'That's right,' her dad said approvingly. 'What you're referring to is Jupiter making up for the effects of Gulian being in the eighth house. Gulian is actually not a planet, but it's a negative influence, and since it's in a negative house, that's doubly bad. However, as you correctly pointed out, Jupiter is more than making up for it. Jupiter is in the fourth house, which has a direct view of the eighth house, where Gulian is. That's why the positive influence of Jupiter can buffer the negative influence of Gulian.'

Sathi digested this. 'Okay, I think I understand. What about the things he said about enemies and the seventh house? I found that part a bit confusing.'

130

'The seventh house is the house of relationships and reveals the relationships your enemies have to you. As Srinivasan said, your enemies are mainly from your own family, and are people who have the same status as parents. This can mean your uncles and aunts, or even cousins of your parents. Venus is feminine, indicating a female enemy, and the Sun is masculine, indicating a male enemy as well.'

'So, Karan could definitely be the male enemy, especially since he is also my mother's cousin?'

'Exactly,' Dad said. 'The female could be an aunt, or even someone else you consider your family. It may even refer to Bhaskar's wife.'

'Srinivasan did say that people who we consider allies have betrayed us,' Sathi recalled slowly. 'There's someone who fits that description perfectly.'

'Susan Roy,' Sathi and Zakiy said together.

'What about Susan?' Amma asked sharply, and Zakiy gave them a quick update on recent events.

'I see. So, she basically threw you under the bus to save herself,' Amma said, her voice cold enough to rival the north pole. 'She definitively seems to fit the bill for an alley-turned-enemy.'

'Yeah, that's what I figured too,' Sathi agreed. 'Although I don't really understand how that relates to this ancestral evil stuff.'

'True,' Zakiy mused. 'That seems to be tied to your family. Srinivasan said it has destroyed multiple generations and is trying to destroy you as well.'

'That's very dangerous, Sathi,' Dad warned. 'I remember you told us that your mother's parents died in a car accident. It's possible that black magic was involved in those deaths as well. I think that's why Srinivasan told you to go to Mookambika and Guruvayur,' he added. 'You will need the help of Mookambika Devi and Guruvayurappan to overcome this ancestral evil.'

Sathi turned to Zakiy and gave a reluctant grin. 'It seems like it's time for another road trip.'

He laughed. 'We wouldn't really be us without that. We just need to make sure we talk to Jayaram about our next step in the police case before we go. 'He paused thoughtfully. 'But can we go back to Karan for a minute? Both Anika and Srinivasan said he has some kind of power and protection that we need to find and destroy. Have you ever heard of anything like that, Dad?'

His father was silent for so long that Zakiy began to doubt whether he had heard him. 'Hello?'

'Yes, you impatient boy, I heard you, now let me think,' Dad ordered.

Sathi started to shake with silent laughter as Zakiy stuck out his tongue at the phone. If they were talking about impatience, it was a classic case of the kettle calling the pot black.

'I think you need to talk to an acquaintance of mine, Raghavan,' Dad said finally. 'He lives in Nelliampathi, and he will be able to answer your questions about Karan's protection. I'll call him and ask for a good time for you to visit.' He hesitated and then added, 'Remember that sometimes you need to use magic to fight magic.'

Sathi frowned. 'Isn't that why we're going to the temples? To get the gods to help us out with their magic?'

'The gods give us their blessings; they don't fight our battles for us. Karan is using major black magic against you, and in order to destroy his power you may need to use magic to counteract his. That's why I want you to visit Raghavan. He's an astrologer too, but he's very different from Srinivasan. He will have contacts who can help you to find and destroy Karan's source of power.'

There was a silence. 'Any other questions, sweetheart?' Amma asked.

Sathi and Zakiy exchanged glances. 'Nope. I think we're good for now. Thank you both.'

'You're very welcome. Let us know if we can help in any other way.'

Sathi assured them that they would, and they said goodnight before hanging up.

132

'Let's talk to Jayaram tomorrow,' Zakiy suggested. 'Then we can figure out our road trip.'

Sathi nodded. 'You know there's another big hurdle to us going on a trip.'

He looked at her, puzzled, and she gave a wide grin. 'We'll first have to convince my father to let us go.'

Zakiy gulped. *Oh shit.*

They all gathered in Zakiy's dining room again the next morning. It was rapidly turning into a sort of conference room.

Jayaram cleared his throat. 'So, I spoke to several of my colleagues yesterday about how to proceed with your case, Sathi. They advised me that since the police have not registered a First Information Report, or FIR, we should approach a Superintendent of Police before we go to a magistrate. So, the next best step is to appeal to the Deputy Commissioner of Police and ask him to put pressure on the local Sub-Inspector to register the FIR against Bhaskar.'

'I thought you said Superintendent of Police first, then you mentioned the Deputy Commissioner?' Sathi asked, confused.

'They're the same,' Jayaram assured her. 'If you're happy with this next step, I'll go see the Deputy Commissioner tomorrow and see if we can get the FIR filed.'

'That sounds perfect,' she responded, and Nakul, Vidhya and Zakiy murmured their agreement.

Jayaram nodded. 'Okay, then. I think we should consider it a small victory if we can get the FIR filed. That will remain as a black mark against Bhaskar, no matter how much he bribes the police to escape punishment.'

Zakiy spoke up hesitantly. 'Since we're not going to go to the magistrate directly, would it be okay for Sathi and me to visit a few temples? We went to an astrologer, and we've got a list of offerings to make. It may take us a few days to make the round trip.'

'Fine with me,' Jayaram said, shrugging. 'God knows we need all the help we can get.'

Taking a deep breath, Zakiy looked at Nakul.

Nakul didn't reply but spent a long time looking between Sathi and Zakiy. Finally, he nodded. 'Yes, it's fine with me too.'

Zakiy barely kept his mouth from dropping open as he stared at Sathi's father in astonishment. What had happened to him?

Nakul stood. 'Zakiy. A word, please.'

Oh damn. Here it comes. He met Sathi's sympathetic gaze for a moment before following Nakul to his doom.

When Zakiy caught up with Nakul, he was in the garden, staring out at the weeds that had infiltrated the once lovingly tended flowers. For a moment, sadness about his abandoned childhood home distracted Zakiy.

Then Nakul turned to face him. 'I'm trusting you with my daughter,' he said without preamble.

Zakiy blinked at him. 'Umm. Thank you, sir.'

'I don't need your thanks. I want to know that you deserve my trust,' Nakul said sternly. 'Sathi has been through a lot, much more than a young girl her age should have had to face. I'm largely to blame for that. I can see that she trusts you, and I know she cares about you as well, even though I'm not sure she realises the depth of her feelings. That means you have the power to hurt her even more.'

Nakul took a step closer, his eyes narrowing. 'She needs you right now, but if you hurt her in any way, I swear to God that I will skin you alive and feed you to my dogs.'

Zakiy felt a bit like he was standing in the path of a fire-breathing dragon. 'I didn't know you have dogs,' he said stupidly.

'For you, I'll get some. Are we clear?'

'Yes, sir.'

'Good.'

As Nakul turned to head back inside, Zakiy could have sworn a smile was playing around his mouth.

134

'Um, sir,' Zakiy said quickly.

Nakul turned. 'Yes?' he barked; all traces of humour gone.

'It's Sathi's birthday soon,' Zakiy blurted. 'I wanted to plan a surprise for her, but I wanted to get your permission first.' Since Nakul didn't look like he wanted to shoot him dead (yet), he hastily explained his idea.

As he spoke, Nakul's expression gradually relaxed until he looked almost impressed.

'So would it be okay?' Zakiy asked nervously when Nakul didn't respond immediately.

Nakul was silent for a moment. 'Alright. But remember what I said about the dogs.'

When Sathi found Zakiy a few minutes later, he hadn't moved from his spot. She studied his face silently. 'That bad, huh?'

Zakiy exhaled completely for the first time since the beginning of his conversation with Nakul. 'You have no idea.'

The next day, they started their journey to Guruvayur, which was about a two-and-a-half-hour drive west of Nelliampathi. After that, they would start the much longer trek up to Mookambika, which was in Karnataka, the state that bordered Kerala in the north-west.

As they pulled into the parking lot of the temple in Guruvayur, Sathi looked around. The temple grounds were packed, with devotees traipsing to and from the main entrance. The two of them got out and headed towards the entrance, with Sathi gawking at the shops on either side of the alley that displayed bright clothes and all sorts of devotional items hanging from hooks and stacked up on the counters.

Sathi noticed that peacock feathers were a common theme; from the embroidery pattern on the white saris and tunics, to the very real-looking feathers tucked behind photos of Krishna, a boyish avatar of Lord Vishnu, the gorgeous teal-blue colour peeked out from everywhere. 'I want that one,' a little boy insisted to his mother as he pointed to a piece of clothing decorated with bright patterns.

After they passed through the metal detectors at the entrance to the temple, Zakiy paused. 'Wait here,' he told her, getting the piece of paper Srinivasan had given them out of his wallet. 'I'll go pay for the offerings.'

Sathi eyed the long queue at the counters. 'Are you sure? I'll come with you.'

'Nah, there's no point in us both getting trampled by the crowd. Just send out a search party if I'm not back in an hour.' He gave her a jaunty salute and went to join the queue.

Sathi settled back against a pillar and people watched. Inside the main entrance, the temple itself had an outer courtyard area surrounding the smaller building that she assumed housed the figurine of the deity. There were large, caged staircases that were already full of people waiting to go inside the main temple to see Guruvayurappan, whose name roughly translated to "The Father of Guruvayur". It was how they called the form of Lord Vishnu who had taken up residence here.

Vishnu was the lord of sustenance, consort to Lakshmi Devi, who was the goddess of wealth. In fact, Sathi could see that there was a smaller pedestal for of Devi in one corner of the outer area of the temple.

She was interrupted in her wool-gathering when a voice right next to her suddenly said, 'Ah, beautiful, isn't she?'

Startled, she turned to see Whitebeard standing next to her and looking dreamily in the direction of the pedestal of Devi. 'You?' What are you doing here?' Sathi had met the old man several times since coming to India, and every time he'd had some vague advice to give her before disappearing as quickly as he appeared.

Whitebeard shrugged and tore his attention from Lakshmi Devi. 'This is my home,' he said, spreading his arms grandiosely. 'It pleases me that you have finally come to see me.'

136

'Umm, I'm actually here to see Guruvayurappan,' she corrected, amused.

'Same difference,' he replied, shrugging.

Sathi waited for Whitebeard to start spouting random advice, but he was just looking around contentedly. Then he caught sight of the little boy Sathi had seen outside earlier, who was clutching a piece of white cloth with a pattern of both peacock feathers and pink lotuses. Whitebeard went over to get a closer look. 'Little boy, can I see that?' he asked, pointing to the cloth.

The boy looked at Whitebeard with distrust. 'It's for Guruvayurappan,' he informed Whitebeard.

Whitebeard stroked his... white beard. 'It's so beautiful. Will you give it to me?' he beseeched.

Sathi buried her head in her hands as the little boy shook his head emphatically. 'No, no, I told you, it's for Guruvayurappan,' he yelled. By this time his mother was looking at Whitebeard with concern.

'But I want it,' Whitebeard argued petulantly.

When the little kid's lower lip began to wobble, his mother took action. 'Baby, give this to him, he's a poor old man. We'll go get another one to give Guruvayurappan, how's that?'

The kid hiccupped. 'I guess.' He reluctantly held out the cloth to Whitebeard, who took it delightedly.

'Thank you, kind lady and generous little boy. A thousand blessings on you both.' He turned to Sathi. 'Don't forget to get the milk pudding afterwards. It's the best.'

Beaming, he waved at them all and walked away, whistling.

The mother and Sathi looked at each other, baffled. Then the mother shrugged and took her son by the hand. 'Come on, sweetheart, let's go get your gift for Guruvayurappan.'

Another ten minutes later, Zakiy found her. 'You survived the crowd,' she said, feigning surprise.

'Yup. Now it's round two, and you'll need to survive too.'

Sathi raised her eyebrows, and he explained, 'We'll need to go inside now to see Guruvayurappan. Ready to get stampeded by the crowd?'

She followed his gaze to the mass of people lining up to go inside the inner temple and gulped. 'Fun.'

As they joined the queue and settled in to wait, Sathi caught sight of the little kid from before standing a few people in front of them. The boy was almost in tears. 'It's not the same,' he wailed to his mother.

'Baby, what's not the same?' His mother hugged him close, bewildered.

'The pattern! I wanted to give Guruvayurappan the mundu with the peacock feather and the lotuses. This one only has the feathers.' The boy had tears streaming down his face at this point.

'Sweetheart, I'm sorry but this is the only design they had left at the shop. Next time we can get the design you wanted,' his mother promised.

Watching the kid's disappointment, Sathi silently cursed Whitebeard. What had he been thinking, taking that kid's gift for the god? She swore Whitebeard was just a big kid himself.

The queue inched forward gradually, people jostling each other in their hurry to see Guruvayurappan. Finally, they reached the inner chamber, from where the statue of the god was visible. He was covered in garlands of fragrant flowers, with multiple lamps lit around him. A white cloth was draped over the statue, its colourful pattern gleaming in the reflected light.

As they drew closer, she overheard a priest asking another, 'Did you put that mundu on the statue?'

The other priest looked confused and stared at the statue. 'No. How did that get there?'

The first guy shook his head, mystified. 'I don't know. It wasn't there a moment ago. I turned my back for a second, and when I looked back it was there. I tried to take it down, but it's stuck somehow.'

'Well, just leave it for now. We can take it down later, after morning prayers.'

Sathi was distracted from the two men by a loud gasp. It was the little boy, who'd come to a standstill directly in front of the statue of Guruvayurappan. Two temple workers tried to vain to shepherd the boy along as he stared in rapture at the statue. 'Look, Amma!' he exclaimed, pointing. 'It's my mundu! Guruvayurappan is wearing my mundu!'

The temple workers turned to the boy's mother helplessly. 'Madam, please move along. You're holding up the others.'

The mother nodded and took her son's hand. 'Come on, baby, let everyone else see Guruvayurappan.' She led him away, still chattering excitedly.

Curiously, Sathi peered into the pedestal, her focus more on the pattern on the mundu draped over the statue than on the god himself.

Sure enough, the white cloth was embroidered with both peacock feathers and lotuses.

Chapter Thirteen

Offence

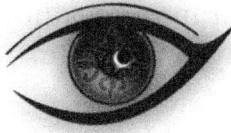

The journey from Guruvayur to Mookambika was extremely long, especially since it involved crossing the border into another state. They decided to drive until Zakiy was tired, and then check into a hotel along the way to rest for the night.

Sathi had just started to nod off when Zakiy's phone rang, startling her awake. She grabbed it from where it was charging in the cupholder and checked the display. 'It's your dad,' she announced.

'Put it on speaker.'

She tapped the screen. 'Hello?'

'Hi Sathi. Did you start your journey?' Narayan asked.

'Yes, we did, Uncle. We got to Guruvayur in the morning, now we're on the way to Mookambika.'

'Thank you so much for updating us, Zakiy, darling.' Maira's usually sweet voice was acerbic as she addressed her youngest son. Narayan must have his phone on speaker as well.

Zakiy winced guiltily. 'Oops. I knew I forgot something.' Then his eyes cut to her. 'Did you update Nakul?'

Her eyes widened. 'Oh crap.' She lunged for her own phone and punched out a quick text.

'Hee hee, you're in trouble, too,' Zakiy crowed.

His mother soon put a stop to that. 'Well, she must be tired from all the travelling,' Maira justified.

'But I'm the one doing all the driving,' Zakiy objected.

'You're older, you should have known better,' Maira rebutted.

His shoulders slumped. 'There's no way I'm going to win this, am I?'

His father chuckled. 'No, so I advise you to stop while you're behind.'

Zakiy opened his mouth, paused, then shut it again.

Narayan cleared his throat. 'Anyway, the reason I called you two is to ask if there's any way you can make a stop in Kannur?'

Kannur was a district in north Kerala. Zakiy thought for a moment and then nodded. 'Yeah, that should be fine, it's on our way. Why?'

'Raghavan, the guy I was telling you about, will be there tomorrow, then he will head back to Nelliampathi. He said he can meet you in Kannur tomorrow, otherwise you'll have to wait until you get back from your trip.'

Zakiy glanced at her, questioning.

'What do you think we should do?' Sathi asked Narayan.

'Well, technically it doesn't matter, but after hearing about the sheer amount of black magic Karan is wielding against you, I think it's better to act sooner rather than later.'

Zakiy spoke up. 'We could easily take a break in Kannur. It's only about five hours from Guruvayur, so we can meet Raghavan tomorrow and then continue the journey afterwards.'

'Sounds good to me,' Sathi agreed.

'Okay, then, I will let Raghavan know.'

'Let us know when you reach Kannur,' Maira ordered.

'Yes, ma'am.'

The call cut off and Zakiy exhaled loudly. 'You're in charge of updating our parents on our journey.'

'Why me?' she protested.

'Because according to mine, you can do no wrong. And your dad doesn't trust me, anyway.'

She softened. 'How about this? I'll update them all from your phone. That way you'll get the credit.'

He brightened. 'Thank you, m'lady! I knew you loved me!' Then his face drained of all colour as he realised what he'd said.

Sathi smiled down at her lap. 'I do,' she said softly, her cheeks feeling several degrees warmer. She peeked at him and was rewarded by his expression of sheer joy.

Content, she closed her eyes and drifted off into a dreamless slumber.

Raghavan offered to meet them at their hotel the next morning.

'I'm visiting family at the moment,' he explained as they made use of the small living room area on their floor. 'There isn't really an office I can use at the moment.'

'We really appreciate you coming to us,' Sathi said sincerely. 'Sorry for taking you away from your family.'

Raghavan waved off her apology. 'No, no, don't worry about that. Narayan is a very close friend of mine, and I'm honoured that he reached out to me.' He paused to take a sip of the tea they had ordered for him. 'So, how can I help? Narayan said it would be better if the two of you explained.'

Sathi nodded and launched into an abbreviated version of all that had happened with Bhaskar and Karan. Zakiy chimed in from time to time with details she missed.

Raghavan was thoughtful when they finished. 'So, you need to find the source of this man's evil power and destroy it,' he concluded.

'Exactly. All we know is that it's tied to his mother in some way,' Zakiy added.

'Alright, let me see.' Raghavan took out a pouch and emptied shells, similar to Sreenivasan's, onto the table. Sathi frowned. Raghavan seemed to be doing the same thing as Sreenivasan. Why had Narayan been so insistent that they see him?

As she kept watching, though, she realised that there were differences between the two astrologers; Raghavan's chanting was harsher, and his tone sent goosebumps down her skin. He also didn't spend much time talking about the planets and seemed to be asking for any clarifications solely in his mind – not out loud.

Finally, he exhaled and spoke. 'This is a very dark piece of magic they've used,' he told them. 'It won't be easy to break it down. It will need a lot of rituals and blood sacrifices.'

Sathi blanched. 'Blood sacrifice?'

Raghavan looked up, and his expression softened. 'Yes. They've made this object with dark magic using the blood of multiple animals, at least five, so we would need to use equal sacrifice to destroy its power.'

Zakiy leaned forward, looking as queasy as she suddenly felt.

'Isn't that...?' He shifted uncomfortably. 'Doesn't that mean we'd be using black magic too?' he asked uneasily.

Raghavan shook his head. 'With magic, intent is what matters most. Magic itself is not good or evil. It's a tool, and its effects depend on the intent of the one wielding it.' When they still looked doubtful, he sighed. 'Have you ever used a knife?'

Confused, Sathi nodded.

'What for?'

She shrugged. 'Chopping up vegetables or meat for cooking, usually.'

'And you?' Raghavan asked Zakiy.

'Well, I don't cook, I only eat.'

She sighed and buried her face in her hand as Raghavan's mouth twitched. 'Well, you'll just have to use your imagination, then. Now say the knife was used in a brutal murder. Does the fact that you used the same knife as a murderer make you evil?'

Wordlessly they shook their heads.

'Now what if someone used that knife to defend themselves or someone they love? Is that knife or the person wielding it evil?'

Sathi blew out a breath through pursed lips. 'I see what you mean.'

Raghavan nodded approvingly. 'Using the blood of animals doesn't mean that the magic itself is evil. Magic is neutral – it's a tool, like the knife, and it can be used for either good or evil.'

'Okay, but I have a question. What's the difference between this kind of magic, used for a good intention, and giving offerings to gods at temples? I mean, we've just come from Guruvayur, and we're on the way to Mookambika.'

Zakiy was the one who answered, looking thoughtful. 'I think the visit to the temples is like our defence – to get the blessings of the gods as protection.' He nodded to Raghavan. 'What you're talking about is offense – we're striking back against the people attacking us.'

Raghavan nodded. 'Exactly. In a war you need to use both defence and offence. A good defence will help you endure, but it will not help you win.' He shrugged. 'Ultimately, it's your choice. Narayan simply wanted me to advise you about the options you have available to you.'

Sathi thought about how she'd felt when she first came to India, as well as her argument with Jayaram just days ago. She'd been prepared to torture and kill her mother's murderers. Now she was being given another weapon with which to exact her revenge; one that she hadn't even known existed. What better way to defeat those wielding black magic than to use magic against them?

She caught Zakiy's eye, and he gave an almost imperceptible nod. She took a deep breath and looked back at Raghavan. 'We're in. Let's launch our offence.'

144

Raghavan left after promising to get in touch soon about their next step. Zakiy and Sathi decided to have dinner at the hotel restaurant before retiring to their separate rooms for the night. In the past, they had often shared a room during their travels, but given the recent tension between them Zakiy had wisely booked two single rooms.

Dinner was a mostly silent affair; both were exhausted. As they walked back to the elevator so they could go back to their rooms, Sathi's phone rang. 'It's Jayaram.' She answered and put the call on speaker.

'There's some good news,' Jayaram announced without preamble. 'The Deputy Commissioner ordered the local CI to register the FIR against Bhaskar.'

Sathi felt her tiredness evaporate as she exchanged delighted glances with Zakiy. 'That's amazing!'

'I agree. He's a very good officer, that DCP. As soon as I told him what happened, he called the CI and asked him why the FIR hadn't been registered. When the CI started blubbering some lame excuse, the DCP cut him off and ordered him to come to his office and made him register the FIR in front of me.'

'Wow,' Zakiy exhaled. 'So good police exist as well.'

'They sure do,' Jayaram confirmed, sounding satisfied. 'So now we just need to keep at it and make sure they investigate properly. Although...' he trailed off, hesitating.

'What?' Sathi asked when he didn't continue.

'Well, I don't mean to discourage you, but the legal system tends to move very slowly here. You won't get justice quickly or easily, especially with someone like Karan on the opposing side.'

She thought back to the conversation they'd had with Raghavan. 'That's okay,' she told Jayaram. 'I have a feeling that Karan won't be a problem for much longer.'

The indistinct figure in the distance crystallised into an all-too familiar shape; the seven-headed dragon. Sathi blinked and corrected herself. The dragon only had six heads now, with just a stump in place of the seventh head.

Suddenly, there was a flash of light. Once Sathi had blinked the spots out of her eyes, her breath caught. Two gods had materialised in front of the dragon. Or more accurately, a god and a goddess had appeared.

Sathi stared; both the gods were half-human and half-lion! The left side of the god's face was that of a handsome man, with one twinkling black eye and a chiselled jaw. The right half had a golden-brown mane and an unblinking yellow eye. Canines protruded from his mouth, the sharp points glinting. His body was that of a human man, except that he had four hands. One hand held a conch shell, and another had a rotating discus spinning around one of his fingers. The last two hands were empty, and they ended in long claws that looked capable of ripping apart human flesh.

At his side was the demi-lion goddess; the lioness-half of her face had a darker mane that merged perfectly with her black hair, making it difficult to know where the lion ended and woman began. She wore a black sari, and instead of flowers, her garland was made of human skulls. She had four hands too, each holding a trident, a drum, another skull, and a serpent that was coiled into the shape of a noose.

Together, the god and goddess stalked forward, stopping only when they were directly in front of the dragon with its six heads and a stump.

With a war-cry, the goddess's eyes burst into flames. She hurled the serpent-noose – which had also caught aflame – at the dragon.

The dragon roared in pain as the burning noose tightened around one its heads. Slowly, the flames encircled the head until it had become nothing but a burnt husk.

146

The noose flew back to the demi-lion goddess, and the fire flickered out, leaving behind the unharmed snake. It curled around the goddess's arm contentedly.

With a satisfied smile that revealed two sharp canines, the goddess shook back her mane, and the two gods disappeared.

Sathi woke up with a gasp, her heart beating out of control. As her pulse gradually slowed, her lips turned up into a smile.

When Zakiy knocked on Sathi's door in the morning, she greeted him with eyes that were bloodshot. Behind her, her laptop was open on the bed, and an empty Coke can rolled around amidst the sheets, forgotten.

'How much sleep did you get?' he demanded, following her into the room and sitting on the desk chair.

'Um... four hours? No, three,' she amended distractedly, picking up her laptop.

'May I ask why?'

She glanced up at him, her eyes heavy with sleep. She looked like she was struggling to remember how to open them after each blink.

'Can I explain over coffee?' she begged. She gestured to the Coke can. 'I ran out of caffeine around five o'clock.'

He raised his eyebrows. 'Alright then, let's go have breakfast.'

After her second cup of coffee, Sathi seemed vaguely more alert. By that time, he'd inhaled a huge plate of scrambled eggs, so she had his undivided attention while she launched into a description of her dream.

'So, another one of seven sins has been defeated,' he said with satisfaction.

'Yup,' she agreed, holding her coffee close. 'Now we just need to figure out which one.' She gestured to her laptop. 'That's what I've been trying to do since I woke up.'

'Any luck?'

'Well, I couldn't really figure out which sin it was, but I did find out that the two lion-gods were Lord Narasimha and Devi Pratyangira.'

'I know Lord Narasimha is an avatar of Lord Vishnu, but I've never heard of Devi Pratyangira before,' he admitted.

'She's Narasimha's consort, and she's also called Narasimhika,' Sathi explained. She opened her laptop and pushed it towards him.

Zakiy quickly scanned the opened Wikipedia page describing the lion goddess. He paused when he read the description, which was almost the same as how Sathi had depicted Pratyangira from her dream. Then he grinned as he read the next sentence.

She blinked, looking up from her coffee. 'What?'

He turned the screen so she could see and pointed. 'It says here that Pratyangira repels and reverses black magic!'

Her mouth dropped open. 'How did I miss that?' she exclaimed, scooting her chair closer so she could read over his shoulder.

'She also punishes people who do evil,' he added, watching her eyes sprint over the short passage. He was intensely aware of how close she was, warmth from her skin radiating across the short distance between them. He was so tempted to close that distance and breathe in the intoxicating jasmine scent of her skin.

He hid his hands under the table and curled them into fists, clenching them as hard as he could to distract himself from temptation.

Sathi turned to face him, her eyes lit up and all traces of exhaustion gone. 'She's exactly who we need to defeat Karan,' she breathed.

He felt his excitement spike to reflect hers. 'I feel like this is a sign that we're on the right track with Raghavan.'

She nodded in agreement, then frowned. 'But which sin was it? I'm still confused by that.'

'Hmm... let's go over them now and figure it out.'

Sathi brought up a Word document on her laptop, on which she'd listed all the seven sins. She'd put a tick next to Pride.

Zakiy tapped it. 'Okay, so we've dealt with Pride. Well, Saraswathi Devi did actually,' he corrected himself quickly. 'So that leaves us with wrath, envy, lust, greed, gluttony and sloth.' He paused, thinking. 'I don't think it's lust. That should have happened when Bhaskar attacked you, but I guess because he hasn't been punished for it yet, that sin hasn't been defeated.' He stopped to read through the list again. 'I don't think its gluttony or sloth, either.'

'Wait,' Sathi interrupted, putting a hand on his automatically. A flash of heat burned through him, and she yanked hers back as though she'd felt the flames too. Their eyes met. Her face slowly flushed, and she ducked her head. 'Um, sorry. I was saying, why did you rule out sloth?'

He tried to bring his mind back under control. Sins. Right. 'Um... isn't sloth like extreme laziness? It doesn't seem to fit, somehow,' he reasoned.

She bit her bottom lip, and Zakiy almost dropped the coffee cup he'd just picked up.

Thankfully, she was too deep in thought to notice. 'Not necessarily. I think sloth could also refer to not doing what you're supposed to, regardless of whether the reason is laziness or something else.'

Zakiy responded articulately: 'Huh?'

Her intent gaze focussed on him; all traces of embarrassment gone as she focused on the puzzle. 'Think about it. We just said Pratyangira Devi is the best goddess to help us with Karan. But what is Karan really doing right now?'

He blinked rapidly, feeling a bit like he was taking an exam he hadn't studied for. 'Well... he created false evidence against you. And he turned Susan against you.'

Sathi made a rotating motion with her hand. 'And...?'

He suddenly straightened. 'And he turned the police against you!'

149

'Exactly. The police are helping Karan and Bhaskar instead of protecting me, the so-called victim. They didn't even file the first information report until –'

'Until yesterday, when the DCP ordered them to do it,' he finished, eyes wide.

'And I had the dream last night – so we defeated the police's sloth, or their unwillingness to do their job, and Pratyangira Devi cut off another head of the dragon.'

'Wow.'

She turned to him, expression turning thoughtful. 'Since I first came to India, I've felt like I was floundering, not knowing what the hell I'm doing most of the time. Now I have so many people to help me in this battle, including gods and goddesses,' she added with a wry smile.

This time he couldn't stop himself; Zakiy reached out and covered her small, warm hand with his own. 'I wish you hadn't had to be alone for so long,' he told her, thinking with a pang of how lonely she must have been. She had spent most of her life believing that her father hated her for being responsible for her mother's death.

He couldn't even begin to imagine what an awful existence that must have been. 'I can't erase your past, but I do promise you that I'll be there for you, no matter what.' He took a deep breath and held her gaze as he said the next words, needing her to understand. 'And I promise that I will be whatever you need me to be.'

Their gaze locked, and he tried to tell her with his eyes that he understood. She needed his friendship, and he would always be her friend first and foremost. No matter what his troubled feelings were for her, he wouldn't let her be alone again.

As he watched, her shoulders relaxed, and her eyes filled with moisture, though no tears spilled. She didn't say anything, but she turned her hand so that now they were holding hands on top of the table. Lips tilting up, she dropped her gaze shyly.

Chest suddenly feeling so light that he felt a bit like a helium-filled balloon – ready to float up into the stratosphere – Zakiy squeezed her fingers. 'Shall we get this show back on the road, m'lady? I believe we have a goddess to visit.

Chapter Fourteen

Mookambika

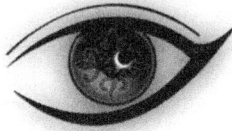

S everal hours later, Zakiy finally pulled up in front of the hotel they'd booked in Mookambika. It was the middle of the night, and he was sore from head to toe from driving for so long.

Sathi was fast asleep, having finally given into his insistence that she needed to rest after her almost sleepless night.

Reluctantly, he woke her up so they could check in, and Zakiy said goodnight to her as she stumbled, half-asleep, into her room. Inside his own room, he collapsed into his bed thankfully, and immediately fell asleep.

It was late morning when they finally woke up, and after showering and getting dressed they headed straight to the temple.

Like always, Zakiy felt at peace as soon as they were inside the temple grounds. The scents of incense blended with the fragrance of the flowers that were offered to the gods (as well as woven into the women's hair) to perfume the air with an intoxicating aroma.

He caught sight of Sathi eyeing the string of white jasmine braided into the dark locks of a woman who was walking by; surreptitiously, she took deep breaths as the lady passed them.

He grinned at her as she met his eyes and jumped sheepishly. Remembering the vendor outside the temple who had been selling strands of woven white flowers, he promised, 'I'll get you some when we leave.' He was rewarded with a smile that surpassed the sweetness of the jasmine.

Zakiy strode ahead to join the queue of people waiting to go into the inner temple, scared that he would start blurting out his feelings if he didn't distract himself. Slowly, he reminded himself sternly. He needed to be patient.

Thankfully, the couple in front of them in the queue were explaining the history of the temple to their daughter, providing a ready-made distraction. Idly, he eavesdropped on their conversation. He felt Sathi move closer to listen in as well.

'Amma, which Devi will be here now?' the little girl asked her mother.

The mother smoothed back the child's hair affectionately. 'Well, baby, you know Mookambika Devi is actually Adi Parashakthi - so she represents Devi Saraswathi, Lakshmi and Parvathi. Different goddesses will be here at different times of the day. Right now, because it's still morning, Devi Saraswathi will be here. At noon, she will assume the form of Lakshmi Devi, and everyone will pray to her in her Parvathi form during the evening.'

'But why does she keep changing?' the little girl asked. 'Why doesn't just one of them stay here all the time?'

Her father smiled indulgently as he answered. 'Because it was all three of them who joined forces to defeat Kaamhasuran.'

'Who's that?'

'He was a demon who'd done great penance, under severe conditions, and gained a boon that he could only be killed by a woman.'

153

'Why?'

'Because he didn't want to die, and he thought women weren't strong enough to defeat a man,' her mother responded with a grin at her husband.

'That's stupid,' the girl observed. 'I bet Amma could beat up Achan any time she wants.'

Zakiy snorted and tried to quickly turn it into a cough, while Sathi was desperately biting her cheeks to suppress her own smile.

The little girl's father was openly grinning. 'And I thank my lucky stars every day that your mother chooses not to beat me up,' he said wryly.

'So? What did Kaamhasuran do?' his daughter pressed.

'Well, after he received this boon, he became very arrogant. He declared himself ruler of all the asuras – the demons – since none of them could beat him. Then he tried to rule over the gods as well. No god could defeat him in battle, so they had to watch helplessly as he tore down all the temples and forbade any prayers being conducted to worship the gods. So, the gods became weaker and weaker since they need the energy from devotees' prayers to retain their powers. The gods were at their wit's end and prayed to Devi Adi Parashakthi to help them.'

'Did she come? Is that why she's here?'

The woman bopped her daughter's nose and she squealed. 'Wait, baby. The gods had to be patient because the goddess didn't come straightaway. You see, Lord Indra and the other gods had become complacent and lazy, and Devi wanted them to first learn their lesson before she saved them from the humiliation Kaamhasuran was inflicting on them.

The girl nodded slowly, seeming to be deep in thought. 'Oh, so that's why you didn't say anything when Leela and I ate too many chocolates last week and then we got sick.'

Her mother's eyes sparkled. 'Not exactly. That was because we didn't realise you two had found the chocolates I'd hidden away. You ate them all before we found you.'

Her father cleared his throat. 'But yes, sometimes the best lessons you learn are the ones no one teaches you,' he concurred. 'Anyway, Kaamhasuran's arrogance grew and grew, until he started making plans to conquer heaven completely so he could become the sole ruler of the universe.'

'Devi wouldn't let that happen,' the girl said confidently.

'No, she wouldn't. But before Devi got involved, Kaamhasuran decided to ask Lord Shiva for another boon, to make sure that not even a woman could kill him.'

'What made him change his mind?' the girl asked, her eyes wide.

'First of all, he got scared because one of his brother demons, Mahishasura, had just been killed by Durga Devi.'

'Ha! I told you he was stupid to think a woman couldn't kill a man!'

Her father pressed a kiss to her forehead. 'You're absolutely right, my darling. So Kaamhasuran went to Lord Shiva and tried to ask for another boon.'

'Then what happened?'

'Well, first he had to do deep penance before asking a boon. Shiva was worried, because if Kaamhasuran asked this new boon, he would become immortal. That would cause the balance of good and evil to be forever disrupted. At the same time, Shiva couldn't refuse a boon earned with hard penance.'

'What did Shiva do?'

'Actually, it was Devi who saved the day. She asked Saraswathi Devi, who is also the goddess of speech, to sit on Kaamhasuran's tongue just as he was about to ask his boon. She immobilised it so that all he could do was make noises – he couldn't talk.'

'After that, he was known as Mookasuran: "The Mute Demon". When he realised that the gods had tricked him, he became so furious that he immediately began his attack on heaven. The gods cried out to Devi for help, and this time she took pity on them.

'Saraswathi, Lakshmi and Parvathi joined forces, and together they killed Mookasuran with their trident. As he died, he realised his mistake in underestimating women and disrespecting the gods. He begged Devi for forgiveness, and she blessed him and allowed his soul to find peace after death.

'After he died, the people begged Devi to stay here and bless them with their presence. She graciously agreed, and became known as Mookambika, after Mookasuran. They renamed this place after Devi.'

As the woman concluded the story, she leaned over to stroke her daughter's cheek. 'And now we'll get to see her for the first time. I'm so happy she called for us.'

The little girl looked puzzled. 'Devi called for us? How did she know our phone number?'

Her parents laughed. 'Baby, she knows how to call us without phones,' her father explained. 'Anyway, no one can visit Mookambika Devi unless she invites them to come. We're very lucky that we got to come.'

By this time, they had reached the door to the inner temple. The small family quieted as they prepared for their first glimpse of the goddess.

Zakiy felt a tug on his arm and glanced back. 'Is that true what she said?' Sathi asked. 'Do people need permission before they can visit here?'

'I'm not sure, but I've heard that before. Being able to come here is a big deal. If you come without the call, your journey ends up being interrupted somehow – like car trouble, for example.'

Sathi nodded and followed him through the doorway. As they approached the goddess, she found that her eyes kept being drawn to the goddess's face. Despite being carved from metal, her eyes managed to exude kindness as well as power.

156

Zakiy took out the sari they'd bought for Mookambika and handed it to the priest standing closest to them, along with the tiny golden locket. The priest took it and passed it to another priest sitting cross-legged in front of the statue of Devi.

The first priest then opened a small gate and ushered them into a square area enclosed with metal bars. He directed them to stand inside so they could watch without being jostled by the crowd. 'Pray hard and tell Devi all your worries,' the priest told them kindly.

The priest inside the pedestal unfolded the deep turquoise sari they'd chosen and draped it over Devi's shoulder, so it looked like she was wearing it. The gold tints in the fabric caught the light reflected from the numerous oil lamps lit around the statue.

Sathi gazed at the goddess and caught her breath at the sudden rush of peace she felt. The hard lump in her chest that had been there since as long as she could remember seemed to loosen its hold, and she reeled with the intense relief its absence brought.

Closing her eyes, she let go of all her pain and worry, surrendering in front of this incredible deity who was surely much better equipped than her to handle it. When she opened her eyes again, she felt as though the goddess had received all her troubled emotions and was telling her to leave it with her – Devi would take care of it.

Beaming, Sathi resolved that she would come back to Mookambika when everything was over – when their battle against evil had been fought and won.

Zakiy opened the little gate so they could re-join the crowd, and they waited to one side to receive the prasadam, which was usually some flowers and fruits that had been offered to the goddess and was subsequently distributed to the devotees.

The priest who'd spoken to them earlier came up to them, holding something covered in a piece of banana leaf. He closed his eyes and prayed inaudibly before dropping the bundle into Sathi's outstretched hands.

She stilled as the banana leaf unfurled to reveal the prasadam.

Zakiy chuckled at her expression. 'I guess Devi beat me to it,' he remarked wryly as he picked up the string of woven jasmine flowers.

Like a mother, Mookambika Devi had fulfilled this small wish of her beloved daughter.

Zakiy pushed for them to get back on the road as soon as possible so they would make it to Alappuzha in time for Sathi's birthday surprise.

Doing so would involve driving much further south, past Nelliampathi, but he was confident that he could pull it off without Sathi realising. She hadn't been in Kerala for very long and wouldn't know the geography well enough to question why he was driving in the wrong direction. At least, that was his hope.

When they were a couple of hours into the drive, Zakiy's phone started to ring. Sathi glanced at the screen. 'It's Raghavan,' she said eagerly.

'Answer it.'

There was a beep, and Raghavan's voice came out, slightly staticky. 'Hello?'

'Good afternoon, sir.'

'Good afternoon. I have some news. I've been trying to figure out what this source of power is that Karan has.'

'And?' Zakiy prompted, pulling his Jeep over to the side of road and turning off the engine.

'I found out a lot more than I was expecting. Prepare yourselves, it's quite gruesome.'

'Go on,' Sathi said evenly.

'This source of power is a kind of talisman... made with Karan's umbilical cord.'

'What?' Sathi exclaimed.

'Wait, it gets worse. The fact that it's made from the umbilical cord makes it an incredibly powerful source of protection for Karan. That means it's also vulnerable and needs to be kept in a safe place where it can't get lost or damaged in any way.'

'Where is that safe place?' Sathi prompted, sounding almost like she didn't want to hear the answer.

Raghavan sighed. 'The talisman is stored inside his mother's uterus.'

Zakiy gelt bile crawl up the back of his throat. Was there no limit to the depravity of that family?

Sathi was making gurgling noises, beyond speech. He himself was kind of stumped on how to respond.

When Raghavan spoke into the deafening silence his voice was hesitant, but with a slight edge of defensiveness. 'I know young people like you probably don't believe in things like this, but –'

'No, no,' Zakiy interrupted. 'This is pretty much in line with our experience so far with this family. We were just shocked.'

Raghavan's voice relaxed. 'Well, people who dabble in evil magic like this tend to have no limits – they believe that they themselves are gods, and don't need to stop for anything.'

'So, what's the next step?' Sathi asked. 'Is it even possible to destroy that talisman when its... you know, up there?'

'Yes, it's possible, but it will be more complicated than I originally thought. I won't be able to do it by myself. I will need to visit some people who deal with this kind of magic and discuss with them about how to proceed.'

Sathi nodded absently. 'Okay. Where do they live?'

'They're mainly tribals and live up in the mountains. They don't have cell phones or anything, and rarely leave their community.'

Sathi's eyes were wide. 'There are tribals here?'

Zakiy couldn't help a smile. A talisman of their enemy shoved up his mother's reproductive system? No problem. There are tribals in India? Stop the presses.

'Of course. They're much more connected to nature and the old ways. They've retained much of the ancient knowledge that modern society has sacrificed in favour of technology.'

'So that's why they're the best people to ask for advice about the talisman situation,' she mused.

'Exactly. My plan is to go there tomorrow and talk to them. I won't be able to get cell service while I'm out there, so don't worry if you can't get a hold of me for the next few days. I'll call you as soon as I have an update,' he promised before ringing off abruptly.

'Wow.'

Zakiy chuckled. 'That about sums it up.'

'I didn't think anything they did would shock me anymore, but then things like this happen.' She turned her gaze to him. 'You don't seem so shocked,' she observed, eyes narrowing. 'Have you heard of this stuff before?'

He started to shake his head and then stopped. 'Well... I have heard of black magic being done with unborn foetuses and placental remains.'

Sathi gulped. 'You mean, they cut open babies...?'

'No, no! I mean, after a miscarriage or an abortion, the hospital is supposed to be very careful to bury the bodies and placenta because depraved people use them for black magic. Sometimes they even go to graveyards and dig up the... you know, the dead foetuses.'

'That's... horrible.'

'Yeah.'

'Why would they target babies, though? What makes them so... so... twisted as to go after foetuses?'

'Babies are the purest form of soul because they haven't lived... so they haven't committed any good or evil. They're a powerful weapon, especially if you bind their power before they've even had the chance to live.'

Sathi was silent for a few moments. 'Do you think Bhaskar and Goudhamy used this kind of magic? With dead babies?'

160

He could only grimace and shrug in response. Unfortunately, this sounded exactly like the kind of thing they would do.

Zakiy parked at the port and stretched, trying to get rid of the ache that driving continuously for hours instilled into every part of your body. He glanced over and smiled when he saw that Sathi was still fast asleep.

They had discussed black magic involving unborn babies until well into the early hours of the morning. Thankfully, Sathi had been so distracted that she hadn't noticed the road signs. Then she'd finally fallen asleep, alleviating his tension that his surprise would be spoilt.

Quietly, he got out of the Jeep and called Unni, the man they were supposed to meet. He confirmed that he was ready for them.

With mounting excitement, Zakiy went around to the passenger side and knocked on the window. Sathi woke immediately, sitting up and opening the door. 'What?' She looked around with wide eyes at the glistening lake, rippling in the sunlight. 'What are we doing here?'

'I'm tired. Let's go for a walk,' he suggested. 'There's a good restaurant around here as well, we can grab brunch while we enjoy the view.'

She blinked sleep out of her eyes and suppressed a yawn. 'Sure. Let's go.'

Zakiy grinned and held the door open wide while she got out. Then he opened the back door and slung the giant backpack he'd carefully packed onto his shoulders.

Sathi watched him with a puzzled frown. 'You're taking that on our walk?'

'Er...' He was stumped for a second, and then a brainwave hit. 'I want to change clothes. I swear I've sweated gallons into this shirt. I'll duck into a restroom to change at the restaurant. It'll look weird if I just carry a t-shirt, though, so I thought I'll take the whole bag.' He realised he was babbling and decided to shut up before he ruined everything.

'...Okay.' She gave him a look that clearly said she had concerns about his sanity but apparently decided to indulge him.

'Come on, let's go this way,' Zakiy said, leading the way along the port. They walked in companionable silence, staring out at the water.

They rounded a corner, and he broke into a grin. He subtly drew back so he could watch Sathi's expression when she realised what they were walking towards.

He wasn't disappointed; she came to a standstill and her mouth dropped open. She gazed at the huge boat docked in front of them, eyes wide. Unni stood in front, smiling, and gesturing them forward.

Sathi pivoted to stare at him. 'You didn't?' she half-threatened, half-marvelled.

Zakiy beamed at her. 'Welcome to your first houseboat trip.'

Chapter Fifteen

Ancestral Evil

Sathi decided this must be what heaven was like.

They'd been given a tour of the boat, which was a double-decker. On the ground floor there were two bedrooms, a kitchen and a living/dining area that opened out onto the water. Upstairs, there was another open area with sofas where they could chill while they sailed lazily through the lake.

The owner and his wife served them breakfast and told them what to expect on the trip. They would sail for most of the day, and he told them they could even take a turn at driving the boat for a while if they liked. Then they would dock at a nearby village, and spend the night moored under the moonlit sky. In the morning they would return to the dock.

Sathi couldn't believe Zakiy had organised all this and driven several hours in the opposite direction just so she could experience a houseboat ride.

'This is incredible,' she gushed; she couldn't look away from the rippling water, her hair blowing back in the breeze.

'Can we swim?' Zakiy asked eagerly, mouth full of delicious idly (rice cakes) and sambar (vegetable curry).

'Of course,' Unni reassured them. 'Just let me know when you would like to swim, and I will stop the boat for you.

Sathi turned to Zakiy, looking crestfallen. 'But we don't have our swimsuits...' She trailed off as her gaze slid to the bulging backpack on the chair next to them. She started to smile.

Zakiy patted the bag. 'I got you covered, m'lady. Vidhya helped me pack extra clothes and toiletries for you and I took our swimsuits from the campsite.'

Her eyes were wide. 'So, everyone back home knows?'

He nodded, helping himself to another idly and drowning it in sambar. 'I even took permission from your dad. I was scared out of my wits, but I knew he would kill me if I didn't ask him beforehand.'

She couldn't believe the effort he'd put into arranging this trip for her. She met his gaze and shyly reached out to lay her hand on his. 'Thank you.'

Zakiy's answering smile was radiant.

They went up to the upper deck to chill and wait for their breakfast to be digested so they could swim. Zakiy, unsurprisingly, fell asleep almost as soon as they sat down on the sofa – he'd driven through the night without sleeping so they could get here on time to board the houseboat.

She let him sleep, gazing at him instead of at the lake rushing past them. Thinking. Deciding. Resolving.

When Zakiy woke up a couple of hours later, he was annoyed with himself for falling asleep.

'You're not a machine. Cut yourself some slack,' she told him as they made their way downstairs again. Zakiy went to ask Unni to stop the boat so they could swim, while Sathi changed into her one-piece swim dress. She wandered out and leaned against the narrow deck at the side of the boat to wait for him. She gazed out at the sunlight gleaming on the water.

As she watched, the sun hid behind the clouds, and plunged the lake into darkness; the previously inviting mass now looked dark and full of murky secrets, and trepidation stiffened her spine.

A warm hand landed on her shoulder, and – like magic – the sun returned. The water became clear and alluring again, and she blinked at the sudden change, wondering if she'd imagined the darkness that had polluted it just moments ago.

'What's wrong?' Zakiy asked quietly, gently turning her around to face him.

'I had a dream while we were driving here.' She saw his expression and hurriedly added, 'Not with the dragon. This was different. I was in a swimming pool, and I was playing with a family of seals. They were so cute, and I loved them. Then they swam away, and I was waiting for them to come back. I felt something coming towards me in the water, and I thought it was the seals, so I put my hands under the water to cuddle them. But my hands touched this... this disgusting mass of something that felt like tarantula legs.' She paused to shudder, remembering.

'I could feel it was an extension of something huge that was rising up in the water, something that felt like a crustacean of some sort. I don't know how I knew that. I also knew without a doubt that it couldn't be allowed to surface fully, because it was so evil that it would destroy me and everything else if it did come out of the water. I used all my strength to push it back down into the depths, and then the dream faded out. The next thing I remember is you waking me up.'

'That sounds gross,' Zakiy said. 'And scary.'

'Yeah. Except...' She bit her lip, hesitating.

'What?'

'Well, the thing was really disgusting, but at the same time I felt like I had some kind of connection to it. Like it was related to me, or something.'

Zakiy was silent for a long time, expression thoughtful. 'Ancestral evil,' he said finally.

She stared at him, and he continued, 'Think about it. It's evil, and it was connected to you... I think that thing was a representation of the ancient evil that's been trying to destroy your family for generations.'

'Huh.'

'But... you won!'

She blinked up at him, her expression a question mark.

'You pushed it back down into the water. You didn't let it rise. So, you won!'

'I hadn't thought of it like that,' she admitted. She gave a decisive nod and faced the water again. 'You're right, I guess I won that particular battle. I shouldn't let it make me afraid anymore.'

The houseboat drew to a stop, and Sathi sat down on the edge of the boat and dropped herself into the water. It was gloriously warm from the sun, and she felt joy rise within her as she tilted her head back and twirled in a circle. With a big splash, Zakiy dived in after her.

They started swimming in earnest, getting a good distance away from the boat before they had to stop for breath.

Zakiy flipped over and floated on his back; eyes closed as he soaked in the sunshine.

Staring at him, she felt her stomach churn as a weird mixture of exhilaration and nerves attacked it. She was going to do it. She was going to tell him how she felt.

She started pedalling the water to move closer to him, and that's when her foot came down on something hairy and disgusting. The sole of her foot connected with something hard and slimy, and she yelled out, rocketing away from whatever it was.

She slammed into Zakiy, who immediately put a hand around her trembling shoulders and pulled her into his chest. 'What? What's wrong?'

She pointed down at the water where she had been moments before, her teeth chattering so hard that she couldn't speak.

Zakiy dived into the water and then came back up several moments later, hair plastered to the sides of his face. 'There's nothing there. What happened?'

She just shook her head and plunged her head into the water herself, frantically looking around for what she had felt. Her lungs felt like they would burst, but she kept stubbornly searching the murky water. But Zakiy had been right; there was nothing there.

Her face broke the surface, gasping for air, and an ear-splitting cawing tore the air. They watched, mouths open, as crows, at least a hundred of them, flew over the sky above them. Their wings beat the air and their cries continued to ring out around them.

Sathi flinched, and Zakiy tightened his hold on her. 'Don't be afraid of them,' he murmured. 'Crows are said to be the spirits of our ancestors. They won't hurt us.'

She gazed up, fear ebbing away at his words. The crows circled around and around, seeming reluctant to leave them.

'I think I was wrong earlier,' Zakiy said, his eyes focused on the crows. 'Remember that statue of Nataraja?' he asked, jumping subjects randomly.

She tore her eyes away from the crows to frown at him. 'What?'

'Nataraja, the lord of dance. He dances with his foot on top of the head of the demon of ignorance. I think just now, when your foot touched that creature, that's when you defeated the ancient evil. That's why your ancestors have come. They're celebrating.'

They remained in the water until the crows disappeared, and then reluctantly swam back to the boat. They showered and went back up to the upper deck while the houseboat continued to sail.

Gazing out at the sky, Sathi strained to catch another glimpse of the crows. She couldn't help wondering whether one of them had been the spirit of her mother.

Zakiy had told her that in India it was custom to conduct a ritual on someone's death anniversary where food was offered on a banana leaf. If crows came and ate it, it meant the ancestor had accepted the offering and was at peace. Had anyone done that for her mother?

Thinking of her twisted family, Sathi shook her head. It was something she would do, she resolved. Hopefully her father would do it with her.

The sound of someone clearing her throat made her turn; it was Unni's wife. She held a tray with cups of tea and freshly fried banana fritters.

Sathi rushed forward to clear the coffee table so that the woman could put the tray down, while Zakiy did his bit to lighten her load by grabbing a fritter and stuffing it whole in his mouth.

'Ow!' He hopped up and down, waving a hand in front of his mouth, presumably because the fritter was too hot.

Sathi rolled her eyes and smiled at the woman. 'Ignore him. Thank you so much!'

She grinned. 'No problem.' She half-turned to go back down the stairs, then hesitated. She glanced back at them, as though trying to decide whether to say something.

'Yes?' Sathi prompted.

'Look... Please don't think I'm intruding, but I couldn't help overhearing you two earlier. When you were about to swim,' she clarified, seeing their confusion. 'You were talking about that dream you had. And then I saw what happened with the crows. I can try to answer your questions if you like.'

'Er... I'm sorry, but how?' Sathi asked. 'Do you know anything about this ancestral evil?'

The woman shook her head. 'No, but I read Tarot. I could read the cards for you, if you like.'

Sathi gaped; she had no idea that Tarot was so popular in India.

'I have a YouTube channel and everything,' she went on. 'I upload videos with general readings every day.' Her eagerness suddenly

168

changed to embarrassment, and she ducked her head. 'Forget I said anything. Sorry.'

She turned to head down the stairs, and Sathi finally found her voice. 'No, wait!' She glanced at Zakiy, who looked a bit like someone had hit him over the head and then ran over him. 'We were just surprised. I'd love it if you did a reading for us.'

The woman smiled. 'I'm Gayathri, by the way. She reached into her pocket and withdrew a box.

Zakiy finally unfroze. 'Oh wow! You read the proper Tarot cards!'

Sathi raised an eyebrow at him, and he explained, 'The cards I read, the Psychic Tarot, aren't really typical. The usual Tarot cards are more like a regular deck of playing cards, except instead of clubs and hearts etc. they have wands, cups, coins and swords for the Minor Arcana. Then there's the Major Arcana as well, of course.'

Seeing that Sathi still looked confused, Gayathri added, 'Each suit – the wands, cups, coins and swords – have 14 cards. Ace, 2 to 10 and then the King, Queen, Knight and Page.'

Zakiy nodded. 'Exactly. It's more complicated to read because each card has a distinct meaning, which you have to memorise from the suit and number. It's a lot more sophisticated than what I do.'

While they'd been talking, Gayathri had sat down and begun shuffling her cards. 'Tell me what you'd like to know, please.'

Sathi thought for a moment. 'We want to know the truth behind the experience we just had out there on the water.'

Gayathri nodded, business-like, and drew three cards from the deck: High Priestess, Six of Wands and Wheel of Fortune.

'The cards are saying that you should trust your intuition,' she said, pointing to the High Priestess. 'It's extremely strong right now, and leading you to your goal. The Six of Wands symbolises victory, especially a moral or spiritual victory.' She glanced at the Wheel of Fortune. 'You're also on the brink of change; something that's been at a standstill for a long time will suddenly mobilise, and you will gain fresh insights.' She looked up at them. 'Does that answer your question?'

They nodded slowly. 'I'd say that was spot on,' Zakiy said.

'Feel free to ask me any other questions you have.'

'The crows... was one of them the spirit of my mother?' Sathi asked.

Gayathri's eyes tightened in sympathy, but she didn't comment. She drew another card from the deck: Empress. 'Yes,' she said immediately. 'Your mother's spirit is extremely strong, and she's looking out for you. She's always with you, even if you can't see her.'

Sathi nodded, her throat too swollen with emotion to speak.

'I have another question,' Zakiy said slowly. 'Recently, I keep getting a card called Deception & Envy. I'm not getting more clarification about that, though. Can you help?'

She nodded and reshuffled before drawing another card: Seven of Swords. 'Hmm.'

'What?'

'This card stands for deception and trickery; it must be the equivalent of the card you were getting.' She took another card: Queen of Swords, upside down. 'I would you say you have a powerful enemy, whose heart is cold as ice and filled with bitterness. He or she is ruthless when it comes to getting what they want. You need to be careful.'

She glanced up at them, shuffling absently. 'Anything else?'

'Do you have any general advice for us?' Sathi asked.

Gayathri drew another card: The Moon. She stared at the card for a while, then looked up at Sathi. 'This card usually symbolises something that's unseen, like how most days of the month at least part of the moon is hidden. Is there something that hasn't been dealt with, something that's been festering in you?'

Sathi chewed on her lip, thinking. 'I'm not sure,' she admitted.

'Okay, let me clarify.' She took out another card: Knight of Wands, reversed. 'I'm seeing a lot of anger, recklessness... does that resonate with you?'

When neither replied, Gayathri looked up and saw their expressions. 'Ah. I guess I've got the answer.'

Irritation rose in Sathi, and she worked to keep it contained. She saw Gayathri watching her carefully.

'I can help you,' she said, holding Sathi's gaze. 'I can see that just talking about it is enough to bring out that rage in you. You do a good job at suppressing it, but eventually it will escape your control. I can teach you to get rid of it so it doesn't affect you anymore.'

Sathi felt hope dilute her irrational anger. She had been doing a better job at keeping her wild emotions under control, but it would be nice not to have to fight so hard all the time. If Gayathri could help her get rid of her anger it would be a huge relief.

Slowly, she nodded.

'Breathe in and out deeply,' Gayathri instructed. 'Try to focus only on the sensation of air moving in and out of your lungs.'

They were sitting face to face in one of the bedrooms downstairs. Gayathri had said it would be better to do this where they would not be disturbed.

'I want you to focus on your heart now,' Gayathri said after they had been breathing quietly for a few minutes. 'Focus on how it feels. Is there pain? Is there anger? Think about what it is that causes you that emotion. Is it an incident, or a person? Think about it and when you feel you have the answer, open your eyes.'

Several minutes later, Sathi blinked her eyes open, feeling a bit like she was resurfacing after a long nap.

'Can you tell me what you found out?' Gayathri prompted gently.

She nodded. 'I think these emotions are linked to my grandparents,' she confessed. 'They're the only link to my mother, and I... I guess I had a lot of expectations about what they would be like.'

Gayathri waited for her to continue, giving her time to gather her thoughts.

'When I first met them they were very loving... or well, they pretended to be very loving. I didn't know that at the time, and I thought their emotions were real. They represented acceptance I've never really had before.' Sathi sighed. 'Then I discovered that they're truly awful people, and that... makes me angry.'

'Is it only anger or is there pain as well?'

She was quiet for a moment. 'I think I transform the pain into anger because it hurts less. Otherwise I would collapse under the agony.'

'That's understandable,' Gayathri said. She exhaled. 'So now I think it's time that you said goodbye to your grandparents.'

Sathi stared. 'You want me to meet them?'

The other woman smiled. 'No. Emotionally, you need to say goodbye to them. You need to release the pain caused by unmet expectations, and when you do that your anger will also disappear.'

Sathi nodded slowly. 'Okay. How do we do that?'

'Close your eyes again. Imagine your grandparents coming in front of you.'

She suppressed a shudder as Bhaskar and Goudhamy appeared in her mind's eye. At the same time, a wave of longing washed over her. She remembered the initial few days she had spent with them in their house, blissfully ignorant of their evil and believing all their honeyed words.

'Ask them to forgive anything wrong that you may have done. And tell them that you've forgiven them as well.'

Sathi opened her mouth to protest, but Gayathri cut her off. 'Trust me. This is about you, not them. They will have to pay for their karma – but that's not up to you. Our goal right now is to release the emotional ties you have to them, and to do that you need to do as I tell you.'

She took a deep breath and focused on her grandparents' repugnant faces. I forgive you, she told them silently. Please forgive me as well.

'Now say goodbye to them. Watch them walk away until you can't see them anymore.'

Sathi waited until Bhaskar and Goudhamy had disappeared from her mind's view. With that, she felt a sudden release, like she'd finally let go of something that had been weighing her down without her even realising it.

Gayathri's voice was soft. 'When you're ready, open your eyes.'

Her eyes focused on Gayathri's. 'How do you feel?' the older woman asked.

Sathi grinned. 'Amazing.'

Gayathri talked her through a few more techniques she could use to manage her rage. Then Sathi thanked her and made her way back up to the upper deck, excited to share what had happened with Zakiy. When she got there, though, he was nowhere to be found. He must be in his room downstairs.

Sathi sank onto the sofa to wait for him. Gazing up at the stars and the crescent moon, she suddenly remembered her resolve to tell Zakiy her feelings. Her earlier nerves returned, battling around in her stomach like wasps on MDMA.

She sat jolt upright at the sound of footsteps on the stairs. This is it. Now or never, she told herself grimly, wiping her sweaty palms on her shorts.

When she saw what Zakiy was holding, all the words she'd been planning to say fled her brain.

He was carrying a small round cake with a single lit candle in the middle. He put it down on the coffee table with a flourish. On the cake, written in blue icing, were the words "Happy Birthday, Sathi!"

She opened her mouth, but no words came out. Silently, she counted days and then glanced at her phone screen. It was, indeed, 12:01 on June 15th. Her birthday.

Like a reflex, her thoughts immediately tacked on, Amma's death-day.

No! Her mother hadn't died on the day Sathi had been born. She hadn't died in childbirth, as Sathi had believed for most of her life. Amma had been killed by her family. *Not my fault. I didn't kill her.*

'Sathi?'

She felt pressure on her arm, and the accompanying warmth of his touch pulled her out of her thought spiral.

She looked up at Zakiy sheepishly. 'Sorry. I just... I'm not used to not spending my birthday hating myself for being born.'

The smile he gave her was full of understanding. 'I know. That's why I wanted you to have this memory for your birthday. To remind you that you have nothing to feel guilty about. To let you know that there are a lot of people who love you and are really, really happy that you're in their life.' He took a deep breath, his cheeks taking on a decidedly pink tint. 'And I'm at the top of that list.'

Nervously, his eyes lifted to meet hers, and their gazes locked. All she could see was him, and she wanted to seize the happiness that he offered. She wanted to try to give him at least a portion of the joy that he shared with her so selflessly.

Not breaking eye contact, Sathi shifted closer so that their thighs pressed together. She reached out and took his hand with both of hers, hugging it to her chest while his eyes widened. 'I'm really glad that you're at the top of that list. Because you're at the top of mine. I am so incredibly happy that you're in my life.'

Overcome with shyness, Sathi dropped her gaze, focusing instead on their clasped hands. She couldn't look at him while she said this; she'd never get the words out.

'You're my best friend,' she told him. 'But I'm tired of pretending that's all you are.' She took a deep breath. 'I'm tired of pretending that I don't have feelings for you.

Chapter Sixteen

Twin Flames

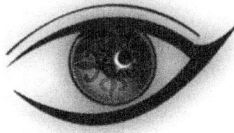

Zakiy gaped at her with his mouth hanging open for at least thirty seconds before her words actually sank in.

She peeked up at him to gauge his reaction, and the vulnerability in her eyes finally jolted him out of his stupor.

'You... you do?'

Obviously, he was still incapable of stringing two words together.

She nodded, her gaze skittering down to the floor as colour bloomed across her cheeks.

Zakiy felt a huge smile take over his face, her admission washing his world in joy. He lifted the hand she was still holding and used it to tilt her chin up, so she had to look at him. Then he brought her hand to his cheek and held it there. 'I have feelings for you, too.'

She exhaled, and all the tension drained out of her body. She spread her fingers so that she was cupping his face; her thumb stroked across his cheek.

Zakiy closed his eyes, marvelling at how good her fingers felt on his skin. Not believing that this was finally happening. 'Will you pinch me?' he asked her without opening his eyes. 'I want to make sure this isn't a dream.'

'Zakiy.' Her voice was quiet with suppressed humour. His eyes opened, and started when he realised that she was much closer to him than he realised. There was barely an inch between their faces. His eyes dropped to her lips, which were just a breath away. Another stroke of his cheek sent his gaze back up to meet hers.

'I have a better way to prove this isn't a dream,' she whispered, her eyes dancing in the reflected light from the candle.

She leaned closer and with a low groan, Zakiy finally, finally pressed his lips to hers.

Zakiy loved kissing. Specifically, he loved kissing Sathi. He wanted to tell her this, but he didn't want to stop kissing her for that long.

Sathi tightened her grip around his neck and wondered why she hadn't done this earlier. What the heck had she been so worried about? Then she told herself to stop thinking and just kiss him some more. So, she did.

Several minutes later, they finally pulled back to look at each other in wonder.

'Hello,' Zakiy said shyly.

She giggled. 'Hello.'

'Why are we acting like we just met?' he whispered.

'I don't know.'

He chuckled and sat back, pulling her with him so she lay across him with her head on his chest. His warm chest, which kept shooting sparks of electricity through her like the world's most comfortable bug zapper.

'Wait!' He shot up, almost sending her flying to the floor.

He caught her just in time and wrapped his arms around her. 'Oh crap, I'm sorry! Are you okay?'

Sathi twisted her head to the side so she could breathe. 'I would be if you stopped squeezing my lungs,' she choked out.

He loosened his grip, and she sat up. He looked so devastated that she smiled and scooted closer, pressing another kiss to his lips.

Zakiy relaxed and kissed her back, taking his time to taste her lips. When he pulled back, they were both breathless.

He tucked her under his arm. 'I'm sorry. As you can see, I'm a complete novice at this.'

She stared at him, eyes wide. 'You've never had a girlfriend?'

He shrugged, embarrassed. 'I've never felt this way about anyone before.'

Sathi laid her head on his shoulder. 'Me neither.'

Their hands found each other, and they sat in silence for a moment.

'So,' Sathi said finally. 'Why did you sit up so suddenly that you nearly toppled me over?'

'Huh? Oh! Your birthday cake – the candle's almost melted down completely! You need to blow it out and make a wish!'

She grinned at his almost manic excitement. She turned to the cake. She'd never had someone buy her a cake and tell her to make a wish as she blew out the candles. She felt that she'd had already got so many wishes granted, without even knowing to ask for them; all because of Zakiy. He always put her first, sacrificing his own happiness for hers. She closed her eyes and leaned towards the cake, knowing what she wanted most of all.

As she blew out the candle to the backdrop of Zakiy whooping and clapping and trying to sing "Happy Birthday", the only thought in her mind was: Zakiy should never lose his smile. His eternal happiness is my only wish.

After they stuffed themselves with cake, they cuddled up on the sofa again and just lay there, gazing at the stars in between kisses. Sathi got him up to date on what had happened with Gayathri.

He looked thoughtful when she finished. 'That makes a lot of sense, actually. Every time you got angry at me it was over your family – either your father or your grandparents.'

She nodded. 'Yeah. With my father, it was more about misunderstanding each other. I think that's pretty much resolved now. With Bhaskar and Goudhamy...'

'It's a totally different story,' he finished. 'I hope this works. I hope they lose the power to cause you pain.'

She squeezed his hand in response and snuggled in closer to his chest. 'Speaking of my father... how on earth did you convince him to let you bring me on this trip?'

Zakiy chuckled. 'He actually didn't need as much convincing as I thought. I think he knew how we felt about each other before we realised it ourselves.'

She winced in embarrassment. Well, at least they'd finally got to this stage. That was the most important thing, right? 'I'm glad he seems to trust you with me now,' she told him. 'It bothered me how he always seemed suspicious of you.'

He ran his fingers through her hair, lifting a few strands to his nose and inhaling when he thought she couldn't see. 'Well, when we go back and tell him about us, I'm sure that trust will disappear.'

She shook her head. 'I don't think so. And anyway, that's one argument he won't win. I'm not giving you up for anything.'

She could hear the smile in his voice when he replied. 'Is that so?' He tapped her nose with a finger.

She blushed and ducked her face, tightening her hold on him. 'I'm very possessive of my things. You're my thing now. Officially,' she declared. Her voice was slightly muffled from being buried in his t-shirt.

Zakiy vibrated with laughter. 'Yes, ma'am.'

She sighed and closed her eyes, content. This has been the best birthday of her life. And she'd gotten the most amazing gift she could've asked for, now that she'd been brave enough to reach out for it.

They woke up to the sound of the boat's engine starting. Groggily, they sat up, untangling their limbs from how they fallen asleep wrapped around each other. They must have dropped off on the sofa sometime in the middle of the night, and now the boat was heading back to the port.

Sathi felt a pang of sadness. She wasn't ready to go back to the real world. She wished they could just extend their trip indefinitely.

Soon Gayathri was calling up the stairs to tell them breakfast was ready. They rushed downstairs to change and pack up their belongings back into Zakiy's backpack.

'It looks pregnant,' he observed, poking a bulging pocket.

Sathi's lips twitched. 'We'd better get back to the Jeep before it gives birth. We don't want to make a mess here.'

He nodded soberly and hoisted the bag onto his shoulder.

Unni kept giving them wide grins over his shoulder while he drove them back to the port but made no comment on their night upstairs. Which, as Zakiy told her, was especially nice of him because it was against the rules. Apparently, some idiots in the past had gotten drunk up there and one had fallen over the railing into the dark water. Thankfully, the splash had woken everyone, and he'd been rescued, but since then it had become a rule that guests weren't allowed to be up on the upper deck during the night.

Sathi had a feeling that Gayathri had convinced her husband to turn a blind eye to last night.

When they got back to the port, they reluctantly said goodbye to the couple. Gayathri gave Sathi her phone number and told her to get in touch if she wanted to continue the meditation or if she wanted private Tarot readings.

Sathi and Zakiy promised to keep in touch and soon they were back in the Jeep, starting their long drive back north to Nelliampathi.

180

They held hands over the central console while Zakiy drove. Sathi only relinquished his hand when he needed to change gear and immediately reclaimed it at soon as he was done, cracking him up.

When they finally drove up to the treehouse it was late evening. They parked and Zakiy turned off the engine, but neither made any move to get out of the Jeep. The last day had a mystical feel; it had been a world with just the two of them, and neither was willing to break the spell.

Zakiy picked up her hand and held it to his cheek again, smiling wryly. 'Come on. We'll have to go in at some point.'

'Why don't we go to the campsite tonight?' Sathi suggested, hit by a sudden brainwave. 'I'll text my dad, and we'll see him in the morning.'

He just chuckled. 'Come on, Birthday Girl. Getting you back here tonight was part of the terms and conditions of the boat trip.'

Her eyes widened. 'Seriously?'

'Yup. You don't want your dad to file a missing person's report, do you?'

Her mood darkened. 'It's not like the police will do anything about it.'

'True. But forget that for tonight. It's your birthday.'

She took a deep breath and nodded, shelving her disdain for the police. Purposely, she lightened her tone. 'If it's my birthday we should do what I want and go to the campsite,' she fake-grumbled, pouting.

She was expecting him to laugh, but when she glanced over, she caught her breath. Zakiy was staring at her mouth, transfixed.

The earlier MDMA wasps attacked her stomach again as he leaned in and captured her pouting bottom lip between his own.

It took another ten minutes for them to finally leave the Jeep. Hand in hand, they climbed the stairs and Sathi used the spare key Dad had given her to unlock the door.

It was dark inside, and she frowned. 'Where's my dad? Why are all the lights off?'

'Maybe he's having a nap?' Zakiy suggested as she groped along the wall to find the light switch. She flipped it, her eyes blinking against the sudden brightness.

'SURPRISE!'

Sathi jumped and made an embarrassing squeaking noise as she took in the packed room. The first person her eyes fell on was her dad, beaming at her. Behind him were Vidhya and Jayaram, sprawled on the sofa and waving. Well, Vidhya was waving, while Jay smiled awkwardly. Manish, the tea stall owner she'd befriended, was leaning against the kitchen counter, and next to him was Rahul, her former co-worker from the resort.

The whole place was decorated with coloured balloons and banners, and a massive cake sat on the kitchen island. Everyone's smile widened when they noticed Zakiy's hand still clasped in hers.

'About time,' Vidhya teased, coming over to hug her.

To Sathi's shock, her father was grinning – yes, actually grinning. He hugged her as well and then clapped Zakiy on the back. 'Thank you for keeping your word and bringing her back in time.'

She turned to glare at Zakiy. 'You knew!'

He just shrugged at her, smiling. 'They wanted to surprise you as well. That's why I was in such a rush to get to the houseboat yesterday.'

Softening, she turned to smile around at everyone. 'Thank you, guys. It means so much to me that you organised all this.'

One by one, her friends came up to hug her and wish her a happy birthday. She cut the cake that Vidhya had baked for her, and soon everyone was happily munching on a slice – or in Zakiy and Rahul's case, several slices – of cake.

Dad came to sit next to her on the sofa, holding out a small box nervously. 'Here. This is for you.'

182

Surprised, she set her plate aside and opened the box to find a thin golden chain with a plain wedding band threaded through it.

'It was your mother's,' Dad explained as she lifted the chain out and turned the ring over in her hands. 'I meant to give it to you on your eighteenth birthday but...' He trailed off awkwardly.

Sathi thought back to that fateful day, exactly a year ago. When she'd discovered that her mother had been murdered, she'd fought with her father and set out alone to India. She'd had to play the "I'm an adult now" card when Dad tried to stop her.

She looked around the room, filled with people who had rapidly become her family... people who valued her more than most of her actual blood relatives.

She knew she'd hurt her father that day, and she felt sorry about that, but she couldn't find any part of her that regretted her decision to come here.

Sathi looked up at her dad, who was waiting anxiously for her reaction. 'Thank you, Dad,' she said sincerely. She clasped the chain around her neck and touched her mother's ring. 'It means so much that you gave this to me. It's the best gift you could have chosen. I love it.'

Eyes looking suspiciously bright, he kissed her forehead and excused himself.

Sathi smiled softly and glanced around the room for Zakiy. He was hovering around the cake (of course), but as though he could sense her gaze he looked up and caught her eye. He came over, carrying a plate stacked high with cake. 'You okay?' he asked, sitting next to her.

She nodded. 'Dad gave me Amma's wedding ring.' She held the chain away from her neck so he could see.

He smiled. 'It's beautiful,' he said, putting an arm around her shoulders. She leaned against him, absorbing his warmth. She couldn't believe how drastically her life had changed since last year. All those years of pain and loneliness had been reversed in just twelve months. It seemed like a dream, too good to be true.

Sathi was so lost in her thoughts that she didn't even realise that Vidhya and Jayaram had joined them.

'Well, don't you lovebirds look adorable,' Vidhya cooed. 'I knew something was going on with you two!'

Sathi blushed and grinned. 'I wish you'd told me – I took ages to figure it out.'

Zakiy bumped her shoulder with his playfully. 'You took ages even after you figured it out.'

She just stuck her tongue out at him, not deigning that with a response.

Surprisingly, Jayaram grinned and joined in. 'Consider yourself lucky, boy,' he told Zakiy. 'You barely had to wait at all compared to what I had to go through with this one.' He nudged Vidhya gently.

'Oh hush, you two,' Vidhya ordered. 'Anyway, Sathi, you have to tell me the whole story someday soon.'

Sathi smiled. 'Definitely.'

Jayaram cleared his throat. 'So we have some good news for you, Sathi.'

She raised her eyebrows. 'Oh?'

'Yes. Anika came to see me at the office a couple of days ago,' Jayaram said after an encouraging nod from Vidhya. 'She's agreed to give a statement to the police in your favour. She'll testify against Bhaskar.'

Sathi's mouth dropped open for several moments as she tried to take this in. 'Wow... seriously? I thought she was too scared.'

Jay shrugged. 'I don't know what made her change her mind. All I know is she's ready to do her part to help bring those bastards down.'

'Yes!' Zakiy exclaimed, punching the air.

Sathi felt relief bubble through her, loosening the knots in her stomach that talking about Bhaskar always brought to the surface. 'I can't believe it. I'd pretty much given up on Anika helping us,' she admitted, feeling bad that she hadn't had more faith in Anika.

184

Obviously, she had just needed a little more time to get her affairs in order.

She reached for her phone, wanting to thank Anika immediately. The call didn't go through, however, and the automated voice informed her that the number she was dialling was out of coverage area. She tried again, only to get the same message.

'Don't worry,' Jayaram said when she gave up. 'She said she would meet us at the police station tomorrow. You can talk to her then.'

Sathi nodded, and thanked him for all his help. Looking embarrassed, he smiled and wandered off towards her father.

Slowly, the party began to break up. Zakiy was the last to leave. She wished they could go to the campsite together, but it was obvious that her father wanted her to spend the night at the treehouse.

She felt too tired and too happy to fight with him tonight; plus, he had been pretty relaxed with Zakiy recently so she could at least try to meet him halfway.

So she lingered by the door to say goodbye to Zakiy, and then kissed her father on the cheek on her way upstairs to her tiny bedroom. She fell into bed and fell asleep as soon as her bed hit the pillow.

Chapter Seventeen

Love is Blind

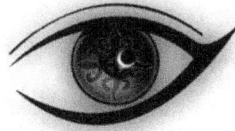

Zakiy turned up early the next morning to drive her to the police station. Her dad had to attend some online meetings for work, so they headed to the station alone. The journey took twice as long because they detoured into a deserted park so they could greet each other properly after being apart the whole night.

When they finally pulled up in front of the police station, Jayaram was already waiting for them. He smirked as he took in their appearance, and she knew he'd guessed what they'd been up to.

'Where's Anika?' she asked, partly to distract him, but also because she'd tried calling Anika again this morning without success.

Jayaram's expression dimmed, and he frowned. 'I don't know. I told her to meet us here at 10 o'clock.'

Zakiy glanced at his watch. 'Maybe she's stuck in traffic,' he suggested, although his expression was uneasy.

Half an hour passed, and Sathi's tension grew into a leaden ball in her gut. She dialled Anika's number for the fiftieth time, and wanted to strangle the annoyingly perky automated voice that kept telling her to try again after some time.

Another twenty minutes passed, and they had to accept that Anika wasn't just delayed by traffic. 'Why don't you two go to her house and check there?' Jayaram said finally. 'I'll go to my office, maybe she got confused and thought we were meeting there.' Even as he spoke it was evident that he was just clutching at straws.

Worry and guilt threatened to rip Sathi apart. Anika had only agreed to speak out against Karan for her sake; she had knowingly put herself in danger for Sathi.

'You don't think...' Sathi hesitated, loathe to give voice to her fears. 'I mean, what if Karan found out that she was going to give a statement supporting us?'

Jayaram seemed to age before their eyes. 'That's what I'm afraid of as well,' he admitted. 'He has spies everywhere, and he just has to give the word to the goons he keeps on his payroll to do his dirty work for him.'

Rage at Karan tore through her veins.

Taking out her phone again, she furiously punched out a message: Start ASAP. He needs to be destroyed.

She looked up at Zakiy, whose eyes were wide from reading the message over her shoulder. 'Let's go,' she barked, stuffing the phone into her pocket. 'We need to find Anika.'

Zakiy was quiet during the short drive to the house Anika had been renting. Sathi's rage left no room for worrying about his silence.

They parked in front of the house and approached the door, about to knock, when she came to a standstill. The door wasn't fully closed, resting a few inches away from the doorframe.

The anger that had been dominating her body yielded to fear. Exchanging looks of trepidation, they pushed the door open further and followed the long hallway into the living room. It has been cleared out and was empty apart from a few dust bunnies and empty boxes.

Heart sinking, Sathi forged ahead into the bedroom and stared in dismay at the empty wardrobes and vacant dresser. A toy car lay abandoned on the floor in the middle of the room.

She picked it up, turning it over in her hands. Arjun. Her six-year-old cousin was missing, along with his mother. A mother who'd painted a target on her own back to help Sathi.

Zakiy wound his arm around his waist, and she dropped the toy. She let out a sob and turned to push her face into his shirt.

'It's not your fault, Sathi,' he murmured. 'You can't blame yourself for this. Karan is the one to blame here.'

His words reminded her of her earlier text to Raghavan. She pulled back to see his face and saw nothing but tenderness there.

'You did the right thing,' he whispered, tucking a strand of hair behind her ear and stroking her cheek.

'Why are you so good at reading my mind?' she demanded, feeling a rush of relief that he understood.

Zakiy grinned and pulled her closer to him. 'Because I'm your partner-in-crime.'

She chuckled and was about to give a pithy reply when they heard the creak of a door opening.

They froze as Jayaram's words about Karan's goons ran through Sathi's mind. At the sound of footsteps, getting louder, Zakiy silently pulled her towards the *en suite*. He climbed into the shower cabinet and gestured for her to get in as well. He slid the door shut as quietly as possible.

Through the crack between the bathroom door and the door-hinge, Sathi could see a man standing in Anika's bedroom. He bent down to grab the toy car she'd dropped earlier, and her fists clenched. How dare this good-for-nothing goon barge into Anika's home?

Making up her mind, she turned and put her lips close to Zakiy's ear to whisper her plan to him. He reluctantly agreed, grumbling under his breath about her obsession with locking people in bedrooms.

She ignored him and glanced around the bathroom for something they could use. She spotted a towel hanging on the hook behind the door and grabbed it. Then she pushed the half-full bucket of water towards Zakiy, bending to drench the towel until it was soaking wet and dripping down her arms.

Zakiy climbed out of the shower cabinet and lifted the bucket. He met her eyes. She mouthed: One... Two... Three... Go!

He yelled out, making the man jump and turn towards them just in time to get a face-full of cold water.

As he spluttered and coughed, Sathi threw the wet towel, heavy with water, over his head. He fruitlessly groped at his face, trying to throw it off, while Sathi and Zakiy slipped out of the bedroom and turned the key in its lock.

The pounding started almost immediately. 'Hey! Hey, let me out!'

'Who are you?' Sathi shouted through the door. 'Where's Anika?'

The noise abruptly ceased. 'What? Isn't she here?'

She snorted. 'Of course she's not here. You and your mates have obviously kidnapped her. Did Karan send you?'

Total silence. 'What are you talking about?' the man asked finally. 'I'm Anika's friend. I've been calling her for days, but she's not picking up. So, I came here looking for her.'

She glanced at Zakiy, trying to gauge the truth of the man's words.

He pursed his lips, thinking. Then his eyes widened. He made a "wait" gesture and rummaged around on the living room shelves. He finally found what he was looking for and brought over a small cardboard box. He turned it over so she could see the label where the name of the sender was scrawled.

Sathi just raised her eyebrows at him, confused.

Not explaining, he asked through the door, 'Are you the same "friend" who sent Anika a special package a few days ago?'

There was a pause. 'You mean the box with the...?'

'The vibrator, yeah.'

Sathi jerked with surprise and stared at Zakiy.

The man's voice was mortified when he finally replied. 'She told you that?'

Zakiy ignored him. 'Tell us your name and address,' he ordered.

The man sighed. 'My name is Jacob Kurian.' He rattled off an address, which matched the one on the box perfectly.

Sathi winced and unlocked the door, opening it to reveal a soaking wet man with a humiliated expression. He had water dripping off his hair. 'Er... right. Sorry about that. I may have overreacted. Let's get you some dry clothes, and then we'll talk.'

Half an hour later, they were sitting in Zakiy's living room and sipping steaming hot tea that Abdullah had made for them.

Jacob had dried off and was now dressed in a pair of shorts and a t-shirt Zakiy had loaned him.

Sathi leaned forward. 'So, you're Anika's boyfriend? Do you know where she is?'

He shook his head. 'No, I told you, I haven't heard from her in days.' He paused. 'But yes, she and I have been in a relationship for years.'

'Years? But she only moved out of Karan's house a few months ago...' Zakiy trailed off and turned bright red. 'Oh.'

Jacob smiled, unembarrassed. 'Yes, we've been having an affair. I was married, too, when I met Anika. I was her college professor, so you can see why we couldn't be together openly.'

Sathi frowned. 'I thought she didn't go to college. She told us that she had to give up her education when she married Karan.' She didn't want to mention the rape and Anika's subsequent pregnancy in case Anika hadn't shared that with Jacob.

Jacob seemed to reflect Sathi's confusion. 'What? No, she finished college. I helped pay most of her fees, because Karan refused to.'

Zakiy held up his hand. 'Wait, can we go back for a second? You two met in college, and then what? You two started having an affair?'

'Well, not right away. She stood out from the crowd from the beginning, though. She was smart and hung on my every word when I was giving lectures. However, she confessed to me that she was struggling a bit because she was married to a man who didn't support her. I started helping her, giving her a bit of extra tutoring after class. Slowly, she started to confide in me about how her parents had basically sold her to her husband's family. She was being continuously raped by Karan, and they even forced her to have an abortion when she became pregnant.'

Zakiy frowned. 'An abortion? But... what about Arjun?'

Jacob set his teacup down. 'Arjun isn't Karan's son,' he said slowly. 'He's mine.'

Sathi and Zakiy exchanged shocked glances as Jacob continued, 'Anika tells everyone, including Arjun, that Karan is his father, but he's mine. Karan doesn't know, and he probably doesn't care – he himself has had countless affairs.'

Sathi tried to digest this. 'So you and Anika have been in a secret relationship for six years?'

'Seven. When I found out Arjun is my son, I decided to get a divorce from my wife so I could marry Anika and save her from that repugnant family. My divorce was long and messy; my ex-wife somehow found out about Anika and shamed me in front of our daughter and all our mutual friends. My daughter was Anika's classmate at the same college where I taught, and she still refuses to speak to me. Of course I had to resign my job as well. The faculty doesn't look kindly on professors having affairs with their students,' he added bitterly, staring at the floor.

Sathi didn't know how to respond. It was so screwed up that he'd slept with someone as young as his daughter, who was also his student. On the other hand, he obviously loved Anika, and had clearly suffered a lot for that love.

Zakiy leaned forward. 'When exactly did you last speak to Anika?'

Jacob looked up. 'On Tuesday. I said goodnight to Arjun on a video call, and then Anika and I spoke for an hour or so. Since then she hasn't answered my calls or texts.'

Zakiy glanced at Sathi. 'Tuesday,' he repeated. 'That's the same day she spoke to Jayaram and promised to give the police statement?'

'Are you sure?' she asked at the same time as Jacob, who said, 'What's that about a police statement?'

Zakiy nodded to answer her before telling Jacob about the police case against Sathi, and Anika's change of mind about speaking out against Karan and Bhaskar.

Jacob seemed puzzled. 'That's strange.'

'What?'

'No, it's just... Well, Anika and I usually talk about everything. But she never told me about any of this. She always said she didn't want to expose Arjun to any bad publicity about Karan, and that's the reason she always gave whenever I tried to persuade her to go to the police and file a complaint against Karan for what he did to her. She's always been adamant on that point. So I'm just wondering why she didn't tell me she was planning to do this for your sake.'

Maybe because she never actually intended to go through with her promise, Sathi thought, meeting Zakiy's eyes. From the grim set of his mouth, she knew he was thinking along the same lines. Especially since Anika had given them a completely different reason for not giving the police statement.

This was the second discrepancy in Anika's story, and Sathi was beginning to shift away from worry that Anika was missing to wondering what the hell kind of game she was playing. Anika had clearly been selective in what she told Jacob as well, a man who was obviously deeply in love with her and willing to do anything for her sake.

192

She wanted to talk this over with Zakiy alone; she'd always felt that he didn't trust Anika, especially after she first refused to help Sathi in the police case.

She thanked Jacob and saved his phone number, promising to contact him if they got any news of Anika. She also made him promise to call them if Anika reached out to Jacob.

After he left, she glanced at Zakiy. 'So what do you think?'

'I think there's something definitely fishy about Anika,' he said immediately. 'I think she left because she doesn't want to give a statement against Karan. Or Bhaskar.'

'But why leave now?' she countered. 'It's not like we were pressuring her to do it. We backed off after that first time. Why go to Jayaram and offer to do it, and then disappear? It doesn't make any sense.'

A strange expression crossed Zakiy's face. 'Yeah, about that... Jayaram told me something weird about her visit.'

She raised her eyebrows. 'Oh?'

'Apparently when she went to talk to him she was... well, she was a bit too friendly, if you catch my drift.'

Sathi blinked, taken aback. 'You mean, she was flirting with Jayaram?!'

He rolled his eyes. 'Well, you know what he's like, he wouldn't know what flirting is if it performed a circus routine in front of him, but he said she was smiling a lot and standing too close to him. He also admitted that she kept touching his arm for no reason. Basically, he was super uncomfortable.'

Her eyes were wide. 'Does Vidhya know?' She paused. 'Wait a minute, how do you know all this?'

'He told me last night at your birthday party. I think he was trying to figure out whether he was just reading too much into it. And no, he didn't tell Vidhya. He was too embarrassed.'

'What did you tell him?'

'I said that from his description it sounds like Flirting 101.'

Sathi stared off into the distance. What was Anika playing at? If she didn't want to testify why go to such elaborate measures? And why flirt with Jayaram, of all people? 'It makes no sense,' she said finally. 'I don't understand why she's doing all this.'

He sighed. 'I think we need to find out more about her,' he said, expression grim. 'She's continuously lied and told half-truths. She told us she has no education and no means to support herself. Jacob just told us that she's graduated from college. Her own boyfriend doesn't know that she promised to help us bring Karan and Co. down.'

'Forget lying to us, okay she barely knows us, but keeping such a big secret from Jacob? That's a major red flag,' Sathi mused.

'Especially since he literally ruined his life over her AND financially supported her through college.'

'Exactly. God only knows how much of her story is actually true.'

Zakiy gave her a meaningful look. 'There is one way to find out. Are you thinking what I'm thinking?'

She just stared back at him for a few moments, eyebrows furrowed. Then her forehead smoothened out with understanding. She smiled.

Chapter Eighteen

Frozen Heart

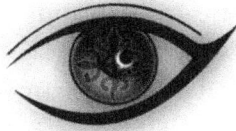

It took them almost an hour, but they finally reached Anika's village just as the sun was setting.

Narayan had told them the name of the village where Anika's parents used to live. Hopefully they hadn't moved house since then.

They kept asking various passers-by for directions until they finally pulled up in front of an old house with a thatched roof.

At the sound of the Jeep, a teenage girl came out onto the porch and stood staring at them.

Sathi smiled at the girl as they got out of the Jeep, but only received a suspicious look in response.

'Who are you?' the girl asked. 'What do you want?'

'Hello!' Zakiy said brightly, ignoring her sullen tone. 'We're Anika's friends. This is Sathi, and I'm Zakiy.'

The girl's lips curled. 'If you're friends of hers, go to the city. She's not here.'

'Oh, well, we're coming from the city,' Sathi jumped in. She decided to make a wild guess and hope it didn't backfire. 'You're her sister, right? She talks about you all the time.'

The girl blinked rapidly, suspicion fading away and surprise taking its place. 'Anika told you about me?'

Sathi knew then that her gamble had paid off. 'Oh, yes, all the time.' She spotted some half-finished drawings on a table nearly and inspiration struck again. 'She talks about how talented you are. She loves your drawings.'

A reluctant smile drew the girl's lips upwards, and it transformed the sullen teenager into a beautiful kid eager for her sister's praise. 'Um... okay. Do you want to come in?' she offered awkwardly.

As she turned and stalked into the house without waiting for a response, Zakiy came up behind Sathi. 'Aaand the Best Actress Award goes to... drumroll please... Sathi Varma,' he whispered, his breath tickling her ear and temporarily short-circuiting her ability to think.

She badly wanted to turn and kiss him until they both ran out of air, but she figured that would undo all the progress they'd made with Anika's sister. So she settled for elbowing him in the stomach and marching into the house after the teenager.

'Er... are your parents here?' Zakiy asked, trying to alleviate the strained silent that had descended once they sat down.

'No.'

'Right. Do you live here alone?' he tried again.

'Of course not. They're just not here right now.'

'Ah.'

Zakiy sent her "help" signals with his eyes.

Sathi chewed on her lip. 'Can we see more of your drawings?' she finally asked.

The girl seemed to thaw a bit. 'Okay.' She got up and retrieved a sketchbook. She brought it over and held it out to Sathi, looking almost shy.

Sathi took it and flipped through the pages. 'Wow. These are amazing,' she said, genuine in her admiration. The girl had sketched mainly trees and flowers, all in intricate detail.

'What's that?' Zakiy asked, pointing over her shoulder. There was a small symbol and a date in the corner of each of the drawings.

'Oh. That's my signature. SRK.'

'SRK as in Shah Rukh Khan? Are you a fan? Me too! High five!' He held up his hand, grinning.

The girl blushed. 'No. I mean, yes, I am a Shah Rukh Khan fan, but SRK is short for my name, Sarika.'

'That's even cooler,' Zakiy said, beaming. 'Your drawings are amazing too.'

'Thanks.'

They fell into silence again while Sathi tried desperately to think of some way to get Sarika to open up.

Then, surprisingly, she herself broke the silence. 'Is Anika coming to visit soon?' she asked, trying but failing to hide the hope in her voice.

Zakiy hesitated before apparently deciding on the truth. 'We're not sure. How often does she usually visit?'

No answer.

'Sarika?' Sathi prompted. 'When did you last see Anika?'

'That's none of your business!' Sarika suddenly shouted, slamming her sketchbook on the table.

They were too shocked to respond. A woman rushed into the room, wiping her hands on her sari. 'Sarika? What's wrong, sweetheart?' She glanced at them. 'Who are you?'

Sathi stood up. 'We're friends of Anika. I'm so sorry, we didn't mean to upset Sarika.'

Understanding underscored with sadness crossed the woman's expression. 'I see. Well, just give me a minute. I need to get Sarika to rest and then I'll come back to you.'

'Yes of course, no problem,' Zakiy assured hastily. 'We'll wait.'

The woman gave them a tired smile and led Sarika from the room. 'Come on, darling, I bet you'd like a nap.'

Fit of anger apparently forgotten, Sarika surrendered to the woman's mothering without complaint.

The woman returned a few minutes later. 'Sorry about that,' she said, closing the door behind her. 'She gets a bit agitated when Anika is mentioned. She's a sweet kid, really.'

'We didn't mean to upset her,' Sathi said apologetically. 'We're so sorry.'

'Oh no, dear, it's not your fault. How could you have known?'

'Er... are you her mother?' Zakiy asked hesitantly.

'Oh no, I'm their neighbour, Rekha. I've known Sarika since she was a baby, though.'

Zakiy introduced himself and Sathi and then asked, 'Are Sarika's parents around? Could we speak to them?'

Rekha frowned. 'So Anika never told you what she did to her family? Typical.'

She sat down, indicating for them to do the same. 'Well, their mother passed away a long time ago, when Sarika was no more than a baby. Their father never remarried, he just devoted his life to Anika, Sarika and their brother, Ajay.'

'That Anika, though, I could tell as she grew up that she was going to be trouble. She only ever thought about herself, and her father could never seem to say no to her. She had him wrapped around her finger, alright,' she added darkly.

Rekha sighed and continued, 'Her father worked hard to keep his kids in school so he could give them a good education, but Anika was a lot more interested in boys than in studying. Then she became obsessed with dancing, and she pestered her father until he gave in to her demands and sent her to a dance academy in the city.

'It wasn't long before she starting making problems there as well. She ended up having an affair with one of the dance instructors. He was married and when his wife found out she publicly humiliated the whole family and made their lives hell.

'Anika's father apologised and got Anika away from that dance academy and back home. That's when she gave him the next nasty surprise: she was pregnant. Despite everything, he loved her and when she said she didn't want the child, he took her to a hospital and helped her get an abortion.

'After the whole scandal no school would agree to have her, so her father started taking her to the city with him, where he worked doing odd jobs for a rich family. He thought he could maybe try to get her a job there, so at least she could become self-sufficient.

'Anika had much better plans for herself, though. She started seducing the son of the rich couple who employed her father. Her father noticed her spending a lot of time with the boy and warned her to keep her distance. She defied him, though, and continued to see the boy secretly. Then she got pregnant again.

'This time her father refused to help her and, like the spoilt brat she is, she left home in a rage. We didn't hear from her for a long time after that. Then we found out that she ended up marrying that boy. She boasted later that she had blackmailed him into it. She didn't invite anyone in her family to the wedding, and never even visited.

'Her father went to visit her once, full of longing to see his eldest daughter. She insulted him in front of all her new family and friends. She even accused him of selling her to his employer's family for money.

'Her father was heartbroken, and on his way home... well, no one knows if it was an accident or if he was overwhelmed with despair, but only his dead body returned to the village.' Rekha concluded her story and stared off into the distance, eyes haunted.

Sathi felt bile crawl up the back of her throat, and a glance at Zakiy's disgusted expression told her she wasn't the only one. Anika really had married into the perfect family. It was a shame that she'd destroyed her own family in the process.

'Sarika...' Zakiy trailed off, obviously at a loss on how to frame his question.

Rekha looked at him. 'She was very attached to Anika, even though Anika never had any time for her. Sarika idolised her big sister... Anika's betrayal, together with her father's death, destabilised her. She's doing a lot better now. She was almost catatonic for a while. At least now she's started going to school again, and she loves her drawing. She only really talks to me and Ajay, though.'

'What does Ajay do?' Sathi asked.

'He works in the city, trying to make ends meet and support himself and his little sister. He leaves at the crack of dawn most days and usually doesn't get home til late. So, I try to spend as much time with Sarika as I can, so she's not on her own all the time.'

She paused and then said, 'Look, maybe it wasn't my place to tell you all I did, but it makes me so angry that Anika pretends that her family are a bunch of villains who ruined her life – when it's really the other way around. I bet she never told you any of this, did she?'

They shook their heads. 'No,' Sathi concurred. 'She told us the same story you mentioned – that her parents sold her to that family and that she's being continuously raped.'

Rekha scoffed. 'Raped? How can she call it rape if she constantly pulls her skirt up for anyone with a penis?'

Zakiy made a choking noise, and Sathi thumped his back. When he was no longer in danger of choking to death on his own spit, she turned back to Rekha. 'That's a very good point. She was obviously playing us right from the beginning.'

'The question is why,' Zakiy mused. 'Why approach us offering to help, if everything she was saying was a lie?'

'Take it from me,' Rekha said. 'Anika doesn't do anything unless it benefits her somehow. Ever.'

Sathi thought back to their initial conversation with Anika. She'd said she wanted help in bringing Karan and his family down. But why, if they hadn't actually been abusing her as she'd claimed?

Her head throbbed. Anika was a far more dangerous enemy than Karan, who at least attacked face-to-face. Anika had pretended to be their ally and then stabbed them in the back.

The reason for Anika's behaviour was still a big question mark. What had been her motive in leading them on such an elaborate ruse? Sathi couldn't figure that part out. They needed more information.

She chewed on her lip, an idea slowly forming in her mind. It was a long shot, but it was better than nothing. She glanced at Rekha. 'Could we see Anika's old bedroom?'

Rekha looked surprised but agreed. She led them towards the back of the house. 'Anika and Sarika used to share a room because there just isn't enough space. Now it's Sarika's room but she doesn't like being in there much. She prefers her brother's room.'

She opened a door, revealing a tiny room. 'Here you are. Will you excuse me, I need to go and put the rice on to boil for lunch. Otherwise, Sarika won't eat anything the whole day.' She hurried out, adding, 'Just close the door behind you when you're done.'

Sathi glanced around the room; there were no personal effects to reflect its owners' personalities. There were no posters on the wall, no make-up on the dresser... no sign, in fact, that this room was in regular use at all.

She walked over to the desk, thinking that was probably the best place to start. There was a thick layer of dust on top. It didn't even have any drawing supplies, unlike those scattered on the living room table. Sarika obviously didn't consider this her room. Sathi wondered if that was because she felt this room belonged to Anika and was keeping it unoccupied for her big sister's return.

Sathi thought of Anika with hate; how selfish would you have to be to trample on such devotion? Could a heart be frozen? If so, that must be how Anika's heart was.

A hand lightly touched her shoulder. 'Sathi? Are you okay?'

She blinked and focused on Zakiy's face, creased in worry. He reached out to stroke her cheek, and his touch momentarily gave respite to her turbulent feelings.

'I'm fine,' she reassured him. 'Just thinking of how cold and twisted Anika turned out to be.'

His expression hardened. 'She really knows how to play the victim role, doesn't she?'

Sathi gave a mirthless laugh. 'Yeah, and we fell for it hook, line and sinker.' Then she frowned, rethinking her words. 'Wait, I definitely fell for it, but I always got the feeling that you never really trusted her. Why not?'

Zakiy absently wound a strand of her hair around his finger as he thought. 'I did believe her story initially, especially about Karan. But I didn't like how she refused to give the police statement supporting you. She was the one who came to us and offered her help. But as soon as we called in her favour, she backed out. I think that's when I started to feel like we couldn't trust her.'

He sighed and focused on her again. 'It was just a feeling, though, and I had no idea she was deceiving us on such an epic level. Anyway, let's look in her desk before Rekha comes back to check on us.'

She nodded and turned to the drawers on one side of the desk. The first held only an old compass and some pens without lids. The second was empty, and the third had a sheaf of dusty papers. She lifted them out and rifled through.

'Looks like old tests and exam score sheets,' Zakiy commented, glancing at the papers over her shoulder.

'Yeah... Oh crap.' Sathi bent down to pick up the paper that had fallen out of the stack. She flipped it over and stared, shocked. 'What the hell?'

Zakiy reached out and gently touched the photo, as though he needed to convince himself that it was real. 'Isn't that...? Why does Anika have a picture of your mother?'

Why indeed. Sathi stared at her mother's teenage face, so much like her own except for the mass of curls instead of Sathi's soft waves.

The most shocking thing about the picture was that it had been desecrated; angry red lines slashed through Amma's cheeks, looking like scratch marks, and something sharp and pointed – maybe the compass they'd found – had been used to punch holes throughout her face.

'What. The. Hell?' she repeated, anger cruising through her like hot lava. How dare she? How dare that bitch do this to her mother's photo? For a moment, her rage masked her vision to such an extent that all she could see were red spots.

'Sathi, look at this,' Zakiy said urgently. She opened her mouth, about to snap that nothing could be more important than the insult to her mother.

Oh God. It's coming back. I'm losing control, she thought in panic. Remembering what Gayathri had told her, she quickly closed her eyes and visualised the rage in her as a cloud of red that polluted her body. She took deep breaths in and out, imagining that more and more of the red smoke was leaving her body with each breath.

When she felt calmer and less likely to snap Zakiy's head off for something that wasn't his fault, she opened her eyes.

He hadn't noticed her near-lapse in control. He was looking through the other papers feverishly. She went over to see why he was so worked up. 'Look,' he said, pointing at an old maths test. In red ink was written 78%, and underneath was a scrawled comment: *Good work. Focus on mastering differentials and integrals, and you will score a higher mark next time.*

The words 'next time' had been crossed out in black marker, and '*NOT GOOD ENOUGH*! *She won again* was written in smaller handwriting next to it, along with another score: 85%

The new score had been underlined twice, so roughly that the paper had torn a little from how harshly the pen had been dug into it.

'There are more of these,' Zakiy said quietly. He showed her a science paper, which had 72% in red and 88% in black, with the words *I WILL beat her*. It was a similar story for old English, Hindi, and Social Science papers.

It seemed Anika had made everything a competition between herself and Amma, making it her sole aim to beat her nemesis. Sathi wondered if her mother had even known about this competition, or if it had existed only inside Anika's sick mind.

'Oh shit,' Zakiy muttered. He wordlessly held up another photograph. This one hadn't been mutilated or graffitied in any way; in fact, hearts had been painstakingly drawn around the edges, and coloured in with pink ink. It showed the side profile of a teenage boy, caught mid-laughter. He was good-looking, with wavy black hair and an infectious smile.

It was also, clearly, a younger version of Sathi's Dad.

PART THREE

Chapter Nineteen

Mistaken Identity

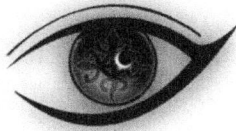

Sathi took a deep breath, held it, then exhaled through pursed lips. She squared her shoulders and rang the doorbell.

It took another couple of rings and several minutes of waiting - during which her stomach churned like a tsunami – before the door swung open.

Karan's eyes widened when he saw Sathi. 'You?'

Sathi smiled at him. 'Good morning, Uncle. How are you?'

'What are you doing here?'

She didn't drop the smile. 'I'd like to come in if that's okay. There's something I'd like to discuss with you.'

Karan snorted. 'What are you up to now? Come with another hidden camera, have you?'

She chuckled lightly, as if this was a ridiculous concept. 'Of course not! I'm not stupid enough to come to the house of a famous criminal lawyer like you while wearing a hidden camera. You can search me if you like,' she offered, holding out her arms like you do at the airport security check.

This seemed to confuse Karan, and he stared at her, speculative. 'I'm not going to search you,' he said finally. 'Because I don't think you're that stupid either. But I'm also not going to let you into my house unless you tell me what you want.'

Sathi sighed. 'Look, I didn't want to say this while standing on your doorstep, but since you're insisting... Uncle, I've come to tell you that I want to withdraw my complaint against Great-Uncle.'

Karan's jaw dropped for a moment before he rapidly recovered his composure. He couldn't hide the triumphant gleam in his eyes, though.

'Well, molé,' he began, the affable uncle once more. He opened the door wider. 'I'm glad to see you've made the right decision at last. Let's go up to my office so we can sit down and discuss this.'

A flash over his shoulder caught her eye, and she had to use all her control to keep her eyes on Karan. She made herself smile at him again. 'Uncle, I would like nothing more than to discuss this further.' Then she delivered the clincher. 'It's time to do the right thing.'

Karan's smile stretched wider. 'Absolutely. Come, let's talk upstairs.'

Still smiling at her as though she was just a favourite niece and not someone he'd been in the process of framing in a false criminal case, he held the door wider for to go through. Then he closed the door and led her up the stairs.

They paused in front of what must be the door to Karan's office. Sathi focused hard on the panelling so that her eyes wouldn't betray her by flicking to another, almost identical, door a few metres to their left.

Karan opened the door to his office and waved her through. There was a large, polished mahogany desk with brown leather armchairs on one side and a matching swivel chair on the other.

Serpent's Dance

Karan gestured her into one of the armchairs before going around to the other side of the desk to take his seat. 'If you don't mind me asking, molé, what made you come to this decision?'

Sathi looked down at the polished wood of the desk. 'I realised that you were right. I took things too far. I was angry with Great-uncle, but your visit made me realise that he is my family, after all. And we should try to let what happens within the family stay within the family.'

'I'm very proud of you, molé. You're being very mature about this.'

Sathi hesitated. 'And...'

He leaned forward. 'Yes?'

'Well... I was also thinking about what you said. You know that education in the UK is very expensive... Then there are the living expenses...' She trailed off, biting her lip.

Smugness threatened to conquer Karan's face entirely. 'Of course, of course! Don't worry at all, molé, I understand. Let's see, where's my chequebook?'

Karan rummaged around under the desk until he found it and opened it to a blank page. He glanced up at her, grinning widely. 'We'll put a nice sum towards your degree, how's that?'

She smiled and nodded.

Zakiy put his ear against Karan and Anika's bedroom door, making sure there were no footsteps heading his way. He breathed out a sigh of relief; he only heard the soft murmur of conversation as Sathi kept Karan distracted in the study.

He turned to examine the bedroom. The bed was unmade, with the sheets twisted and hanging half on the floor. One side of the bed was noticeably neater, and the bed-side table was bare except for a notepad and pen. Zakiy went over to flip through the notepad, but it was just full of old grocery lists.

He checked the drawers next: nothing. It was the same story for all the other cupboards and the dressing table drawers. He headed over to the wardrobe. He opened it, noticing that Anika had left a few sets of clothes behind. He rifled through them, even checking the bottom of the wardrobe, but there was nothing there either.

Zakiy flopped on the bed, stumped for ideas. Sathi had been convinced that they needed to search this room after finding out about Anika's obsession with Nakul. He'd known better than to argue, but he had argued – and won – when he insisted that he would be the one to search the room, not her. The last thing she needed was another case against her. He'd convinced her to distract Karan instead while he searched.

Of course, he had no doubts that Karan would march him straight to jail if he found Zakiy in here, but that was a risk he was willing to take – especially if it meant keeping Sathi out of prison.

It would all be for nothing, though, if he couldn't find anything useful in this room.

He groaned and fell back onto the bed, blinking at the ceiling. A flash of colour caught his eye. One of the panels above the wardrobe had a splash of red standing out in stark contrast to the wood. He stared. There weren't panels, but more cupboards!

'And this should be the last of the paperwork,' Karan said, passing her yet another pile of paper.

As he explained the mass of legal jargon, Sathi did her best to keep her breathing even and pretend to pay attention. She hid her sweaty palms in her lap and tried to nod along. She really hoped Zakiy had found something by now. She wouldn't be able to stall Karan for much longer.

'What about the case against me?' she asked, putting the right amount of worry into her voice. 'You said the police have a text message...?'

Karan waved away her concern. 'Oh, I can make that disappear don't you worry.'

210

'But what about Susan's statement?' she pressed. 'She gave a false statement against me,' she said, real indignation leaking into her tone.

He smiled. 'If I can convince her to give a statement like that, do you think I'll have any trouble getting her to retract it?'

Sathi tried to smile back convincingly, and surreptitiously checked her phone. There was still no message from Zakiy. She suppressed a groan. That meant he hadn't found anything yet.

She was about to text him to abandon the search and get out of there when Karan suddenly rose from his chair and came up behind her. Sathi hastily dropped the phone into her lap.

'Now, if you could just sign here, molé. This is a letter saying that you are withdrawing your complaint.' Karan patted her shoulder, and she only just managed to suppress a shudder.

Karan cleared his throat. 'While you're signing that, I'll just go and get my seal from the bedroom.'

'No!' she blurted, shooting up. Her phone clattered to the floor. She ignored it, panic rising in her throat. 'I mean... I don't quite understand this terminology, could you just explain it again before you go?'

Karan was already at the door. 'I'll explain it in a moment, just sign it,' he said impatiently over his shoulder as he left.

She swore and scooped up her phone. *Get out now!!* she texted, not daring to call in case the ringtone gave him away. Also knowing that it was probably too late anyway.

Devi, please let him have gotten away, she prayed as she raced after Karan.

Zakiy dragged out the stool in front of the dresser and balanced on it to yank open the cupboard. A red sari fell out immediately; it was what had been caught in the cupboard door and attracted his attention.

He reached his hand into the cupboard and groped around blindly. His fingers touched the handle of a bag. He pulled it out; it was a black laptop bag, its heaviness indicating that there was a laptop inside.

Zakiy was just about to unzip it when the door to the bedroom was yanked open.

He nearly fell off the stool in shock. Then he saw that it was just Sathi.

'Oh my God, you scared me,' he rebuked, getting off the stool with the laptop bag in hand. 'Look what I found–'

'Zakiy,' she cut him off, brushing a curl out of her face impatiently. 'You have to leave right now. Karan is coming.'

'Oh shit!' Zakiy scrambled to chuck the sari into the wardrobe and then dragged the stool back to the dresser.

Sathi was peering out the door. 'Zakiy, come on!'

'Okay, okay.' Zakiy slung the computer bag over his shoulder and hurried after her. She led him down the stairs and out the front door, closing the door softly behind them just as a voice above was saying, 'Just sign it.'

They sprinted around the back of the house, only slowing when they reached his Jeep.

Zakiy's phone beeped with an incoming text message. Sathi had texted him: *Get out now!!*

Bloody Indian cell phone towers. 'Your message only just came through,' he grumbled, holding up the phone to show her.

He looked around. 'Sathi?'

Where had she gone? He texted her. *Where are you?*

A moment later: *Did u get out?*

He was still blinking at the message when another arrived. *Be at jeep 2 mins.*

Zakiy shook his head. The messages must still be delayed. He waited, and soon Sathi was running up to him. She threw her arms around him and buried her face in his chest.

He chuckled and wrapped his arms around her waist, the adrenaline high making him feel giddy. 'It's okay,' he murmured to her, brushing a kiss against her hair. 'We're okay,' he repeated.

She didn't reply, just lifted her lips to his. For a moment, they just drowned in the relief that they had both gotten out safely.

Sathi pulled back and gazed into his eyes. 'I was so scared you wouldn't make it out in time.'

He traced his thumb across her bottom lip. Sathi shivered and closed her eyes. He kissed her eyelids, then the tip of her nose. 'I nearly didn't,' he murmured, staring intently at her lips. 'If you hadn't come when you did, Karan would've caught me.'

Her eyes snapped open, and she stiffened in his arms. 'What?'

Zakiy's gaze was still fixed hungrily on her lips. 'What?' he asked absently, leaning in to touch his lips to the corner of her mouth.

She pushed against his chest. 'Zakiy! What are you talking about?'

'Huh?'

Sathi snapped her finger in front of his face. 'Focus! How did you get out of there in time?'

He frowned at her. 'Why are you asking me that? You're the one who came to warn me that Karan was coming.'

She stared at him, mouth hanging open. 'Zakiy, I didn't come to warn you. I couldn't! There wasn't enough time, he left the room too quickly. I texted you and went after him. He went into his bedroom, and then I got that text from you. So, I figured you got out, and I ran out of there.'

'But... but you... the texts... the cell tower...' he spluttered. 'You were right there with me! We left the house together!' Zakiy stared at her increasingly worried expression, aghast, and his eyes took in something he'd noticed about her earlier in Karan's room, and then promptly forgotten in the panic of escaping.

He reached out and threaded a strand of Sathi's hair through his fingers. Her silky waves slipped and slid over his hand. 'Your hair...' he breathed, realisation stealing the air from his lungs.

'What about my hair?' she demanded, bewildered. 'Zakiy, you're scaring me! What the hell is going on?'

He blinked and focused on Sathi, *his* Sathi. He cupped her face in his hands. 'It was your mother,' he told her gently. 'She looked exactly like you, but she had curly hair. She came to warn me because she knew you couldn't. It was your mother,' he repeated in awe.

Sathi had become a statue under his hands. He kept stroking her hair, staying quiet so she could process what had happened.

He knew the moment it sank in because she collapsed into him. The howl that broke through her lips was barely human; it was a guttural release of pain.

Zakiy hugged her tight, holding her together until she was strong enough to do it on her own.

They had just reached Zakiy's house when his phone rang. He answered one-handedly, keeping his other arm securely around Sathi. 'Hello?'

'Where are you?' Jayaram barked.

'At the house. Why?'

'I'm coming over,' Jay responded before hanging up.

Zakiy stared at his phone. Now what? He shrugged and told Abdullah to make tea before pulling Sathi to the sofa. Her skin was like ice, and she stared blankly in front of her, unseeing.

He got a blanket and wrapped her in it like a burrito, and then sat next to her so his body heat would help warm her up. Abdullah soon came in with the tea, and together they coaxed her to take a few sips.

After a few minutes she stopped shivering and some colour finally returned to her cheeks.

'Would the little madam like some banana fritters?' Abdullah asked, hovering over them.

His obvious concern touched Zakiy; for all his cantankerous ways, he really did care about Sathi.

214

She managed to smile up at Abdullah, even though her eyes were still a little glassy. 'I'm okay.' She put her hand on Zakiy's knee. 'Really, I'm okay now.'

He covered her hand with his own and leaned in to press a kiss to her forehead. Then he glanced up at Abdullah. 'I wouldn't mind some fritters,' he hinted.

Abdullah sniffed. 'I need to check whether we have enough bananas.'

Zakiy's mouth dropped open as the butler turned and trotted away.

Sathi giggled at his expression, and the sweet sound pulled him out of his indignation.

He gave her a rueful look. 'Do you see the double standard here? When it was for you, he would've made fritters even if he had to go out and forage for bananas in the wild. When I ask for them...'

She giggled even harder. 'It's probably because he knows that he'll need a whole plantation's worth of bananas to fill that bottomless stomach of yours,' she teased.

'I don't know what you mean,' he claimed staunchly, hiding his relief that she seemed to be back to her normal self. Then he sobered. 'Are you okay?'

She nodded, smile fading. 'Yeah. I wish I could've seen her... but I'm glad she came to get you out. I wouldn't have been able to bear if it Karan caught you. She probably knew that.'

Zakiy picked up her hand and started playing with her fingers. 'She must love you a lot... why else would she come to warn me?' he asked rhetorically.

She wacked him on the back of the head with her free hand. 'You don't think she loves you?'

'Well, of course she does,' he retorted, rubbing his head. 'How could she not?'

Sathi chuckled and rolled her eyes. 'Indeed. So, did you find anything?'

He nodded and got up to retrieve the computer bag from where he'd dumped it next to the door. He handed it to Sathi and sat back down.

She unzipped the bag and pulled out an iPad. Eagerly, she pressed the home button but was met with a prompt for a passcode.

'Hmm...' Pursing her lips, she tried 1234 and then 0000 with no luck. 'Damn it. I guess those would have been too simple.'

'May I?' She passed it to him, and he tried a couple more combinations. He was staring in frustration at the incorrect passcode – please try again message when the doorbell rang. 'Oh! That must be Jay.'

Sure enough, a moment later Abdullah showed in Jayaram – and Jacob. An extremely dishevelled Jacob. When he turned his head, they gasped; there was a red mark under one eye, like he had been punched.

'What happened?' Sathi exclaimed, jumping up.

Jay's eyes were flint. 'It's a long story.'

Zakiy got up as well and gestured towards the dining room. 'Let's all sit down. I'll get you some ice,' he told Jacob.

'I will fetch the ice, Master Zakiy,' Abdullah said, hurrying out.

Jacob sat down gingerly. 'I found Anika.'

'Hold on,' Jay interrupted. 'Maybe you should tell them how you ended up at the police station first.'

Sathi and Zakiy gaped at the two men. 'Police station?' Zakiy repeated finally.

Jacob grimaced and then winced as the motion stretched the skin around his eyes. 'Anika filed a complaint against me.'

Abdullah opened the door, holding a tray in his hands. 'Coffee, freshly made banana fritters... and ice,' he announced.

Chapter Twenty

Accomplice

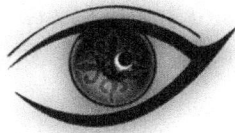

Jacob held the ice to his cheek, and visibly wilted with relief. 'That's better. Anyway, as I said, I found Anika. She's with this fraud salesman. He's been sniffing around her for months, and she didn't chase him off because he gave her free samples from the cosmetics company he worked for. I didn't like it, but she assured me that she didn't care about him, only about the products her gave her for free. Then, recently, he told her that he embezzled a lot of money from the company.'

He paused and his eyes filled with pain. 'I think that's around the time that I noticed Anika was becoming a little colder in her attitude towards me. She didn't want to meet up as often as before, and she kept making excuses that didn't really make sense. Her phone was always busy whenever I tried calling her.

'Anyway, I figured out she's with him because I bought her the sim she's using, and I had a friend of mine trace the location. I sent her a message telling her that I know where she is and that I want to talk. I knew she'd ignore that, like she's ignored all my other messages, so when I didn't get a response, I went to that fraud's house. She was there, and so was my son. I tried to talk sense into her, but she was beyond reason.

"I don't want you anymore,' she said, her eyes cold and uncaring. 'You need to leave me alone. I'm someone else's wife now.'

'At first, I thought she meant Karan – then I realised she'd married that fraud! After all her promises to me, after making me go through a divorce and estrange myself from my daughter... after making me pay for her education and all her expenses, she was just throwing me aside for that bastard.'

Jacob paused, his hands trembling. He took a long drink of his coffee before continuing, 'I told her that she may not want me anymore, but she couldn't stop me from seeing my son.'

His hands clenched into fists. 'That's when she sneered and said, 'Arjun isn't your son."

Jacob looked up at their stunned expressions. 'I don't know what she's talking about. We were together when she became pregnant, and she told me he's mine. Now... I don't know if she's lying or if Karan...' He shrugged helplessly. 'I don't know. I sort of lost control then. I picked up Arjun and started to walk out.

'Anika cried out, and that fraud husband of hers came running. He saw Arjun in my arms and punched me in the face.

'I was about to hit him back when I noticed Arjun's expression. He was crying, afraid... When I looked at his face, I couldn't bring myself to do anything that would scare him anymore. So, I left.'

Sathi shook her head. 'She really is a psychopath. I can't believe she said Arjun isn't your son.'

'Yeah,' Jacob said bitterly. 'And that's not all. The police called me in for questioning today because they got a complaint that I was harassing her.' He shook his head, disgusted. 'That's when I called Jayaram and asked him to go with me. I needed legal advice, especially since it was clear Anika wouldn't stop at anything to get her own way.'

'When we explained the real story, the policeman we spoke to became more sympathetic towards Jacob,' Jayaram said grimly. 'He said Anika had clearly been honey-trapping him. He told us to put together all the evidence – text messages, receipts of everything he paid for – and file a complaint against her.'

'Yeah, because the police are so good at delivering justice,' Sathi said sarcastically. 'Look at the complaint I filed – they just made me the villain. That's what will happen to Jacob, too. People like Bhaskar and Anika will win if we go down that route again.'

'Sathi,' Jay began.

'No,' she cut him off. 'I'm sorry Jayaram, but I think we all need to accept that the justice system isn't going to help us here.'

Jacob stared frantically between them. 'But I need my son! I gave up my family for that bitch – he's all I've got left.'

Zakiy pursed his lips. 'The only way for you to get custody of Arjun is by discrediting Anika as a mother.'

'How do we do that?'

Silence. Jacob looked around helplessly, and then frowned when he caught sight of something. He put the ice down and went over to the sofa, picking up the iPad Zakiy had abandoned there earlier.

'This is... How do you have Anika's iPad?' he asked, turning to stare at them.

Sathi shifted guiltily. 'Er... we kind of stole it.'

Now both Jacob and Jayaram were staring, wide mouthed.

'We had to!' Zakiy protested. 'We needed to find out more about her.'

Sathi nodded. 'She's done nothing but lie to us.'

Jacob gave a grim smile. 'Join the club.' He turned the iPad in his hands. 'I bought this for her, you know. She told me she was finding it difficult to get access to all the textbooks she needed, so I bought her this iPad and got her digital versions of the textbooks.' He sighed. 'So, did you find anything useful on it?'

'No. It's locked, and we don't know the passcode.'

Jacob opened the lid of the iPad case. 'Well, unless she changed it since we were together, I should be able to unlock it.' He touched the screen a few times. 'Ah, there we go. Wait, what's this?'

While he frowned down at the iPad screen, Sathi went to peer over his shoulder. It was a textbook written in Malayalam.

'So, it's not only college textbooks she was reading,' Jacob said in disgust. 'This is a book on black magic. She must have gotten it from her mother-in-law.'

Sathi froze. 'Mother-in-law? You mean, Goudhamy?'

Jacob looked up. 'Yeah. She's a master at this black magic, and she used to teach Anika. I hated it, but Anika always said she was just humouring the old woman. She would never actually do anything...'

He trailed off as Sathi and Zakiy exchanged significant glances.

'Can I borrow that for a while?' Zakiy asked, holding out his hand for the iPad.

Jacob surrendered it to him. 'Keep it. I don't want it.' He turned to Jayaram. 'So, what should I do now?'

'Well, even if you don't file a complaint against her, I still think the policeman's advice was good – we need to put together a file with all your communications with Anika and any receipts you've kept. It's important to have it ready in case she escalates this harassment claim.'

Jayaram started to go over what Jacob needed to do in more detail, but Sathi tuned them out. This new information about Anika's interest in black magic meant she was a much more dangerous enemy than they'd thought. What were they supposed to do next?

'Sathi.'

The tone of Zakiy's voice caught her attention immediately. Silently, he held out a piece of paper.

She took it, and her insides started to writhe as she read the letter. 'Guys!' she barked.

Jayaram and Jacob stopped mid-conversation to stare at her. She silently passed them the letter.

220

'I found it in the iPad cover,' Zakiy said.

Dear Anika,

I was so happy to get your letter, even though I wish it contained happier news. I cannot believe you were suffering in silence for so long. I feel disgusted to call Karan my brother.

Of course, I will come back to help you! I hate to leave Sathi, but she will be safer with her father. I could not bear it if I put her in danger.

But you are important to me, too, and I cannot tell you how glad I am that you reached out for help.

I will book my flight soon and send you another letter with the details. Stay strong, dear, and I will see you soon. I will do everything I can to get justice for you. My best friend, Vidhya, has a friend who is a lawyer, I'm sure he will help us as well.

Love,
Madhu

'This is why Amma came back to India,' Sathi said bitterly. 'Anika lured her to her death with the same sob story she used to buy our pity.'

'That woman needs to be stopped,' Jay said through clenched teeth. It was obvious that Madhu's indirect mention of him had hit him hard.

There was a pause. 'So, what are we going to do?' Zakiy asked.

Silence.

Sathi's phone started to ring. She retrieved it, and her eyes widened at the caller id. 'Um. Excuse us a minute,' she muttered, pulling on Zakiy's arm to drag him out of the house.

'It's Raghavan,' she told him quickly before answering and putting the call on speaker. 'Hello?'

'Hello, my dear. I'm calling to tell you that the ritual to destroy the talisman is scheduled to start tomorrow.'

'That's great news,' Sathi began, before Zakiy suddenly started jumping up and down and pointing at the phone. She raised her eyebrows at him. What? she mouthed.

He just pointed at the phone again. Rolling her eyes, she held it out to him. 'Say whatever it is before you explode.'

Zakiy grabbed the phone. 'Raghavan, there's another enemy whose power we need to destroy. Can you add them to the ritual tomorrow?'

She just stared at him while Raghavan replied, 'Hold on, let me grab a pen. Okay, who is it?'

'Her name is Anika.'

As soon as Raghavan hung up, Sathi threw her arms around Zakiy's neck. 'You are a genius!'

'You ever doubted?' he asked in a fake injured tone before drawing her to him in a kiss.

Several minutes later, they reluctantly turned to head back inside. The sound of an autorickshaw had them glancing back in surprise. The rickshaw's headlight shone in their eyes, temporarily blinding them. Someone got out and paid, their figure just a silhouette.

The rickshaw turned in a wide arc and drew away, finally revealing the identity of its passenger.

It was Susan Roy.

'I know you must all be angry with me,' Susan said.

She didn't look at Jayaram, whose jaw was clenched so tightly that it was a wonder it didn't break. 'I'm so sorry. I was scared and I let myself be bullied into betraying you,' she told Sathi, eyes filled with remorse. 'I didn't want to give that statement against you, but they threatened my daughter. Karan's goons said they would kill her if I didn't do it. I don't ask for your forgiveness, but please try to understand the position I was in.'

Sathi's arms were crossed tightly across her chest. 'Why are you here now?' she asked bluntly. 'Did Karan send you?' He must have realised it had all been a ruse when she ran out of the house.

'What? No!' Susan shook her head emphatically. 'No, I came because I couldn't live with what I did. I feel disgusted with myself, and I want to stop feeling like a coward.'

'What about your daughter?' Zakiy asked, his expression carefully neutral.

Susan's shoulders straightened, and pride took over her expression. 'She's the one who helped me to make this decision. She said that if we live in fear, then we might as well be dead already. She wants me to do whatever I can to help you.'

Jayaram hit the table with his fist. 'How the hell are supposed to trust anything you say?'

Susan flinched and finally met his gaze. 'I deserve your anger,' she admitted. 'You are my friend, and I betrayed you. But I swear to you, on my daughter's life, that I'm telling the truth.'

There was silence as Jayaram glared at her, unconvinced.

'Prove it.'

Everyone's gaze turned to Sathi, who kept her eyes fixed on Susan. 'If what you're saying is true, prove it.'

Susan met Sathi's gaze unflinchingly and nodded. 'What should I do?'

'Do you think she'll do it?' Zakiy asked quietly as he drove her to the treehouse.

Sathi sighed. 'I don't know. I want to believe her, but after Anika, I feel like I can't trust anyone anymore.'

He felt for her hand blindly and lifted it to his lips. 'You can trust me.'

She smiled and cradled his cheek. 'Obviously. Trusting you is like trusting myself.' She paused, reconsidering. 'Actually, I think I trust you more than I trust myself.'

He groaned. 'Don't say things like that when I can't kiss you,' he moaned dramatically.

Sathi laughed and leaned forward to press her lips to his cheek. 'There? Is that better?'

'Hmm... maybe if you do it again.'

She obliged, grinning.

'Once more.' Then: 'And again.'

She peppered his face with kisses until they were both laughing so hard that the Jeep nearly veered into a bush. Thankfully it was late, and the roads were empty.

'Sathi.' His tone was suddenly shy.

'Yeah?'

'I'm in love with you.'

Silence.

'Zakiy?'

'Yeah?'

'I think you should stop the Jeep.'

'Why?'

'Because you told me not to say things like this when you can't kiss me.'

The Jeep rolled to a stop and Zakiy pulled up the handbrake. He turned to her, eyes shining. 'Things like what?'

'I'm in love with you too.'

Chapter Twenty-One

Just Desserts

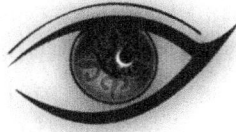

The temple was filled with soft evening light as the sun bid goodbye; hundreds of oil lamps with flickering wicks of flame waited for their light to be needed, playing tag with the breeze as they illuminated the indulgent faces of the idols of the gods. Garlands of flowers wreathed their necks in bright colour and bells rang out as the puja began.

Soft music floated on the air as a female voice sang praises to the goddess. A man chanted Sanskrit mantras as he held a lamp lit with multiple wicks of flame. As he chanted, he started moving the lamp clockwise in front of Devi's idol.

Once he finished there, he started going around to each of the other pedestals one by and one and repeated the ritual. He finally finished back at the main pedestal by raining flowers on the statue of Devi.

He pressed his palms together and bowed his head in prayer. He opened his eyes and picked up a large conch shell. Pressing it to his lips, he took a deep breath and blew.

Sathi's eyes jolted open, the sound of the conch ringing in her ears.

She lay there, thinking, for a good half an hour or so while her bedroom filled with pre-dawn light.

Finally, she sat up and dug in her drawer for her deck of playing cards. She hadn't used her cards to make a significant decision in a while, but it felt right for her to use them for this question, rather than the Tarot. After all, it had been her cards that revealed the truth that brought her to India on this momentous journey.

The sun rose higher and became warmer and warmer as it greeted the earth. Sathi kept playing, her question clear in her mind, until she had four kings – 2 red and 2 black – smiling up at her.

Decision made, she reached for her phone. Narayan picked up immediately, and she explained her dream and what needed to happen. He was reluctant at first, but after some persuasion, he finally agreed.

She was about to hang up when he said, 'I spoke to Srinivasan again, about that woman who is your enemy.'

'Anika?'

'I thought you said it was that reporter?'

She shook her head, even though he couldn't see her. 'No, it must be Anika. She's the one who manipulated my mum into coming back to India after I was born.' She paused. 'So did Sreenivasan say something else about her?'

Narayan's voice was disturbed when he replied. 'He said that she is continuously doing black magic against you. Apparently recently she went to a temple where they used to do human sacrifice thousands of years ago.'

Bile crawled up her throat. 'Do they still do that? Human sacrifice, I mean?'

'Oh no! It's illegal, of course, but for her to go to a place like that... it suggests she won't stop at anything to achieve her goal.'

226

Sathi silently thought of all the lives Anika had ruined. 'Well, I'm not going to argue with that.'

'Anyway, Sathi, be careful. I'll do everything I can as well, to get the gods' protection.'

'Thank you, Uncle. Think about what I said.'

Narayan promised he would, and she hung up. She noticed that she had received an email from Susan while she'd been on the call with Narayan. She clicked on the attachment and quickly scanned through the document. She smiled.

Someone knocked on her door. 'Come in,' she said, gathering up her cards and putting them back into her drawer.

'Good morning,' Zakiy said, his hair sticking up in different directions as it always did in the morning.

Her dad had let him stay over last night on the condition that he slept on the sofa downstairs.

She jumped up and thrust her phone in his face. 'Look!'

He read the email, smile growing until it took over his face. 'It's perfect.'

'Right?' she crowed. 'Shall I tell her to go ahead?'

'Er... actually, wait, there's something I want to show you first. Susan may be able to use it as well.' He took out Anika's iPad and opened it. 'Here,' he said, handing it to her.

Sathi flinched when she saw the photos. There were hundreds, some identifiable as Anika, but others that were just close ups of her breasts, thighs and private parts.

'Keep scrolling,' Zakiy said grimly.

There were a lot more, and even more disturbingly there were also some pictures of Arjun without any clothes. He was just a kid...

'This is disgusting,' she said, trying to keep her nausea under control.

'That's not all. She's been sending these to a lot of people, a lot of men, with all these disgusting messages. Jacob isn't the only one she's been conning money from. Her other admirers are happy to send her money, too.'

Her hand accidentally brushed the screen, and a video started playing. Cheeks flaming, Sathi hurriedly tapped the screen, but it still took a while for the sounds of a woman masturbating to fade.

'Oh my God,' she breathed, throwing the iPad on the bed.

'Sorry,' Zakiy said, wincing guiltily. 'I should have warned you about that.'

She glanced up at him, noticing his bloodshot eyes for the first time. 'Were you going through this crap last night?'

'I wanted to find something to nail that bitch. I don't know if these will help, but we should send them to Susan.'

She threaded her fingers through his and laid her head on his shoulder. 'Did you sleep at all?'

The muscles in his shoulder shifted under her cheek as he nodded. 'For a few hours. Dad woke me up, actually. I just got off the phone with him.'

Sathi glanced at him guiltily. 'Oops. I didn't think he'd call you right after. Sorry.'

He waved off her apology. 'They're coming to Nelliampathi?'

She nodded and described her dream. 'I think it was a sign. The gods want him back at the temple. They want him to take his rightful place and perform pujas for them.'

'But... isn't that risky? What if Bhaskar and Karan cause problems again?'

Sathi smiled and ran her hand through his hair, trying to flatten it. It just sprang back up like a slinky. 'After Susan's article comes out, they'll have too many other things to worry about.'

He grinned and grabbed her hand, pressing a kiss to her palm. 'You're diabolical. I like it.'

The New Power Couple: Black Widow and a Lawyer on the Wrong Side of the Law

228

By Susan Roy, Investigative Journalist

We all know Karan Bhaskar, the renowned criminal lawyer that all public prosecutors have learned to fear facing in court. Today, however, we have showing new evidence that may find this lawyer taking his own turn on the stand soon enough.

Ajay Rajan, an autorickshaw driver forced to do dirty work for Karan and his family for years, speaks out against the notorious lawyer.

'Karan pays strangers to act as witnesses and trains them to lie on the stand to win his cases,' Ajay says. 'He also gets his goons to threaten real witnesses for the prosecution and forces them to give false testimony.'

I myself have been forced to give a false statement to the police by Karan. He and his goons threatened to hurt my daughter if I didn't lie to protect his father from the dowry scandal.

Sathi Varma, Karan's niece, is another victim of Karan's misuse of the legal system. She was framed for extortion and blackmail when she dared to file a complaint against Bhaskar for trying to rape her. Karan first attempted to bribe her, switching tactics to blackmail when she refused to give into his games.

Where's the proof for all this? I hear you demand. Well, I'm glad you asked.

Ajay Rajan kept records of all the underhand procedures Karan ordered him to do over the years. He has turned all those documents over to me, and they will be given as evidence to the magistrate in the case against Karan.

That's not all. I have a voice recording of Karan and his goons threatening my daughter and forcing me to give false evidence against Sathi Varma.

Finally, Sathi Varma has video evidence of Karan bribing her with money in exchange for withdrawing her complaint against Bhaskar. Karan admitted on camera to tampering with police evidence and to forcing me to give a false statement against Sathi. Sathi also has a letter written by Karan, in his own handwriting, requesting the police to drop her complaint against Bhaskar, as well as the cheque he wrote her as payment.

With all this mass of evidence against him, I think Karan can count himself lucky if he doesn't end up in prison along with all his criminal friends.
And now for the Black Widow: Anika Karan, *née* Anika Rajan, went missing several days ago. Even though Karan himself doesn't seem bothered by her absence, Jacob Kurian, the man with whom Anika has been having an affair for the past seven years, is beside himself with worry.

'I don't know where she's gone,' Jacob says tearfully. 'And worst of all, she took my six-year-old son with her.'

Delving deeper into Anika's life to find her, I uncovered some showing truths about this housewife.

While still at school, she seduced the decorated classical dancer, Shankaran Pillai, and blackmailed him. 'She nearly ruined my life,' the dancer says. 'She wanted to get into the film industry through dance, and I had contacts in that field. I've even helped talented dancers become actresses before. That's why she pretended to love me, but the truth is she didn't have the talent or looks to make it in the film industry. When I told her I couldn't help, she became furious. She told my wife about our relationship and humiliated me in front of everyone in my society. No one would send their children to my dance school after that. I know I was wrong to get involved with a student, but she's not exactly an innocent victim in all this. She was just using me to get what she wanted.'

Jacob Kurian's story is, unfortunately, like Shankaran Pillai's. Anika manipulated Jacob, her college professor, into paying for her education. 'I divorced my wife and lost my daughter's respect because of Anika. I need justice.'

Jacob isn't the only one deserving justice. Anika's brother, Ajay Rajan – yes, the same Ajay who was forced to do dirty work for his brother-in-law – reveals disturbing truths about his sister's childhood. 'When she was fourteen years old, she was approached by some agent who promised to take her to Mumbai and help her become an actress. Even though she knew what they wanted in exchange for their trouble, she was willing to do anything to become an actress.

'She sneaked out of our house one night, and even worse, she persuaded two of her friends from school to go with her to Mumbai,' Ajay says. 'Thankfully, one of the girl's parents found out and stopped them just in time. The girls had no idea what Anika was leading them into. My father had to sell everything he owned to compensate the girls' families and persuade them not to go public with what Anika almost did. He moved us back to the village after that.'

What makes a girl so twisted as to be willing to sell herself – and her friends – to become famous? I guess a leopard never changes its spots, because we have just uncovered Anika's iPad, which contains disturbing nude photos and videos she had taken of herself and sent to her many admirers.

I was recently accused of being a sex trafficker – a "madam" – by Karan when I exposed his father's dowry scam. It seems like Karan got his inspiration from his own wife!

Let us hope that the dark reign of Karan and Anika ends now, and that all their victims find justice.

Sathi finished reading the article aloud and flung herself at Susan. 'You. Are. Amazing!'

Zakiy was dancing around the room with Susan's daughter, an adorable girl of twelve, while she grinned shyly and let him spin her around.

Jayaram and Vidhya sat with their hands clasped, beaming.

Dad held Amma's letter to Anika, reading it for the fiftieth time, eyes moist.

Ajay stood awkwardly, not quite sure what to do with himself. Sathi finally let go of Susan and went over to him. 'Thank you,' she said sincerely, clasping his hand. 'We couldn't have done this without you. I know it couldn't have been easy for you.'

He shook his head. 'We protected her for too long. We should have let her face the consequences instead of always shielding her from them. Maybe then she wouldn't have caused so much damage. And–' Ajay hesitated.

'Yes?'

Ajay closed his eyes for a moment, as though for strength. 'I think she's the one who set you up to be raped,' he said quickly.

Sathi inhaled sharply. 'What?'

He nodded miserably. 'She asked me to drop her off at your resort that morning. I swear I didn't know what she was going to do. But later I heard her tell Karan that she'd done what he wanted.'

Zakiy was instantly by her side, putting his arm around her shoulders.

'She must have sent that text,' Sathi realised. 'Anika must have taken my phone and wrote that text to Bhaskar, the one Karan used to frame me.'

Zakiy nodded. 'That was probably a signal to Bhaskar, telling him that you were alone in your room.' His jaw was clenched angrily.

Sathi shook her head. Anika was pure evil. She and Karan truly were a match made in hell.

Zakiy laced his fingers through hers. 'Well, she'll get what's coming to her.'

'Thanks to Susan's kickass article,' she said, purposefully lightening the tension. 'How many people read the local paper?' she asked Susan.

'Millions,' she replied. 'And that's not all, it's been printed online on their website as well. I've also posted it on all my social media sites. It's already been reposted lots of times. They're getting their just desserts, don't worry about that,' Susan added in satisfaction, hugging her daughter close.

Ajay cleared his throat. 'Speaking of just desserts... did you hear about Bhaskar?'

Everyone stared at him. 'No. What about him?' Sathi asked.

'Well, apparently his' – he glanced at Susan's daughter – 'private parts got infected from the burn wounds. Apparently, the doctors are saying they'll have to cut it off.'

Silence. Then they all started laughing.

At a small village medical clinic two months later

A policewoman holding a small child in her arms walked along the hallway, prodding a woman in handcuffs in front of her to walk more quickly.

She stopped a nurse who was walking by. 'Is Dr Geetha free?' she asked.

'She has a patient now, but she should be finished soon.' The nurse eyed the woman. 'What's the case?'

The policewoman rolled her eyes. 'Prostitution. Except she tried to sell the kid for sex as well.'

The nurse gasped in horror. 'Oh my God.'

'Yeah. The villagers found out and they started throwing stones at her. She's lucky someone called us, otherwise she'd be dead by now.'

'I hope you go to hell, you miserable hag,' the nurse spat at the woman.

The woman turned to stare at the nurse, her face and neck covered in small cuts. She didn't respond.

A door opened near them, and an elderly woman left the room, staring at them curiously.

'The doctor should be free now,' the nurse told the policewoman.

She nodded and nudged the handcuffed woman into the examination room. 'Good morning, Dr Geetha,' she said, sticking her head around the door and addressing the woman behind the desk. 'Can I speak to you for a moment out here?'

The doctor looked unsurprised and nodded. 'Wait inside,' she told the prisoner, before stepping out and closing the door behind her.

The policewoman briefly repeated the history of the woman. 'I just need you to check her injuries and make sure there's nothing seriously wrong before I take her to the station.'

The doctor nodded. 'No problem. Wait a minute, please.' She went back inside while the policewoman made herself comfortable on a chair outside the examination room. She absently bounced the little boy on her lap; he seemed content to sit there quietly.

About half an hour later, the doctor came out. 'Handcuff her to the bedframe or something,' she told the policewoman. 'We need to talk in private.'

Bewildered, she did as the doctor said and when she came back outside, she found that the doctor had persuaded the earlier nurse to babysit the child for a while. The policewoman followed the doctor to her office on the first floor.

'What's wrong, doctor?' she asked, sitting down.

'That woman's vagina is infested with maggots,' she said bluntly.

The policewoman's mouth dropped. 'What? Maggots? How...?'

The doctor's mouth was twisted in disgust. 'Apparently, she uses things like carrots and cucumbers when she... well, when she masturbates, or during sex with all those men, if they ask for it. I asked her if she at least washes the vegetables properly before she sticks them up there and she didn't answer.' She rolled her eyes. 'If I had to guess, some flies must have laid eggs on the vegetables and got inside her body when she stuck them inside her.'

The policewoman shook her head, struggling to take this in. 'I didn't even know something like that was possible.'

The doctor shrugged. 'I've reached a point in my career where nothing really surprises me anymore. This is a first, though. Do you know who she is?'

The policewoman nodded. 'Yes, you know that lawyer who was debarred a few weeks ago?'

The doctor's eyes widened. 'You mean Karan Bhaskar?'

'Yes. She's his former wife, Anika.'

Chapter Twenty-Two

Final Battle

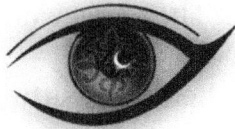

Sathi was back at the meadow. The dragon, now with only five heads, blew red hot flames into the sky. Eagerly, Sathi looked around for the gods.

One by one they appeared; first came a boar-headed god and goddess. Next, a man with a lightning bolt in his crown materialised, and next to him was a woman with a matching, smaller tiara.

A younger-looking god appeared next, holding a spear in one hand, and at his side was a beautiful woman with long black hair. Next arrived a gorgeous man with dark skin, garlands around his neck and a rotating discus spinning around one finger. With him was a woman whose body had gold jewellery glinting everywhere.

Last to materialise was a man dressed in tiger skin and holding a trident, with a goddess at his side who reminded Sathi so much of her own mother that her eyes filled. Devi.

Together the gods watched the dragon, their expressions unreadable. Devi then nodded to the boar-headed couple. 'Lord Varaaha and Devi Varaahi. Please rid the world of asooya, or envy.'

They bowed to her and strode towards the dragon. Devi Varaahi raised her hand, and a golden stick appeared in her hands. With the danda, she hit one of the dragon heads with such force that it instantly separated from the body. The dragon writhed in agony, now down to only four heads.

Devi's face was expressionless. 'Lord Indhra and Devi Indhraani. Please destroy mathsarya, or competition.

The couple with lightning bolts in their crowns stepped forward. Devi Indhraani lifted her hand, and a bajrao materialised. Lightning blasted out from it and hit another head, charring it until it detached and fell to the floor.

Three heads left.

'Lord Karthikeya and Devi Kaumaari. Please vanquish moha, or illusion.'

The young, long-haired god grinned at Devi. 'Yes, Mother.'

The couple went up to the dragon, and a spear appeared in Devi Kaumaari's hands. With a war cry, she struck at a head, and it became skewered on the end of the spear. She pulled on the shaft, and the head detached from the body. She closed her eyes, and head and blood disappeared, leaving the vel clean once more.

Two heads left now.

'Lord Vishnu and Devi Vaishnavi. Please get rid of lobha, or covetousness.'

Lord Vishnu nodded respectfully. 'As you wish, Sister.'

He and the goddess covered in gold moved forward. A serrated discus appeared on Devi Vaishnavi's lifted finger. She flicked her finger, and the spinning chakra sailed through the air to decapitate the dragon before it spun back to her finger.

One head left.

Finally, Devi looked at the god standing calmly next to her. 'Shall we, my Lord?' she asked him.

He smiled at her. 'After you, my Devi.'

All the gods turned to face them, and together said, 'Lord Maheshwara and Devi Maheshwari. Please erase krodha, or wrath.'

Devi held out her hand, and a trident materialised. Holding the staff in her right hand, she lunged forward and separated the last head from the dragon's body.

The dragon let out a last ear-splitting roar of pain, and then went silent. Its body kept writhing, as though it was refusing to accept the loss of its heads.

'I'll take care of it, Mother,' Karthikeya said, lifting his spear.

'Wait, Son,' Devi said, stopping him. 'There is another matter to which we should attend first.'

She looked at Lord Vishnu. 'Brother, please call Lord Adhishesha.'

Lord Vishnu closed his eyes and concentrated, and a moment later a massive cobra rose from the ground. The cobra spread its gigantic hood, which was balancing nine different coloured spheres, over Vishnu and Vaishnavi. In a deep rumble, Lord Adhishesha spoke. 'Devi, how may I serve you?'

Devi smiled at the god of snakes. 'My friend, I need your blessings. You know that a grave perversion of nature has taken place. A mother has used her umbilical cord for black magic. That magic needs to be destroyed, but it is protected by two coupling snakes.'

Adhishesha bowed. 'I understand your predicament, Devi. You cannot hurt the snakes for fear of insulting me.'

'Exactly,' Devi said.

'Devi, with your permission, I will call on my half-brother and my Lord's vehicle, Garuda. He will be able to remove the snakes from the cord without it being an insult to me.'

Devi's smile was incandescent. 'Thank you, Adhishesha.'

'It is my pleasure to serve you, Devi.'

He closed his eyes, and a moment later a massive eagle appeared on Vishnu's shoulder.

'Welcome, Lord Garuda.'

Garuda inclined his beak in response to Devi.

238

Devi concentrated, and a writhing mass appeared in the air. It was a long, sickly white cord, and two snakes slithered around it, so entwined that you couldn't tell where one ended and the other began.

The snake god hissed. 'Devi, these serpents hold no allegiance to me. They are allied with evil, and you have my blessings to destroy them.'

Devi nodded. 'Lord Garuda.'

With a screech, the massive eagle flew over the writhing snakes and grasped them in his claws. He wrenched them away from the cord and flew away, the snakes hanging limp from his claws.

Devi momentarily disappeared before reappearing seated atop a massive lion. A double-edged sword was in her right hand. The lion growled, and Devi brought down the sword on the exposed cord, shattering it in two.

The two severed ends began to spew blood. Bhadrakaali materialised in the meadow. She drank the drops of blood before they could reach the ground, then put the two ends of the cord into her mouth, in between her canines, and sucked them dry.

As the cord shrivelled up, a ball of dark energy burst out from it. It formed a humanoid shape made of black smoke. The pulse of energy concentrated in the chest of the smoke figure.

Devi nodded to Karthikeya, who touched his mother's feet for her blessing before thrusting his vel, now glowing red-hot, into the frozen chest, splintering the ice there.

The warmth spread out from the spear-tip, and the creature tried to escape the heat by fleeing up to the eyes.

Lord Shiva held out his hand, and Lord Bhairava appeared. Bhairava bowed to Lord Shiva and then plunged his trishul into the eyes.

Panicking, the dark energy made a last bid for freedom and flew down to the kundalini. Before it could find respite there, Lord Agni materialised and sent his flaming darts to set the loin on fire.

Lord Ganapathi appeared as the flames died down. The elephant-headed god used his noose and goad to guide the creature up to the throat.

'This is your last chance,' Devi told it, her voice ringing out through the meadow. 'Lord Ganapathi's noose is helping you to face your own ignorance. Face what you are and the damage you caused. Think of all the lives you ruined. Will you repent? Or will you choose to continue in your ignorance?'

She gestured to Lord Indhra, and he sent his lightning bolt to illuminate the crown of the humanoid form of smoke. 'Ascend to the sahasra chakra, and you can finally begin to repent.'

The creature, instead of ascending, darted up to try and exit via the mouth.

Devi made a signal, and Lord Vishnu directed the sudharshana chakra to cut off the head of the smoke form. As it collapsed, the body of the dragon combusted.

Cawing ripped apart the quiet of the meadow, and a hundred crows flew overhead.

Devi looked up at them and smiled. 'Come, celebrate. You have had to wait for a long time, but the ancestral evil that has been tormenting your family for generations has finally been defeated, once and for all. Your descendants are safe now.'

The crows banked towards the ground, and as soon as they landed, they turned into human form. Sathi stared out at the crowd of familiar strangers: her ancestors.

One crow landed at Devi's feet. Devi bent down, and when she straightened again, she was holding a sobbing woman in her arms. The woman's mass of black curls cascaded down her back.

Sathi's breath caught as her mother turned to look at her, pride and longing warring in her expression.

Devi kissed Madhu's forehead. 'Go to her now, Daughter. She has been waiting for you for a long time.'

Tears still streaming down her cheeks, her mother ran towards Sathi and took her daughter into her arms. 'Oh, my darling,' she breathed, stroking her hair.

Sathi hugged her mother tightly, unable to believe her eyes. She knew this was a dream, it had to be, but she also knew that everything she was seeing and experiencing in this dream was real. Maybe not on the earthly level, but on some other plane of existence that she was being allowed to visit during her sleep.

Behind her mother's shoulder, the other gods disappeared one by one. Devi was the last to leave, and she was watching Sathi. Just before she vanished, the supreme goddess looked at Sathi and winked.

Her mother drew back to look at her, eyelashes wet with tears. 'My baby,' she breathed in wonder. 'I'm so proud of you, sweetheart.'

'Amma?' Sathi managed before her voice broke. 'Is it really you?'

Amma tucked a strand of Sathi's hair behind her ear. 'Yes, baby girl, it's me. Your mother.'

Sathi was scared to blink in case her mother disappeared. 'Are you...? Are you okay? Are you in heaven?'

Amma's expression softened. 'I'm fine, vavé. I'm with Devi, and my parents and all our ancestors. I'm okay.'

She stroked Sathi's cheek. 'Sweetheart, I want you to listen to me. Cherish your time on earth. Love your father and your friends. Be happy.'

She seemed to anticipate Sathi's next question, and sadness crossed her features. 'When you've lived a long, full life, you can join me. But not before then. It already wounds me beyond words that you were so unhappy for most of your life. Every tear you shed was like acid burning through my veins. Now let me be happy by seeing you enjoy life. You deserve happiness, darling. Now promise me.'

Sathi was crying so hard that she could barely breathe, but she managed to nod and whisper, 'I promise.'

'That's my girl. Now, one more thing...'

She wiped her face. 'Yeah?'
'That Zakiy of yours... he's a keeper.'

Epilogue

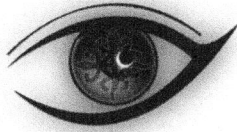

I can't believe this,' Sathi said, peeking out from behind a pillar. 'It's finally happening!'

Zakiy grinned at her excitement. He put his hands on either side of her waist and gently drew her towards him. 'It's about time those two made it official.'

She smiled and draped her arms around his neck. 'Vidhya looks so beautiful,' she said happily.

'So do you,' he responded before drawing her into a kiss.

They broke apart reluctantly, not wanting to let go of each other. Despite their outward cheerfulness, the looming separation clung to them both like a bad odour.

They had returned from Mookambika two days ago, with just enough time to prepare for the wedding. Tomorrow Sathi would return to the UK with her father. On Monday she would be starting college in London.

Zakiy took a deep breath. 'I need to talk to you.'

She raised her eyebrows, but before they could say any more, they were interrupted by one of Vidhya's sisters.

'Sathi, there you are! Come on, it's almost time.' She turned to Zakiy. 'Your father's looking for you.'

He rolled his eyes. 'Of course he is.' He kissed Sathi's forehead and whispered, 'To be continued.'

He watched her get dragged away and then went looking for his father.

Every time he saw the temple he was amazed anew. Gone were the old ruins. Now every single lamp was lit, and incense filled the place with sweet-smelling smoke. All the pedestals and statues of the gods had been scrubbed clean and decorated with fresh flowers.

His father stood at the main pedestal, arranging all the ritual offerings used in Hindu weddings. Zakiy walked up to him. 'You've done an incredible job, Dad. I'm impressed.'

Dad smiled. 'Thank you, son. Have you seen your brother?'

Zakiy nodded. 'Yeah, he was back there talking to Raghavan and Jacob. He seems to be getting on well with Arjun.' His smile faded and he lowered his voice. 'Did you find any snakes when you cleared out the temple?'

Dad looked surprised, then he turned thoughtful. 'No, I think the snakes were guarding Devi so they wouldn't uproot her statue for treasure.'

Zakiy smiled in satisfaction. 'So now the gods are happy because the rightful priest has returned.'

His father looked pleased. 'I've missed being here,' he admitted, looking around. 'It feels right to tend to the gods again.'

'Good. You're all moving back to Nelliampathi now, right?' he checked. 'Back to our house?'

'Yes. Especially since Girish has written the deed to this temple in my name. He and Maya moved down to Kollam, where Maya's family lives.'

'And Jacob was finally given custody of Arjun,' Zakiy added.

Dad nodded. 'Anyway, what about you?' he asked. 'Have you told Sathi yet?'

He sighed. 'Not yet. I will, after the ceremony.'

His father was about to respond when Jayaram and Vidhya walked up, smiling. They pressed their palms together and bowed to Devi, praying, before turning to Dad.

'Ready?' he asked them.

'Definitely,' Jay replied. 'I've been waiting for this moment for twenty years.'

Vidhya giggled, gorgeous in a midnight blue sari with gold trimmings.

Dad picked up a metal platter with a golden chain on it and held it out to Jayaram.

Amidst the sound of trumpets and drums playing the Indian wedding march, Jay clasped the chain around Vidhya's neck.

Sathi, holding Vidhya's hair back for Jay, caught Zakiy's eye and winked.

Everyone rained flower petals on the couple, and they took turns to place a garland of flowers around each other's necks.

They prayed to Devi again and then beaming, they were passed from one hug to another as everyone took turns to congratulate them.

A warm hand slipped into his, and Sathi leaned up to kiss his cheek. 'That was beautiful.'

Zakiy squeezed her hand. 'Yes, it was.' He caught his father's eyes, and Dad looked at Sathi meaningfully before walking off in the opposite direction.

Making up his mind, Zakiy pulled her behind Devi's pedestal, where they had a bubble of privacy.

'Sathi, I need to tell you something.'

She looked up at him in concern. 'What is it?'

He took a deep breath and blurted, 'I applied to an MBA course some time ago. I got the acceptance letter yesterday.'

She looked surprised, then she beamed. 'That's great news! Congratulations.'

He stared at her, punctured. He'd expected a bit more enthusiasm. Then he replayed his words and wanted to smack himself on the forehead. In his haste, he hadn't told her the most important part.

'It's at LSE.'

Sathi blinked up at him. 'LSE? You mean...' Her hands flew to her mouth, eyes widening. 'London School of Economics?' she shrieked. 'You're coming to London?!'

She threw herself at him, and he chuckled, holding her close. 'Yup. I've talked to my parents, and they're okay with it. I won't be able to come with you tomorrow, but I should be able get there before the end of the month. I'm going to stay in London until you graduate, and then we can come back here, if you like.'

'Of course I want to come back here!' she exclaimed. 'Oh my God, I can't believe you're coming to London!'

Zakiy brushed the hair out of her face and traced the shape of her lips with his thumb, watching as her eyes fluttered shut involuntarily. 'Then, later on... maybe... one day... in this temple... in front of Devi... and all our family and friends... maybe we can...'

Zakiy didn't finish, simply leaning in and brushing her lips with his own.

He took her enthusiasm as acceptance of his unspoken offer.

The End

Glossary

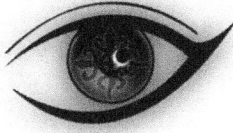

Malayalam terms:
Malayalam is the native language spoken in Kerala, south-west India.

Malayali/Keralite – someone from Kerala/someone who speaks Malayalam.

Achan – father
Amma – mother
Asooya – envy
Asura – mythological demons that inhabit the Underworld, usually depicted as being evil.
Bajrao – lighting bolt
Chakra – discus
Churidar – Indian clothing consisting of long flowing top, leggings and shawl
Danda – stick
Idly – rice cake
Kaivisham – literally "hand-poison", a form of black magic
Lobha – covetousness
Kalathilakam – accolade given to someone who excels in the arts like dance, music or drama
Krodha – wrath
Kundalini – latent female energy coiled at the base of spine

Manthram – magic
Mathsarya – competition
Moha – illusion
Molé – term of endearment, like "dear" (female)
Mundu – cotton wraparound garment worn tied around the waist
Puja – prayer
Prasadam – flowers and fruits offered to the gods and then distributed to devotees
Raashi = Moon sign
Sahasra chakra – crown chakra, seventh primary chakra
Sambar – vegetable curry with lentils
Sari – traditional Indian attire for women, composed of six metres of cloth wrapped artistically around the body
Sudharshana chakra – divine discus, typically Lord Vishnu's preferred weapon in Hindu mythology
Thali – wedding chain (equivalent of wedding ring in Hinduism)
Trishul – trident
Vavé – baby
Vel – spear

Acknowledgements

Heartfelt thanks to my parents for always supporting me and having implicit trust that I'll get exactly where I need to be, no matter how bumpy the ride. I hope you know how much I appreciate you guys.

Iqbal Uncle, you have been our rock. Thank you for everything.

Thank you Vishwalatha chechi, for your Tarot wisdom. You are an inspiration. In more ways than one.

Anitha chechi, your meditation techniques were invaluable to me. Thank you.

A special thanks to Shaatish Rajendran for letting me use your Sheshnag for the cover – I fell in love with it and cannot imagine using anything else.

Unnikrishnan Uncle and Prabhakaran Uncle – I have no words. Thank you.

Mummy's Daddy, Mummy's Mummy, Suresh Uncle and Salim Uncle – love you so, so much. I wish I could tell you in person, but I know you know my heart.

Vishnu – Whitebeard? How cool is he? Or should I say, how cool are you? *wink*

Mookambika Devi – you rock. Seriously. You know what I mean.

More by Shivon Mirza Sudesh

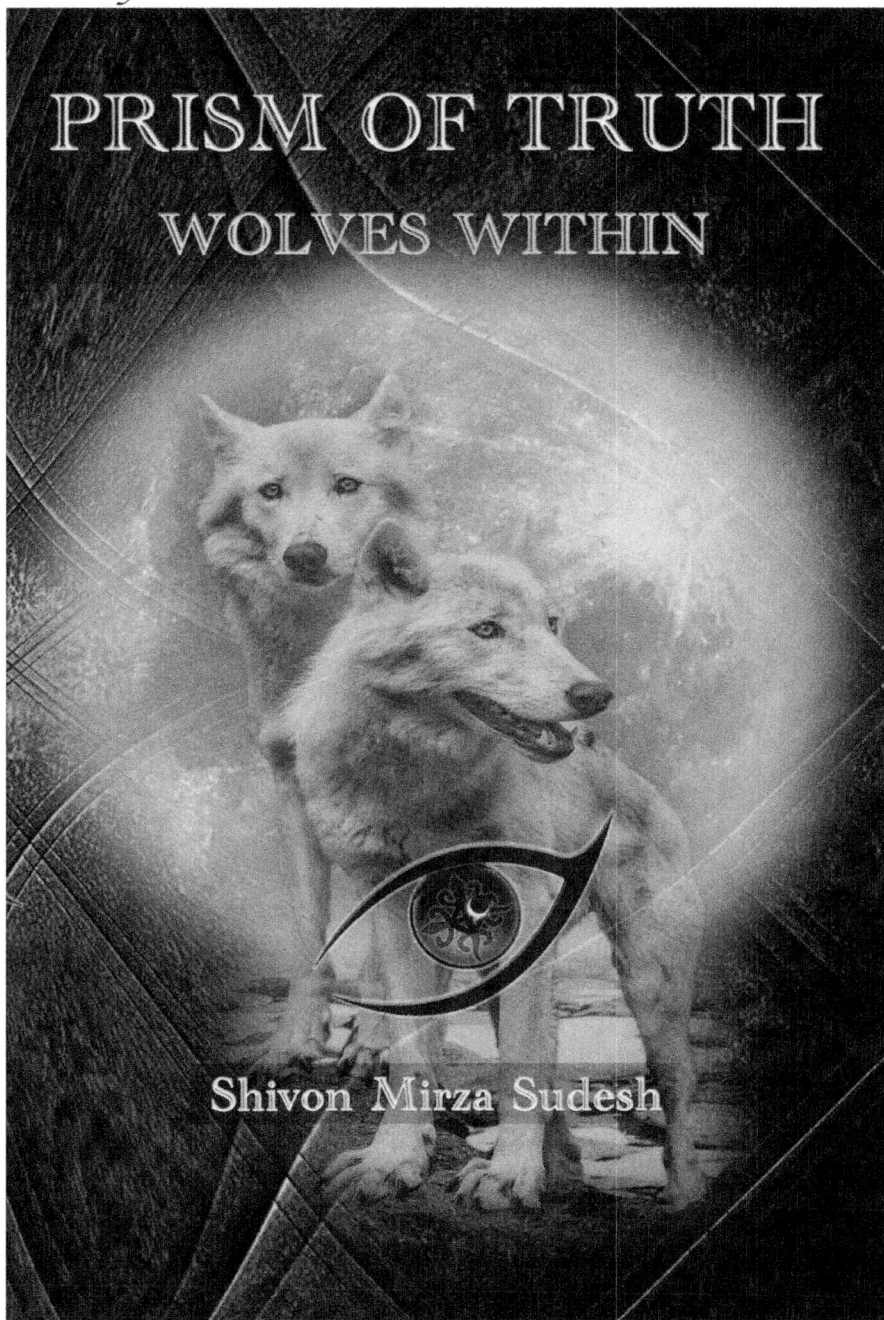

PRISM OF TRUTH
WOLVES WITHIN

Shivon Mirza Sudesh

More by Shivon Mirza Sudesh

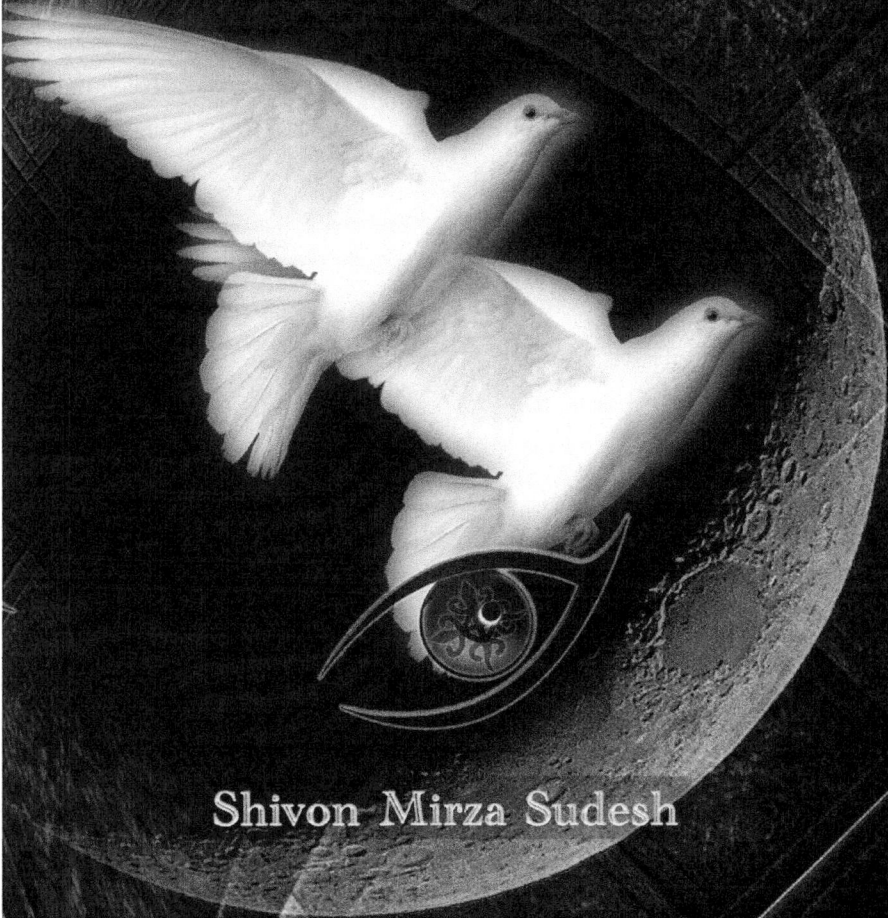

PRISM OF TRUTH

DOVES IN FLIGHT

Shivon Mirza Sudesh

Printed in Dunstable, United Kingdom